"I'M SORRY, GORDON, BUT I CAN'T GET INVOLVED WITH YOU RIGHT NOW."

"Why not?" he demanded.

"Because I have to concentrate on my career. I've saved and worked for this chance to be on my own for ten years and I just can't afford any distractions, no matter how tempting they may seem."

"You're so damn stubborn," he said, his voice rough with annoyance. "You say you have to concentrate on your career, that a relationship would be distracting."

"It's true—"

"Only because you want it to be true," he cut in. "You're denying the obvious attraction between us."

"I don't know how you can be sure of that. You hardly know me."

"This is why," he murmured against her cheek, her mouth. "And now tell me I'm wrong."

CANDLELIGHT ECSTASY SUPREME

9 NEVER LOOK BACK, *Donna Kimel Vitek*
10 NIGHT, SEA, AND STARS, *Heather Graham*
11 POLITICS OF PASSION, *Samantha Hughes*
12 NO STRINGS ATTACHED, *Prudence Martin*
13 BODY AND SOUL, *Anna Hudson*
14 CROSSFIRE, *Eileen Bryan*
15 WHERE THERE'S SMOKE . . . , *Nell Kincaid*
16 PAYMENT IN FULL, *Jackie Black*
17 RED MIDNIGHT, *Heather Graham*
18 A HEART DIVIDED, *Ginger Chambers*
19 SHADOW GAMES, *Elise Randolph*
20 JUST HIS TOUCH, *Emily Elliott*
21 BREAKING THE RULES, *Donna Kimel Vitek*
22 ALL IN GOOD TIME, *Samantha Scott*
23 SHADY BUSINESS, *Barbara Andrews*
24 SOMEWHERE IN THE STARS, *Jo Calloway*
25 AGAINST ALL ODDS, *Eileen Bryan*
26 SUSPICION AND SEDUCTION, *Shirley Hart*
27 PRIVATE SCREENINGS, *Lori Herter*
28 FASCINATION, *Jackie Black*
29 DIAMONDS IN THE SKY, *Samantha Hughes*
30 EVENTIDE, *Margaret Dobson*
31 CAUTION: MAN AT WORK, *Linda Randall Wisdom*
32 WHILE THE FIRE RAGES, *Amii Lorin*
33 FATEFUL EMBRACE, *Nell Kincaid*
34 A DANGEROUS ATTRACTION, *Emily Elliott*
35 MAN IN CONTROL, *Alice Morgan*
36 PLAYING IT SAFE, *Alison Tyler*
37 ARABIAN NIGHTS, *Heather Graham*
38 ANOTHER DAY OF LOVING, *Rebecca Nunn*
39 TWO OF A KIND, *Lori Copeland*
40 STEAL AWAY, *Candice Adams*
41 TOUCHED BY FIRE, *Jo Calloway*
42 ASKING FOR TROUBLE, *Donna Kimel Vitek*
43 HARBOR OF DREAMS, *Ginger Chambers*
44 SECRETS AND DESIRE, *Sandi Gellis*

SILENT PARTNER

Nell Kincaid

A CANDLELIGHT ECSTASY SUPREME

Published by
Dell Publishing Co., Inc.
1 Dag Hammarskjold Plaza
New York, New York 10017

ISBN: 0-440-17856-8

Printed in the United States of America
First printing—October 1984

To Our Readers:

Candlelight Ecstasy is delighted to announce the start of a brand-new series—Ecstasy Supremes! Now you can enjoy a romance series unlike all the others—longer and more exciting, filled with more passion, adventure, and intrigue—the stories you've been waiting for.

In months to come we look forward to presenting books by many of your favorite authors and the very finest work from new authors of romantic fiction as well. As always, we are striving to present the unique, absorbing love stories that you enjoy most—the very best love has to offer.

Breathtaking and unforgettable, Ecstasy Supremes will follow in the great romantic tradition you've come to expect *only* from Candlelight Ecstasy.

Your suggestions and comments are always welcome. Please let us hear from you.

Sincerely,

The Editors
Candlelight Romances
1 Dag Hammarskjold Plaza
New York, New York 10017

CHAPTER ONE

He was standing at the other side of the room, laughing with a beautiful woman. Laura hadn't been able to stop looking at him since she had first arrived at the party half an hour ago. She was sure he was a television star, since the party was peopled mostly with men and women from that industry, but she just couldn't place him.

It was his eyes that were the most striking: dark and intense, shaded by thick lashes. He was definitely leading-man material, but she couldn't think from what show. He was athletic enough to star in a detective or action-adventure series, but Laura thought of the few she watched and knew he wasn't in any of them. And he seemed well-built in an offhanded rather than a studied way, naturally sleek and long-limbed rather than brawny from hours of working out in a gym.

Laura didn't want to stare; he hadn't even noticed her, and he seemed to be deep in conversation with this other woman, so Laura went off to find the friend who had brought her to the party.

"Laura!"

She turned and saw her friend Robert moving through the crowd. He was a free-lance stylist, someone who chose props and just the right accessories for everything from one-time fashion photo sessions to long-running TV series, and he had brought Laura to the party so she could meet some "useful people," as he had put it.

He breezed up to her with a grace that hinted at the years of dance he had taken before becoming a stylist. "Do I see the light of success glittering in those blue eyes of yours?" he asked. "Have you met the man of your dreams, or anyone halfway interesting at least?"

"No and yes," she answered, sipping at her champagne. "I've met a few interesting types, but no one *you'd* want me to meet."

He smiled. "You can't bear the idea of using anyone, Laura, but that's what makes the world go around—particularly that strange part of the world called show business. Connections are what it's all about, darling, and if you're going to be a *successful* makeup artist, you're going to have to realize it and realize it quickly."

"Oh, I know," she said, brushing her straight honey-colored bangs back from her face. "Believe me, I know. It's my least favorite aspect of being my own boss and being responsible for getting business, but I know I have to do it. It just always strikes me as so calculating." And it always brought back unpleasant memories of her ex-boyfriend Matthew. He was the first person she had ever met who was always thinking about what people could do for him. Whether he was at a party or with friends or even with family, he was constantly thinking about how he could use them to benefit himself in some way. And Laura's distaste for what Matthew did used to infuriate him, because he'd correctly point out that in terms of business, seeing what people could do for you was simply the way of the world.

Laura knew he was right, but it had always bothered her.

Suddenly, Robert nudged Laura and brought her thoughts back to the party as he nodded his head in the direction of the tall stranger Laura had been looking at. "There's someone you'd do well to know."

"Who is he?" Laura asked, once again unable to stop staring at the man. He was talking to someone else now —a young man who was talking very fast and laughing nervously every few seconds. But the tall man was just barely smiling, and it was a smile that looked forced rather than genuine.

"That's Gordon Chase," Robert said quietly. "Head of CTC—the whole network. And, honey, if you could get to know *him*. your whole career would be made."

Laura frowned skeptically. "Oh, come on, Robert, I believe in making contacts as much as the next person, but I really don't believe one person can make or break your career. From what I've heard, those days are long gone. And don't look at me with that 'you're such a hick' expression."

"I can't help it." Robert laughed. "Sometimes you are, Laura. You may come from a small town in Connecticut where things like that don't happen, and the salon you just left may not have taught you this, but there *are* still people who are that important. And if my eyes aren't playing tricks on me, it looks as if Gordon Chase is heading right this way. So make me proud, Laura; I'll be watching." And he moved off into the crowd before she could say anything more.

Gordon Chase was indeed coming toward her, having shed the talkative and nervous young man, but he seemed more intent on hors d'oeuvres than Laura as he approached the table.

Laura glanced at him as he put some oysters and

cheese puffs on his plate. He was even handsomer up close, with a certain athletic vitality she hadn't noticed from afar. His hands looked strong and capable, and his profile was firm and decisive, with a ruggedness that was enormously appealing.

"Are these as good as they look?" he asked, looking not at Laura but at some stuffed mushrooms.

"What? Oh, I don't know. I haven't tried them."

He smiled. "Then will you join me?" He put some of the mushrooms on another plate and offered it to her, then refilled her glass of champagne and set it down on the table. "There. Now you can't claim you need to refill your drink or get more food."

"Am I going to need to get away from you that quickly?"

He raised a brow. "Perhaps. Haven't you ever heard that the prettiest woman in the room is also the most elusive? And you can't deny you're that, can you?"

She laughed. "Oh, come on. Elusive, maybe. Prettiest . . ."

"Then it's an illusion?" he asked with a smile. "You're telling me that those aren't the prettiest blue eyes I've ever seen?"

"Oh, you don't know what miracles are possible when it comes to looks," she said. "That's my business—I'm a makeup artist—and I can promise you that half the top models today are women you wouldn't even look twice at if you passed them on the street. My eyes are blue-green, and I can make them look either blue or green depending on makeup. And in terms of my general look—"

"If you're trying to tell me you're an expert illusionist with others, Miss Dawson, that's one thing, but—"

"How did you know my name?"

"I have my sources," he said easily. "I know that you just left Gleason and Gibbs to start your own business, and I know that you're the prettiest woman in the room whether you admit it or not," he added, battling a smile.

"How did you know about my business?"

"I told you I have my sources. Which I take full advantage of when I see a woman like you. And I also know that your charms have been slightly wasted on this party so far."

"What do you mean?"

"That man you left a few minutes ago—Bill Atkinson. He was quite taken with you. Thought you might be an actress, and since he's a director he thought he could be of some help."

"Hmmm. I didn't know he was a director."

"My point exactly," he observed. "What are you talking about with all these people?"

"Whatever comes up," she answered honestly. "Whatever we seem to have in common at that moment. Is that so terrible?" she asked with a smile.

"That depends on why you're here."

She shook her head. "I think I just heard this lecture from someone else not five minutes ago. What is it about me that makes people feel they have to explain how I should be acting at this party?"

"Well, I can't speak for anyone else, but I thought you might welcome some friendly advice. I knew you were going into business for yourself, and I thought this was a natural place for you to make some contacts."

"Well, you're right—it is. But I really *was* planning to make them on my own, maybe at a slightly different pace than what you're suggesting. And I'm not too worried about my new business. I have a lot of clients from the salon."

"Sounds interesting," he said, pouring more champagne for both of them. "But come—let's talk where it's quieter," he added, and gently led Laura through the crowd out onto the terrace, to a softly cushioned chaïse facing Central Park and the whole East Side. The view was lovely, the city glittering below in the haze of the night, and the spring evening air smelled wonderful.

"So tell me about these clients," he said.

She shrugged. "Oh, they're just women who've come to me at Gleason and Gibbs for years."

"And you expect every one of them to keep her word?"

"Sixty or seventy percent, I imagine. Around that number."

"Try twenty or twenty-five percent if you're very, very lucky, Laura. Don't you understand that when you tell people something like what you've told them—that you're starting a business—they're naturally going to say they'll come see you? Most of them even mean it. But getting them to actually do it is an entirely different proposition. They've gone to Gleason and Gibbs for years and they're going to continue to go. So I suggest you don't count on them; you should concentrate on other people."

"Like who?" she asked.

"Producers. Directors. Women who use makeup artists every time they go to a party. Photographers."

"I *was* planning to tap all those possibilities," she said dryly, "believe it or not."

"Then start tapping. Would you like me to introduce you to that man over there? He's another director."

She looked over at a heavyset red-haired man standing over by a fig tree at the edge of the terrace. He was talking to a tall, very pretty, raven-haired woman, and Laura was certain he wouldn't want to be interrupted. "I'll go talk to him myself—later, thank you."

Gordon Chase tilted his head. "Then you really don't want my help?" He sounded genuinely surprised.

"No. Thank you, Mr. Chase, but I really don't think I need it."

"Gordon."

"Gordon, then."

"I didn't get where I am today without help from a tremendous number of people," he said.

"That's fine for you. But aren't we at rather different levels?"

He shrugged. "I don't know what you mean."

"Oh, come on. You have to be one of the most highly paid men in America if you run CTC. How can you compare yourself to someone like me who's just starting out?"

"I can compare us because at one time I was just starting out too."

"Mmmm," she said doubtfully.

He looked at her closely. "I detect a rather large dose of skepticism in there somewhere."

She shrugged. "Well, I just think that when people reach your level, they're really in a different world. I've never actually understood why anyone deserves to make that much money for *any*thing. My parents have both worked themselves to the bone all their lives, and they're still as poor as church mice. It isn't for lack of trying, either; they just can't make the kind of money other people make. And then when you start talking about the kind of salary the head of a network makes—"

"Are you expecting me to apologize?" he cut in.

"Whether you choose to believe it or not, I do work hard, and I've worked damn hard to get where I am. And I imagine that if you had the chance to make that kind of money, Laura, you wouldn't turn the opportunity down."

"Well . . . yes, that happens to be true. But I do feel I know what I'm doing."

"All right, I have a suggestion," he said quietly. "I'll agree to put a halt to my advice if you agree to dance with me."

She smiled. "But you were the one who said I should use my time here wisely, making contacts," she teased. "I already know you."

"Not well enough," he said softly. "Now come on. This can be our song," he whispered as the band began to play "As Time Goes By."

She didn't protest as he led her back in and onto the dance floor. In the soft glow of candlelight flickering against peach walls, with the achingly romantic music setting a dream-smooth rhythm, Laura gracefully slid into Gordon Chase's arms and forgot about everything but the intoxicating scent of his neck and the warmth of his gentle hold on her.

"You dance beautifully," he murmured into her ear, his breath warm and stirring. He drew back so he could look into her eyes. "Maybe I should push you into dance instead."

She laughed.

"And I'm sorry if I came on as some sort of know-it-all," he continued. "All I really wanted to do was meet you."

She smiled. "Well, *I'm* sorry if I was rude. I just have

this automatic resistance when anyone tries to tell me what to do."

She rested her head on his shoulder as they danced some more, and he held her close, inhaling the scent of her hair, loving the feel of her, wanting her.

When the song ended, they looked into each other's eyes and smiled. "What are you doing for the rest of the evening?" he asked softly.

"Circulating, I guess." She slipped out of his grasp and began walking with him to the edge of the dance floor. She turned and looked up at him. "Maybe I'll even take your advice and go talk to that director you pointed out. What's his name?"

"Jason Higgins," Gordon said. "But why not let me introduce you?"

She shook her head. "No, thanks. I have my own plans." And she gave him a wink and a wave and was lost in the crowd a moment later.

Gordon smiled. Laura Dawson was clearly giving him a small slap in the face, showing him that all his advice could backfire when he least expected it. Now that he wanted to spend time with her, she was following his orders and making contact with one of the very men he least wanted her to speak with. For he knew that Jason Higgins was a ladies' man of the first order, one on whom Laura's beauty wouldn't be wasted. Telling her about Jason Higgins and promising to introduce her were entirely different from having her strike out on her own. But he had realized his mistake too late.

He drifted off toward the corner where Laura had headed, and out of the corner of his eye he saw Laura talking and laughing with Higgins.

Damn you and your damn advice, he said to himself as

he saw Higgins slip his arm through Laura's and lead her off toward the dance floor.

And a half hour later, when he had extricated himself from an excruciatingly dull conversation with a casting director named Jack Hepburn, he looked everywhere for Laura—on the dance floor, on the terrace, in the living room, the library, the halls. But she was gone.

Laura, meanwhile, was wondering whether Gordon's advice was as good as his dancing. She had dutifully gone up to Jason Higgins and charmed him into a dance, charmed him into talking about his work and where she might fit in, charmed him into forgetting—or not noticing—that she was more interested in Jason Higgins the Director than in Jason Higgins the Man.

Yet at some point he had turned the tables on her. For clearly he was more interested in Laura Dawson the Woman than in Laura Dawson the Makeup Artist. And she didn't know how to turn the tables back again toward the kind of relationship she wanted to develop.

They had left the party and gone down the block to the bar at Café des Artistes, a wonderful restaurant Laura had heard of but had never been to before. Though she hadn't wanted to leave the party, he had gotten her out so smoothly and so quickly that she barely noticed what was happening. With the ease of all springtime leavetakings, she had left the party without having to get coat, hat, or anything else, "for a drink in the loveliest restaurant in the city," Higgins had promised.

And the restaurant was indeed lovely, with flowers everywhere and magnificent murals covering all the walls.

But Laura realized she had left the party on a whim—partly to demonstrate teasingly to Gordon Chase that she could take his advice as well as anyone could. Only now, Jason Higgins was the last person she wanted to be with.

"You can go far," he said, his eyes twinkling as he pressed his knee against hers. "But you know that, I'm sure. My only question, Miss Dawson, is why you chose to be a makeup artist rather than a model or an actress. You're certainly pretty enough to do either."

"Well, thank you," she said, shifting on the barstool so there was some distance between her leg and his. "But I'm not at all right for modeling, actually. My eyes are much too close together, my hands are too big, I'm not a standard size anything, and . . . well, you don't want to hear all the reasons."

"What about acting?"

She quickly shook her head. "I'd die of fear. And anyway, I happen to love what I do. *And* it can give me the kind of financial security I want. Actresses have to wait around for parts, sometimes for years. If I can build up a steady clientele, I'll be set."

"Which is where people like me come in," he said softly, putting a hand on her knee. "I suppose if you develop a loyal group of producers, directors, and models who swear by your work, you can have anything you want."

She put her hand over his and firmly removed it from her knee. "It *would* be nice," she said calmly. "But if I'm good enough, that should come in time, without my having to force it."

"You're very confident," he said with an edge of malice in his voice. "Maybe too confident for someone so new in the business."

"I may be new at running my own business, but I'm

not inexperienced," she said evenly. "Which should be all that counts."

"It's easier to make friends than enemies," he said softly. "Do you understand what I'm saying?"

She finished her Scotch and looked Jason Higgins in the eye. "I wish I didn't, but I do. And I liked you until you made that statement, Mr. Higgins." She stood up. "Thank you for the drink."

His eyes flashed angrily. "You're leaving?"

"Yes, if that's all right with you." And she turned and left without a backward glance.

Gordon Chase left the party early. With Laura gone, he felt alternately irritated and angry, annoyed at himself for having let her slip out of his grasp, irritated at her for leaving.

And if she had left with Jason Higgins, there wasn't too much he had to guess at: virtually every woman who went off with Jason Higgins spent the rest of the night with him—at least that was true of every actress he had ever known.

Damn it, he knew the syndrome well himself; it simply couldn't be avoided. When you were in a position in which you could literally change someone's life, where one yes could mean the difference between failure and success, between being a waitress for another year of unsuccessful auditions or being a star actress on a new series, almost everyone you met was someone you could choose to help in some way—or not. And he remembered how, in a certain period of his life, he had heartily taken advantage of the situation, bedding a new woman whenever the need struck him—for opportunity knocked in the form of a lovelier woman every day.

And he had finally outgrown the situation, finding the pleasure empty and leaving him more depressed each day.

But Jason Higgins wasn't like that. And Laura was with him.

And what amazed him was that he was bothered so much. But damn it, he couldn't help it. Long ago he had sworn off the kinds of affairs that left him feeling strangely lonely—the one-night stands that were for one night because he just couldn't get interested, the brief flings that were nothing more than draining.

He didn't know Laura—at least, not well. But suddenly the fact that she had gone off with Jason Higgins was eating away at him like an ulcer.

And he knew he wouldn't sleep until he thought of a way to see her again.

CHAPTER TWO

The next morning, when Laura awakened in a fuzzy, painful haze, she realized she had drunk a tremendous amount of champagne the night before. It had gone down easily—too easily—but now she remembered the state of mind she had been in when she'd left the party, and she cursed herself for having drunk so much. Jason Higgins was the kind of man she could normally spot in a minute as someone she'd like to stay away from; yet she had breezed out of the party with him as if he were the most interesting and exciting person she'd met all evening.

And without question the most interesting and exciting man she had met in a long, long time was Gordon Chase.

She had resented him at first for presuming to know so much about her work. But the fact was that his advice had been good, and not very different from Robert's. And her resentment had dissolved as soon as he took her in his arms.

Laura dragged herself out of bed and stumbled into the bathroom. No sense lying in bed fantasizing about a near-stranger when there was work to do.

But when she looked in the bathroom mirror, she saw there was more to be done than she'd thought: before she could make up anyone else's face, she was definitely going to have to do an awful lot on her own. Her eyelids were puffy, her skin creased from sodden sleep, her cheeks pale and gray. She smiled as she imagined going to the house of her afternoon customer like this. "Hi, I'm Laura Dawson, the makeup artist," she'd say, and the woman would probably slam the door in her face.

The ringing of the phone in the bedroom was so loud and jarring it made Laura's head hurt as she walked over to answer it.

"Hello?" she said listlessly.

"I was going to say good morning but that doesn't sound very accurate in your case. What's wrong?"

"Who's this?"

There was a pause, but when he spoke again, it sounded as if he were smiling. "I'm insulted. Here I had hoped you'd spent all night and all morning thinking about me, and you don't even know who I am. This is Gordon Chase."

"Oh, hi," she said.

"You sound half-asleep. Don't tell me you just got up."

"Well—"

"It's nine thirty!" he cried.

"I needed my beauty sleep. And actually, if you saw me now, you'd tell me to go right back to bed. I must have drunk a lot more than I realized last night."

"Good," he said firmly.

"Why is that good?"

"Because then I can console myself with the thought that the only reason you left with Jason Higgins was because you were wildly drunk, and that otherwise you would have left with me."

"Well, I wasn't wildly drunk, but I was pretty hazy."

"Hey, come on," he complained. "I keep trying to make myself feel better and you keep bursting my illusions. Let me at least think we might have gotten together last night, all right? Even if it's just a pipe dream."

She laughed. "All right, go ahead and think it," she said happily, silently adding to herself, *I wish I had left with him.*

"Anyway," he said, "I called for a reason other than just wanting to hear you laugh, which is awfully nice, and wanting you to admit you were thinking about me as much as I was thinking about you last night. I have a project for you."

"Oh, really?"

"Mmmm. Do you watch our seven o'clock news?"

"Uh, sometimes. Not too often."

"Do you know Sandra Strachan?"

"I think. A blonde, right? She's one of the two women on the show that has two anchorwomen?"

"Right. The brunette is Jocelyn Croft. Anyway, I need you to make Sandra Strachan look better than she has been lately."

"I didn't know network presidents got involved in that sort of thing."

"Network presidents who want to get to know certain makeup artists do. But that's really not the only reason I'm calling you, Laura. You need work and I need a makeup person. And for the first time in two weeks, which is how long Sandra has been looking like death warmed over, I'm glad I need to hire someone, because I want to hire you."

"Who's doing her now?"

"Victor Marcel is doing them both. Jocelyn looks like a million bucks and Sandra looks like hell. I want to see what you can do."

"Well, I have an appoint—"

"Hey, I don't want to hear *any* excuses, *any* foot-dragging; I don't want to hear anything but yes. You hear me?"

She laughed. "I hear you. And I wasn't going to say no. Just that I have a four o'clock appointment. I was just thinking out loud."

"When can you get here, then?"

"Where are you?" she asked.

"Rockefeller Center. Fiftieth and Fifth."

"Hmmm. Six at the latest, I'd say."

"Then be here, Laura. Thirty-second floor, and I'll see you then, okay? Whether you like it or not, whether you resist or not, you are on the road to success."

She smiled. "I'll see you later."

When she hung up and caught a glance of herself in the mirror, she cursed the champagne once more and then got down to the serious work of making herself look halfway decent.

Her four o'clock appointment was a pleasure—a woman who had heard about her from a good friend. She had never hired a makeup artist—or anyone, for that matter—and was so thrilled at the idea of having someone come to her house to do her makeup that Laura couldn't have done anything wrong even if she had tried.

And then, at six on the dot, Laura announced herself at CTC headquarters at Rockefeller Center. The offices were sleek and relaxing, with light gray walls, dark gray carpeting, and black leather furniture, the restful grays and blacks interrupted here and there by bursts of bright bouquets in graceful floor vases. On the walls, framed publicity shots from CTC's spring lineup boasted of the network's triumphs, and nowhere did Laura see any indication that the network had ever been in any position but its current number one. Though she could think of several shows that CTC hadn't done all that well with, they were most definitely absent from the photos and posters and pamphlets everywhere. And all the employees who passed through the reception area, whether they were mail boys or secretaries or executives, looked as if they were heading straight for the top with no plans to linger anywhere else.

Laura wanted to be blasé, like a jaded New Yorker who's seen everything there is to see, but part of her couldn't help being impressed by the atmosphere. As a girl growing up in a small town in Connecticut, she had dreamed of such places for years. Since she had first begun going to the movies and watching TV, she had dreamed of going to work at just this sort of place and performing some sort of magic—perhaps acting, perhaps directing, anything that could make her life glamorous and exciting.

"Miss Dawson? Mr. Chase is ready to see you now," the receptionist said. "His secretary will be out in a moment."

"Thank you," Laura said, noticing the open script on the receptionist's desk. Like everyone else at the network, she was probably just waiting for the day when she'd be discovered, and was developing every contact she could while she waited until that day came.

An attractive young woman emerged from behind smoked-glass doors and asked Laura to follow; a few moments later Laura was announced to Gordon and then the two of them were alone in one of the most magnificent offices Laura had ever seen.

But it was Gordon she stared at. He was smiling a

slightly crooked smile, one that seemed to express both pleasure and surprise.

"Last night I wouldn't have thought it possible I'd actually see you in here today," he said, coming forward.

He reached out and firmly shook her hand, and for a moment he was tempted to pull her into his arms, to feel the softness of her body against his, to relight the fires that had just begun to kindle the night before. As he looked into her lovely eyes, he thought she just might be hoping for the same thing, that she was waiting for him to bring her against him, waiting for him to cover her lips with his.

But he resisted and forced himself to break the contact. She had run off last night with Jason Higgins—not with him. And while he wasn't sure what had happened between her and the director, he *was* sure that if she had wanted something to happen with him rather than with Jason, she would have stayed at the party, not left.

Yet her eyes told him—or seemed to tell him—that she wanted him.

She turned away and stepped quickly to the window. "Well," she said loudly, as if she were nervous, "you have an appropriately magnificent view."

He smiled as he came up beside her. "Don't tell me I'm going to have to start justifying my position to you again."

Her eyes flashed as she looked up at him. "No, don't worry about that. You're doing me a favor with no strings attached. Which is more than a man like Jason Higgins is willing to do."

He said nothing, searching her eyes.

"I left a very angry man back at Café des Artistes, Gordon."

He laughed, a wonderful laugh that seemed to hold back nothing. "You don't know how glad I am to hear that."

"Oh, come on! Do you really think I'd sleep with a man like that just for a vague chance at some future jobs? Or even for the greatest job in the world?"

"I don't know you very well, Laura. I—"

"Obviously not," she cut in. "And I don't want to sound sanctimonious or naive. I don't see anything wrong with *anything* if both people are willing. I just happened not to be. Anyway, Gordon, he was such a sleaze bucket! What kind of taste do you think I have?"

He smiled. "All right, I get the message. You did not go home with Jason Higgins and you probably never will. There's just one problem, though."

"What's that?"

"How do I do a favor for you *and* ask you out without your thinking I'm another Jason Higgins?" His eyes were dark with desire as he spoke, and he moved forward until he was so close he was almost touching her, the heat from his body sending a powerful message of need. "Although I'm not really doing a favor for you, Laura—I want you for this job. But I did stay up half the night trying to figure out how I could see you again as quickly as I could."

She caught a hint of the lemony scent of his cologne, felt the warmth flood through her veins as he took her in his arms, lost her voice as his eyes held her in thrall. "I can't stop thinking about you, Laura," he said huskily. "When I realized you had left that party . . . I know we've just met, but I also know . . ." His voice trailed off as he brushed his lips against hers. He moved his mouth gently, tentatively, as she wrapped her arms around his neck and pulled him closer. The thrusting strength of his hips and hard thighs aroused her immediately, his masculine flesh promising pleasure she had been missing. "Laura," he murmured against her lips. "I thought about you last night and I wanted you so much I couldn't sleep, couldn't think. And now . . ." He teased her lips with playful silken bites, trapping her hips and buttocks beneath his strong hands. And then with a moan of hoarse desire, he parted her lips and found the inner recesses of her mouth with his tongue, teased her till she was awash with desire.

From somewhere nearby a bell softly rang, and Gordon drew back, almost drunkenly, from Laura's arms. "Damn," he muttered. "I have to get that." As he left her arms and walked to the desk, Laura took a deep breath, dizzy and off-balance after the embrace.

"Yes," he said into a speaker on his desk. "What is it, Vera?"

"Jake wanted to know if you'd made a decision about Hal Arnstein's new script."

"Not yet. Tomorrow. But don't tell him that; I don't want him hanging on the decision. Tell him we'll let him know when we let him know."

"Right," Vera said. "I'll take care of it."

"Thanks, Vera."

When he turned back to Laura, he was smiling. "All this work," he said, shaking his head. "You have a rather amazing effect on me, I've discovered. I actually forgot I was at the office."

"Me too." She laughed.

He glanced at his watch. "Well. You're going to be late unless I talk fast."

She smiled. "Okay. But you don't have to tell me

much. I have all the equipment I need right over there in my makeup case, and I'm going to make Sandra Strachan look as great as she can."

"Well, great but not too too, all right?"

"Not too glamorous, you mean," she prompted.

"Exactly. I don't want the viewers to think they're getting the news from a starlet."

"I understand; you don't have to explain."

He took her into his arms again and held her close. "I know, I know," he murmured. "But I do have to explain one thing to you, Laura."

"What's that?"

"I'm not another Jason Higgins. I can't let you walk out that door thinking I scrounged up this job as a way to get you to go to bed with me. I want you, Laura, more than I've wanted anyone in a long, long time." His eyes darkened with need as he brought her against his hard length, and like wildfire she was aflame inside at a touch that was subtle yet part of a deep and primitive message. He was a man who had a potent ability to give her pleasure, and they had a connection that worked beneath the surface, without words, through the power of touch, scent, nearness.

"I should go," she said softly.

"Come back when you're finished . . . ?"

She hesitated only for a moment, but he felt the need to persuade her. "I want to be sure you'll come," he whispered, raining kisses on the smooth length of her neck. The tip of his tongue teased a hot message in her ear, and she fell deeper and deeper under his spell as his hands began a slow ascent up from her hips. Just as they warmly cupped her breasts, she pulled away. "I really have to go," she murmured, and she shakily picked up her makeup case and purse and left without looking back.

A few moments later, as she carried her bags down the hall to the receptionist, who was supposed to show her where the news broadcast was taping, she realized her body was still tingling and aglow from the embrace with Gordon. That the man obviously had an effect on her just couldn't be ignored.

On the news sound stage, a simple set designed for the two anchorwomen of the seven o'clock world news, she was introduced to the crew members. And she took a few moments to observe the women she'd be working on.

Sandra Strachan was actually the prettier of the two anchorwomen, with more delicate features, prettier eyes, glossier hair. But what Gordon had said was true. She looked washed-out and pale.

In contrast, Jocelyn Croft positively glowed. Her dark eyes flashed a sparkling energy, and she looked vibrant, alive, and healthy next to Sandra Strachan. Her cheeks were rosy, her lips well-defined and full, and her dark brown eyes with their lavender shading and beige highlights made Sandra's look like mere shadows.

The two women were at their seats reading over what was obviously the copy for the upcoming broadcast. When Laura approached, only Sandra looked up. "Are you Laura Dawson?" she asked.

"Yes, hi. Sandra Strachan, right?"

"Thank God you're here," Sandra said with a smile. "I've been looking positively green lately."

Jocelyn Croft looked up from her reading with a glint in her eyes. She looked as if she were about to say something as she studied Laura, but then seemed to think better of it, returning to her copy without another word.

"All right, I think I see the problem," Laura said, looking from the lights to Sandra's face. "We're going to need a lot more color, that's all."

"Victor tried that," Sandra said doubtfully. "I looked like a clown that night, or as if I had just come out of an oven."

Laura laughed. "Then that was Victor's problem—not yours. You've got a lovely face and beautiful hair, and there's no reason you shouldn't look absolutely spectacular on the air."

She started from scratch with Sandra, instructing her to wash all her makeup off so they could start fresh. Then it was a simple matter of highlighting her cheeks and brow bones, using a foundation that brought out some color, emphasizing naturally pretty features—something that should have been simple for Victor Marcel to accomplish.

As Laura looked up at Sandra on one of the monitors at the edge of the studio, Gordon came up beside her. "You did a beautiful job," he said quietly.

She smiled. "Thanks. I would have had to do Jocelyn under protest, so I let her do her own blotting, which was all she needed anyway."

Gordon nodded. "They both look great. How'd you like the job forever?"

"Forever?"

"You know what I mean. Permanently. I'll give Victor the heave-ho tomorrow."

"You're a very precipitous man. You'd do that on the basis of what I did tonight?"

"He's already on notice, Laura. And I know talent when I see it, which I do with you. Plus I know when something strange is going on. I don't know whether it's because Victor Marcel dislikes Sandra or likes Jocelyn too much, or that he's incompetent, but I do know that it's time to fire him."

"Well, don't fire him on my account," she said quickly. "Because I wouldn't take the job even if it was available."

At first he looked surprised, then angry. "Why not? You'd have to be here a minimal amount of time every day, and you'd get a damn handsome salary—as you know."

"I got a damn handsome salary at my last job, Gordon. I don't want another full-time job where I'm—"

"It wouldn't be full-time," he cut in.

She smiled. "All right, not full-time, but a commitment every day. I don't want that. If I have to be here at six thirty every evening, what's that going to do to the afternoon and evening appointments I hope to be making soon?"

"Make them later," he said simply.

She shook her head. "That's like my telling you to put the eleven o'clock news on at midnight. Late afternoons and early evenings will probably be the busiest parts of my day when my business gets going; I'm going to have to leave them open. And more than anything else, Gordon, I want to be my own boss—not an employee all over again."

"We'll talk about it over dinner."

She smiled. "Who said anything about dinner?"

"I'm saying it now."

"Oh, you are . . . ?"

"And if you say no, Laura, you're going to find yourself being followed all week—'dogged pursuit,' they used to call it. I'll call you every morning and every afternoon and every night until you say yes."

She laughed. "I'm not that hard to get. I'm starved and I'd love to come."

Fifteen minutes later, after Gordon had wrapped up his business at the network and left an amazed secretary who couldn't believe he was leaving so early, Gordon and Laura walked out into the cool spring air and out onto 50th Street.

"Do you want me to get rid of the limo?" Gordon asked, gesturing at the sleek black Cadillac by the curb.

"Why would I want you to do that?" she asked with a smile.

"Oh, just an instinct," he said quietly. "But I guess I was wrong. After your rather severe lecture on executives who make too much money, I thought you might want to take the subway—anything but this."

"You must think I'm crazy," she said with a laugh.

Just mysterious, he said to himself. It had been a long time since he had consciously tried to impress a woman, and an even longer time since he hadn't known how to do it. Laura was a complete mystery to him—at one moment interested in all the trappings of success, and in the next, almost critical of those same trappings. And he didn't know which was the real Laura Dawson, if either one was.

All he was sure of was that he wanted her more than any woman he had wanted in a long, long time. And he wasn't at all sure he'd succeed.

CHAPTER THREE

Gordon took Laura to a small French restaurant on West 56th Street, and as he talked with her, he found she was unlike anyone else he had ever met. She knew exactly what she wanted from life, and she wasn't about to let anyone get in her way, yet she didn't have the hard edges he had seen in so many other women and men who possessed her ambition.

"How long have you lived in New York?" he asked over coffee.

"Oh, I guess eight years now. I came a couple of years after I graduated from high school."

"No college?"

She quickly shook her head. "I didn't need college for what I was interested in, and not going gave me four years of a head start. Most of the people I know who went to college just wasted their time anyway, so I really don't feel it was a mistake."

"You don't have to be defensive about it," he said gently. "I couldn't agree with you more."

Her eyes flashed. "I wasn't being defensive. I was just stating a fact."

"But I'm sure you've met a lot of people who do think you should have gone to college."

She shrugged. "I don't pay any attention to them."

He smiled. "You like to do things your own way, don't you?"

"Oh, I wouldn't make a big deal out of it. I mean, if you go around saying that you're 'fiercely uncompromising,' or whatever, it just sounds silly."

"But you *are* different from most of the people you grew up with, I imagine. You told me you're from a small town in Connecticut. Didn't most of your friends stay there?"

"Yes, but that doesn't make me any better than they are. Just different. What are you trying to say?"

"I'm trying to understand you. I've never met a woman who confused me as much as you do. And that wouldn't matter if I didn't want you so much." He smiled. "And don't look so surprised. How can you be surprised after what happened in my office?"

She set her coffee down and smiled. "I'm sorry. I'm not surprised. I just don't know how to react to someone like you—someone I just can't get involved with at the moment."

"Why not?" He hesitated, and then said, "Are you seeing someone else?"

"No, I'm not, and for the same reason I wouldn't want to get involved with you, Gordon. I have to concentrate on my career right now." She looked down at the table and then into his eyes. "And I know that sounds corny and like something that can't really be true, but it is. I've saved and worked for this chance—a chance to be on my own—for ten years now, and I just can't afford any distractions. No matter how tempting they may seem."

Gordon said nothing, calling for the check and finishing his coffee in silence.

"Gordon?" Laura finally said.

"We'll talk in the limo."

When they walked outside, Gordon's driver opened the rear door for them and Laura stepped in. Gordon looked tense and angry as he sat down beside her. Once the driver closed the door, it was as if Laura and Gordon were in a world of their own, silent and isolated from everything else because of the curtained divider between the rear and front of the car and the dark glass windows.

"I'm sorry if you're angry," Laura began, not sure Gordon was going to say anything at all.

"Just tell me where you live," he said flatly.

She gave him her address and he told the driver through a speaker phone. Then he sat back and continued to scowl.

"Gordon?"

"You're so damn stubborn," he finally said, his voice rough with annoyance. "You say you have to concentrate on your career, that a relationship would be distracting."

"Because it's true—"

"Because you want it to be true," he cut in. "You're denying an obvious connection between the two of us."

"Then wait for me," she challenged. "You hardly know me, so I don't know how you can be so sure anyway, but if you *are* so sure, wait for me until I *am* ready for some kind of a relationship."

"Don't you know why I'm so sure?" he asked softly.

"No. I—"

"This is why," he murmured hoarsely against her cheek, her mouth. "So tell me I'm wrong." But how could she deny his words when, deep inside, she agreed as she opened her lips to his, as she plundered the recesses of his mouth with an urgency that equaled his. At some level she had known—and hoped—he was going to kiss her, and she'd known exactly what he meant by saying he was sure.

And she couldn't ignore that truth. For she was sure too—sure she had never felt such pleasure in a mere kiss, sure that no one's lips had ever felt so right on hers, sure that no one else's softly spoken words could reach her so deeply.

And she knew what making love with him would be like. He'd be powerful and deeply arousing, caring and tender and bold all at the same time. His hands found their way to her knees and gently parted her legs, and began a provocative and achingly slow course upward. She wanted him to stop but she wanted him to go on, melting for the touch she knew he could give. His fingers were as persuasive as his words, suggesting a thousand pleasures with every touch, coaxing her as she had to admit she wanted to be coaxed. With his other hand he began another potent onslaught, finding the fullness of her breasts beneath her blouse and daring them to swell beneath his touch as he swirled around her nipples and teased them to hardness. She was lost in a warm swell of desire that was growing. . . .

But suddenly she was annoyed. It was easy for Gordon to be so smooth, telling her to forget her resolves and think only of the chemistry between them. He *had* what he wanted; he didn't have to concentrate on anything special in his life; he was one of the most successful men in his field. But she was starting out on her own in an almost equally competitive field. And she couldn't afford the kind of emotional distraction Gordon would certainly demand. He would dominate her thoughts and moods and dreams at a time when she had to think of nothing but work. His gain would be her loss, pleasurable as it would seem at the time.

She drew back from his hold and looked up into his stormy dark eyes.

"What's wrong?" he murmured, his gaze searching hers.

"You don't listen," she said quietly.

"*You* don't listen, Laura. To me *or* to yourself."

"That's too easy for you to say, and this is too easy for both of us," she said, straightening up in the seat and smoothing down her dress. "And I'm not playing some kind of teasing game, Gordon. *You* have nothing to lose in this. I do."

"You don't think that being happy could make you more productive in your work? I'm not saying I *could* make you happy; I don't know yet. But it's an idea you don't seem to have considered."

She glanced out the window and saw that they were only a few blocks from her house—which was a relief since she felt more confused than anything else. She was sure her principles were sound. But what force did they have when challenged by something as strong as her attraction to Gordon Chase? And the attraction wasn't just physical, either. She liked his confidence, his enthusiasm, the pleasure he seemed to take in everything he did; and at some level she liked his persistence as well.

"Well, what about it?" he asked, interrupting her thoughts. "Have you ever considered the possibility that feeling good in general—even if that meant some time spent *not* working—might make your work go much better? You'd be happier and your customers would like you better, and they'd tell their friends, who'd also like you, and before you knew it, you'd be rich and famous and successful and happy, all at the same time."

She laughed. "I see a smile behind the serious 'you must listen to what I'm saying' expression."

He grinned. "Well, you're right. But I am serious."

The limo glided to a smooth stop in front of Laura's building.

"I'll talk to you soon, okay?" Laura said.

"Soon? What does that mean?"

"Soon means soon."

He shook his head. "I'm not letting you off that easily. You'll talk to me tomorrow."

She smiled in spite of herself. "All right."

"Oh, and one more thing."

"What's that?"

He pulled her into his arms and kissed her. "That's so you won't forget me."

She gazed into his eyes, feeling as if she never wanted to leave their hold.

"I'll walk you to your apartment door," he offered.

She quickly shook her head. "That's okay. Really."

"Oh, don't be silly," he said, reaching past her and opening the door.

They got out of the limo and walked up to the front steps of the building and he said a quick good night and went back to the limo. Laura turned and watched him drive off as she stood on the front steps of her building.

Had it been earlier in the evening, the stoop would have been filled with people—children, babies, old men and women—most of whom had lived in the building or on the block all their lives. But even now, with the block empty and quiet, Laura wondered what Gordon and his driver must have thought when the limo pulled into a block in the West 80s that was made up almost exclusively of run-down old buildings.

Of course, Gordon hadn't said a word about the building or the neighborhood, but she was sure she knew what he must have been thinking—that it all looked terrible and poor and neglected, that she had to be something of a failure if she still lived in a place like this. People like Gordon Chase were *always* quick to judge, even if they pretended they weren't. She could always sense it even if nothing was said.

As Laura let herself in the building's front door and began walking up the familiar and slightly dirty marble steps that led to her third-floor walk-up, she didn't feel any of the impatience she usually felt when she came home. She wanted to move to a better apartment in a better building, but she also felt some pride at having gotten as far as she had. People like Gordon Chase tended to look on where she lived as some sort of sign of defeat, but they were wrong to assume everyone wanted what they had. Laura was obligated to no one, completely on her own for the first time in her life. Maybe she didn't live on Park Avenue or have a chauffeur-driven limousine; but she was her own woman.

The feeling lasted only a few moments, though. When Laura walked into her apartment, the first thing she saw was a pile of bills on the living room table—none of them paid, all of them too large for her to begin to consider paying any of them in full. She had a certain amount in the bank, but her start-up expenses had been higher than she'd expected, and she had to make the bank money last as long as she could—even if that meant paying twenty or thirty dollars each month on credit-card bills of a thousand dollars and paying much too much in interest.

Gordon Chase obviously never had to worry about paying his bills. Money to him was something to enjoy rather than to worry about, something that was always there when you needed it.

And Laura couldn't help resenting him for that.

But as she sat down at the table and searched for the phone bill, which absolutely *had* to be paid the next day—she suddenly realized it was silly to resent Gordon. He had done nothing wrong; in fact, he had tried to help her in every way possible with her business.

It wasn't Gordon she resented; it was the situation she had created for herself. In her strong desire to be free, to set herself up in a business that would depend only on her abilities and good fortune, she had pretended she was much more confident than she really was. She had decided that with enough savings to live on for six months, she would have enough time to set up and run her business properly. But she hadn't counted on the fear and uncertainty, both of which made the money in the bank seem like something that she simply couldn't afford to touch.

She found the phone bill and reluctantly wrote out a check, promising herself that next month she wouldn't spend so much on long-distance calls.

And she went to bed so worried about her finances that she didn't think about Gordon at all.

The next morning Laura just managed to pull herself out of a dream in which she had been evicted by her landlord and given a terrible write-up in *West Side Living* magazine. When she woke up, she was sweating and her heart was pounding, and she sat up and stared at the clock: 5:00 A.M., and she'd never get back to sleep. Not with her heart like a drum in her chest. And not with the worries she had.

And she knew one thing with certainty: She had to take Gordon up on his offer of the network makeup job. Turning him down had been an act of utter stubbornness and conceit. For while it was true that being tied down at that hour was inconvenient, it was *also* true that at this point the job wouldn't be keeping her from anything better. And the money would be good; the union saw to that.

At nine fifteen on the dot she called Gordon's office and was connected with him quickly.

She could sense the smile on his face as he said, "Good morning! I thought *I* was going to have to call you!"

"Well, I didn't want to be predictably stubborn, since that seems to be what you think I am. And I also wanted to talk to you about something. I'd like to take you up on your offer about the makeup job."

There was a pause, and for a moment she thought he hadn't even been listening. But then he said, "Are you sure?"

"Yes. I gave it a lot of thought this morning."

"What made you change your mind?" he asked. There was an odd note of caution in his voice that she couldn't quite figure out.

"Well, money, actually. It's all well and good for me to say that I can't afford the time, but when I'm looking down at a nearly empty calendar in the weeks ahead, the picture changes."

"Hmmm."

"Is there anything wrong?" she asked. "You don't sound particularly enthusiastic."

"I know you won't be staying with the network long. Not when your business picks up."

"That's true," she said. "Is that a big problem?"

"No, no, whatever's good for you," he said musingly. Now that she had asked, he saw that that wasn't the problem at all. He wanted Laura around, whether it was going to be for a minute or a month or a year. If only he hadn't heard that damn rumor this morning about Jerry Manning. . . . "Actually," he continued, "it doesn't have anything to do with you at all, Laura. The minute I got in this morning, I heard some bad news—that's all."

"Is it serious?" she asked quickly. "Is it something I can help you with?"

"It's nothing personal—just an ugly rumor I heard about someone at the network. I'll tell you about it when I see you, if you come early."

"I will."

"Great. I'll tell my secretary you're coming, then. And, Laura, even if I didn't sound it before, I'm very glad you're coming on board even if it's just for a short time. For what should be obvious personal reasons as well as professional ones."

She smiled. "Good. I'll see you later."

And she was indeed looking forward to seeing him, even admitting to herself that she *was* playing something of a game by saying she didn't want to become involved with him.

But when she walked into his office at three, Gordon hardly seemed happy to see her. He looked furious and utterly distracted as he paced the length of his office.

"What's the matter?" she asked, coming over to where he had stopped by the window. "Is it the same problem as this morning?"

"Yes, but it's worse than I'd thought. It's . . . it's just so damn seamy." He clenched his jaw as he looked out over the skyline, then turned to Laura and sighed. "I've been at this network for a year now, and in the business for almost ten years, and I don't have any illusions about what goes on. Show business has a way of attracting some pretty sleazy types. But that doesn't mean I have to have them working for me. And one of them apparently is."

"What happened?" Laura asked.

"We don't know for sure and I haven't yet figured out exactly how we're going to find out. But as it stands now, it looks as if this young man in the Sales department, whose only job is supposed to be assisting his boss to sell spots, has a very unattractive sideline as some sort of agent. Apparently he's made certain promises he couldn't possibly keep, and he might have even taken some money from at least a few innocent people."

"You means he's promised people acting jobs?"

Gordon nodded. "That's what the rumor is."

"*Does* he have pull?"

"Well, anyone at the network who's at a high enough level does have a certain amount of pull, yes. You see, networks, even though certain people don't like to admit it, have a tremendous amount of power when it comes to casting. In fact, we have the ultimate power, because we can simply say we won't buy a pilot, or that we won't go to series after a pilot has done well, unless we get actors of our liking to star in it. But someone on Jerry Manning's level doesn't have that kind of power. And if he's using the network's name in some kind of scam, I damn well want to know about it."

"How are you going to look into it?" Laura asked.

He shook his head. "I really don't know. Stu Whelan, his supervisor, spoke to him about it, and he denied it."

"Just like that?"

"Oh, he had some story. This guy always does, from what I hear. He said the rumor must have come from a girl he had just broken up with. Hell, maybe it did. But I'm going to check into it anyway. He's too damn fast-talking for this network anyway, in my opinion. But you don't fire someone for being fast-talking, especially when they're a damn good sales assistant." He sighed. "But all this doesn't have anything to do with you," he said softly, taking her in his arms.

She smiled. "Aren't you forgetting something?"

"What?"

"Our discussion last night."

He nodded. "I have. I've forgotten everything except this," he whispered, brushing his lips against hers. "And your beautiful eyes, and that great laugh, and a woman I'll do anything to get to know better."

She smiled. "You remember an awful lot for such a forgetful man."

"What I've forgotten, I've chosen to forget. But I'll never forget this." He lowered his mouth to hers, and she reacted the only way she knew how to react to this man who exerted such a powerful physical influence over her. She welcomed him, tasting his tongue, his lips, imagining as he rubbed his rough jaw against hers, as his breathing quickened, as he grasped her more fully, what it would be like to be naked against his lean form, to feel his male nipples harden beneath her touch, to feel his thighs and hips urge her on, to feel him explode inside her with thrusting strokes of pure satisfaction.

As she caught a glimpse of his eyes, heavy-lidded and

dark brown, she wondered how she'd ever thought she could resist them. There was a connection that flowed from him to her every time their eyes met, and the connection always heated and burst into flame on a level that was beyond reason or logic.

And deep down, she had known she wouldn't be able to resist those eyes.

"Tell me you've changed your mind," he said softly. "Tell me what your lips have already told me." He grinned. "I love that sly smile of yours," he said. "Just one corner of your mouth, as if you don't think you're really smiling."

"Am I?" she teased.

"That looks like a smile to me, which sounds like a yes that you've changed your mind."

She didn't want to talk about them, about her feelings, about anything so complicated, and her mind grasped for an idea, an answer, something she could say that would get her away from that dangerous subject he kept harping on.

"I have an idea," she said.

He raised a brow. "Go on."

"It's about the Jerry Manning thing."

His smile faded. "I thought we were talking about us."

"I don't want to talk about us. Don't you want to hear my idea?"

"I don't think I have any choice," he said with a sigh. "Although a man could get an inferiority complex if he thought your mind was always on other things when he was kissing you."

"Believe me, I wasn't thinking about Jerry Manning when I was kissing you. But something made me think of this: I know how I can help you."

"All right," he said, sounding less than fully interested. "How?"

"Well, I could pretend to be an aspiring actress. I could ask Jerry Manning for help."

He shook his head. "That would never work. People are beginning to know you around here from yesterday alone. If you're going to be doing the news team's makeup—"

"Which is the key word," she cut in. "Makeup, Gordon. I can make myself look like a totally different person when I want to. I mean so different that *you* wouldn't even recognize me."

He smiled. "This is beginning to sound pretty interesting," he said. "Although I'd have to give it a lot of thought. But tell me—just speaking hypothetically: if we went ahead, how would you contact him? You can't just look him up in the phone book and call him at home. He'd wonder where you had gotten his name."

"Why couldn't I meet him here?" she asked. "I could bump into him. . . ." She frowned. "No, that wouldn't be any good, because how would I know he was an agent or a pseudo-agent or whatever he is?" Her face lit up. "Unless I pretended I *didn't* know."

"I don't understand."

"Look. Let's say I was working here—pretending to work here as something other than a makeup artist—as a secretary or a receptionist or something I could passably pretend to be. Then I could just conveniently tell Jerry Manning, if I got to know him, that I wasn't *really* a secretary or a receptionist, that I was really an aspiring actress but having no luck at all—"

"And you'd let *him* mention his work," Gordon finished.

"Exactly."

"Can you type?" he asked.

"Sixty-five words a minute. I was a temp at about a hundred companies when I first came to New York. I was a secretary before I even got my cosmetician's license."

Gordon said nothing.

"What's the matter?" she asked.

"I'm just thinking," he mused. "If you were an employee of the company, there'd be a good chance you'd *know* Manning didn't have the power he says he does."

"So I could be a temp," she said easily. "Here for a few days and then gone forever."

"You should have been a detective," Gordon said with a smile.

"Oh, I love my work too much. But it's something I've always been interested in."

"And you'd do all that for me?"

"Are you kidding? I'd love to. My only question about the idea was whether you'd let me do it."

"I'd want you to do anything that would keep you near me," he said. "But there *is* a problem: your safety."

"Oh, come—"

"I mean it," he cut in. "How do we know it's safe?"

"How do we know anything's safe?" she asked. "I could walk out of this office and get hit by a car this afternoon, Gordon. You never really know. But I do know how to take care of myself."

"I really don't know—"

"Come on," she insisted. "We'll talk about everything I'm going to do and everything I'm going to talk about with him, so I really don't think there should be a problem. And I don't want to do anything dangerous any more than you do."

He sighed. "Well, I suppose. As long as you agree you might have to pull out sooner than you want. If I hear *anything* risky is going on—"

"I agree, I agree."

He smiled. "All right. But only on one condition: You come out to dinner again with me tonight."

"That's blackmail," she said with a smile.

"It's only fair. You get what you want, I get what I want."

And as he took her in his arms once again, Laura wondered what had happened to her resolve. What was generally considered an iron will was the anchor of her life, something that allowed her to trust in her instincts and move ahead in the face of uncertainty. And she knew that going out to dinner with Gordon Chase was absolutely minor in the context of her life—even in the context of a week. Yet it bothered her that she felt almost as if she were in a trance, as if she simply couldn't say no to this magnetic man. He was a man she knew little about, yet she couldn't help being powerfully attracted to him emotionally as well as physically.

He made her forget her troubles, he set her sense of adventure free without even being aware of what he was doing, he made her feel alive and pretty and liked, and he made her feel unpredictable with the flashes of surprise and pleasure she sometimes saw in his eyes.

Damn it, she liked him. In the two short days she had known him, she had resented him for all sorts of things. But the fact was that she liked him. And she wanted him. And as she gazed up into his eyes, she knew the famous will of iron that her friends kidded her about was melting fast, too quickly to control in any way.

CHAPTER FOUR

"I hear you did a beautiful job this afternoon with Sandra and Jocelyn," Gordon said as he sipped an after-dinner brandy.

"Mmmm. Thanks. I found out something interesting too. Victor Marcel is having an affair with Jocelyn Croft."

Gordon stared. "That's why he was making Sandra look like hell, then."

"That's what I assume. But you can't prove that."

"I can thank God I fired his butt, though. What kind of unprofessional crap is that?"

"Well, he may be unprofessional, but I don't think Jocelyn realized what he was doing."

"Damn it, that woman gets paid too damn much money to—"

"I really don't think she knew," Laura cut in. "I heard about the relationship through Angela Vandenberg, the hair stylist. And she was just speculating. Anyway, Victor's gone, so—"

"Why are you jumping to his defense?" Gordon asked.

"I'm not jumping to anyone's defense. I just don't like seeing people accused of things they haven't necessarily done. I was once fired from a waitress job on Fourteenth

Street because the boss swore I had taken thirty-six dollars from the cash register."

"And he didn't believe you when you denied it?"

"Nope. I was the girl from a rural pocket in Connecticut who nobody knew, just arrived in the city and desperate for work, and they knew I needed the money. I hadn't even gotten work as a temp yet then. Anyway, there was no way I could convince my boss that he was wrong."

"But you didn't rise to Jerry Manning's defense," Gordon pointed out. "I'm accusing *him* of something he may or may not have done."

"Well, that's true," Laura admitted, "but it sounds like it would be really interesting to look into. And anyway, he's someone who might be hurting other people. I think that falls into a special category. Innocent young actors and actresses who are led on by some con artist—I don't like that and I'd love to have a hand in stopping it. What are you smiling at?"

Gordon covered her hand with his. "You," he said softly. "You're always looking out for the underdog. Crusading. You're so different from other women I've known."

"Oh, come on. I'm not that much of a crusader. You just happen to have caught me at a certain moment."

He shook his head. "No, that's not it, Laura. Most of the women I've gone out with—ever since high school, actually—have been from the same background. Christmas in Palm Beach or Switzerland, summers in the south of France, the right schools and apartments and jobs and clothes. But with all that privilege usually comes a definite arrogance. They can do their Junior League activities, playing Lady Bountiful to those 'less fortunate' than they are, but I promise you that most of them think it's only right they're in that position, giving to people they really think aren't as good as they are."

"It sounds as if they *never* appealed to you, Gordon!"

"No, no, they did, until recently. But you're different," he said softly, squeezing her hand.

Laura smiled, but suddenly she had the unpleasant feeling that she was an example to him, a symbol of an idea he had about what sort of woman he could be interested in.

And later on, when Gordon brought her back to her building, she had the same feeling as he came upstairs with her and complimented her on the building. "These old places are great," he said as they started up the last flight of stairs. "I'll bet you know everyone in the building."

"I do," she said quietly. "But you really don't have to search for compliments, Gordon. I know what this place is, what it must look like to you."

"What do you think it looks like?"

"It's just an old broken-down brownstone. Not exactly the kind of place you shower with compliments." She unlocked her door and flicked the light on, and she started to turn to face Gordon.

But he finished the turn for her, taking her by the shoulders and holding her tightly. "I want you to listen to me," he warned, "and to understand me. I've never said anything to you that I don't mean and mean a hundred percent. If I tell you I like something about you or your life, you can't tell me I'm lying. And if you think there's a problem in terms of our backgrounds, Laura, that's a problem that's in *your* mind—not in mine."

"I don't think so," she said, wresting her shoulders

from his grasp. She stalked into the living room. "Do you want a drink?" she called.

"Sure. Scotch if you have it," he said, following her in.

She poured out two glasses and handed him one without looking up.

"Tell me what's wrong," he said softly.

"I've told you. I feel as if I'm part of some plan of yours, or some philosophy or idea that says 'women of a different background have to be better than the women I've been seeing.' Something like that."

"But you *are* different," he insisted, walking with her to the couch. "Every time I think I'm getting to know you, you surprise me. And every surprise is nicer than the last. What's so terrible about that? You're refreshing, Laura. But you're not a symbol." He took her glass from her hand and set it on the table. "If you could see through my eyes instead of your own, if you could see you and hear you and know what you are to me, you wouldn't question anything. And I can't stop thinking about you."

He reached out and cradled her cheek in a warm hand, then drew her into a kiss that deepened quickly, drawing her faster and faster into a pleasure that was satisfying but tantalizing as well. Every time he gently edged her lips with his teeth, she knew what that kind of teasing would feel like against the sensitive skin of her thighs, the tingling tips of her nipples, and she wanted him; every time his tongue danced with hers, she wanted him inside her, his virile strength stroking and bringing her closer and closer to ecstasy; and as his fingers found her breasts through the silk of her blouse, a small cry escaped her and he claimed her mouth with his once again. His tongue promised endless pleasure, endless passion, and his quick, teasing fingers sent urgent messages of need to the warm center of her soul.

"Let's make love," he whispered into her ear, giving small, wet nips to the tip of her earlobe, teasing with his warm tongue. "I want you so much, Laura."

"I—no—I can't," she murmured, amazed that those words had come out. She was melting beneath his touch, swept up in the heat of an embrace that seemed like fantasy come alive, and she had thought her will was gone, that when she was in Gordon's arms, thoughts were impossible. But she had been wrong.

"What's the matter?" he asked, drawing away and stroking her honey-blond hair back from the fair skin of her forehead.

"I'm just not ready," she said quietly. "I want to, but I'd be really annoyed with myself if I did."

"Because we don't know each other well enough," he supplied.

"That's it."

"But this isn't good-bye," Gordon said half questioningly. "I really will understand, Laura, as long as you tell me this isn't good-bye."

She smiled as he tenderly ran his fingers through her hair. "No, it isn't good-bye. I promise you that. And anyway, you *have* to see me at the network, whether you like it or not."

"That's right. You're our new temp in Programming."

"I still don't know how you arranged things without anyone noticing."

"Oh, there are a *few* good people I can trust at the network," he said with a wink. "When I ask them to put the daughter of a friend of a friend in the Programming department for a few days and that department has a secretary who was just promoted anyway, it doesn't raise any eyebrows. Believe me."

"I'm supposed to be the daughter of a friend of yours?" she asked with a frown. "You didn't tell me that. Why didn't you tell me that? Whose daughter?"

"Don't get so excited. You don't have to know that. This was a conversation that's never going to go anywhere, between me and one of my most trusted Personnel people. As far as everyone else is concerned, the company has you in its temp floater program, and that's all anyone will know or think about."

"Is there anything else you haven't told me?"

"Well, your name is Laura Hoover—"

"Laura? Why am I still Laura?" she cut in.

"Because Laura is a common enough name that no one's going to think anything about it—and I want you to answer if someone calls your name. In the position you'll be in, a lot of people will be asking for you and I don't want any hesitation."

"I guess that makes sense. What about Hoover?"

Gordon smiled. "It was late in the day and one of the cleaning women was vacuuming down the hall. Just be glad she wasn't using a Eureka."

Laura laughed. "You're a nut."

"No, just enjoying this little plan."

"Well, I am too," she said, "but I don't think I have quite as much confidence as you seem to. All these things you haven't told me. Is there anything else? Like where I come from, or what my experience is?"

He shook his head. "You are a suspicious young woman," he said with a smile. "Suspicious but extremely lovely and extremely distracting. What was it that you wanted to know?"

"Come on. You know—is there anything else you haven't told me?"

"No, there isn't. But if you're getting nervous—"

"I'm not. I really can't wait. The only thing that might be a little difficult is changing my appearance at the end of the day for when I do the news team's makeup. I think I should leave the building and come back."

He smiled. "I can't wait to see."

The next day Laura surprised even herself at the transformation she had engineered. The pretty young woman with flashing blue-green eyes and honey-blond hair that fell softly to her shoulders was gone, replaced by someone with a ponytail and almost no makeup, and bangs held back by a barrette. She looked much as she had in high school. She dressed differently, too—in a slightly younger fashion, with clothes she had been meaning to give away for months: pants that were just a little too tight, a plaid shirt she hadn't worn in years, and shoes with heels she felt were too high for the outfit. And she looked younger, taller, and altogether different when she walked into the offices of CTC Television and reported in as Laura Hoover at the Office of Personnel in order to be processed. This was the part that Laura felt would be more nerve-racking than anything else, because she'd have to give a false social security number and false biographical information.

But the young woman who took down the information was so condescending and supercilious that Laura took great pleasure in giving her false information.

"You do realize this is a trial period," the young woman—named Ms. Plunkett, according to a plaque on her desk—said with a threat in her voice.

"Yes, of course," Laura said.

Ms. Plunkett shook her head. "Your experience is much lighter than that of most participants in the program," she warned. "You know, it isn't just a matter of being able to type, Miss Hoover. There's a certain amount of comprehension involved. You have to concentrate and stay alert."

"I *have* been a secretary before."

Ms. Plunkett shot her a triumphant glance as she looked up from her résumé. "Yet you've never held a permanent position."

"I haven't wanted to."

Ms. Plunkett blinked and closed the folder. "Well. You're already late, and Mr. Wakefield won't like that a bit. Twenty-eighth floor, Suite 2832."

Laura rose. "All right, I'm on my way. And if Mr. Wakefield says anything about my lateness, I'll just explain I was talking to you." She flashed a smile, turned, and left.

She would be working in Programming, right next door to Sales—the department Jerry Manning worked in —and if all went as expected, there would be ample opportunity to meet when the coffee cart came around or when Laura was delivering memos.

But when Laura stepped out of the elevator at the twenty-eighth floor, she realized she had her work cut out for her in terms of just meeting Jerry Manning. Gordon had told her where Manning's desk was, but it all looked like a maze. She walked down a gray-carpeted hallway and found Suite 2832, a vast area with dozens of desks, and she walked up to a large one at the front of the room, where a receptionist greeted her and showed her to her desk. She handed Laura an enormous pile of folders that had to be filed and said Laura would meet Mr.

Wakefield later. And then Laura was left alone with her work, feeling not at all like someone playing a part and very much like a temp—boredom making her sleepy as she looked at the giant pile of memos that had to be filed.

She worked through the morning, filing and taking messages for Mr. Wakefield, whom she met midmorning and liked well enough, but she was impatient about getting on with the real reason she was there: meeting Jerry Manning.

In the afternoon she typed over a dozen memos, and, annoyingly, all she had to do was put them in her Out box and a mail boy came to pick them up and distribute them. Finally, though, she typed a memo that Mr. Wakefield wanted her to deliver by hand to Jerry Manning's supervisor, and she decided to speed things up a little by making a detour past Jerry Manning's desk.

Gordon had described Manning as a dark-haired, good-looking young man, well built with a short, trimmed beard and mustache and green eyes, and Laura spotted a man who fit his description at the far end of the room, just as Gordon had said. She passed him once and then circled back to his desk and hovered nearby, as if lost.

Manning looked up immediately, and his eyes told Laura he liked what he was seeing.

Laura smiled. "Sorry to bother you, but can you help me? I'm looking for Stu Whelan's office."

Manning smiled. "This must be your first day," he said in a voice that was low-pitched and surprisingly seductive.

Laura looked surprised. "Yes, it is. Why? Did I walk past a huge sign that says Stu Whelan?"

"No, no, nothing like that. Just that I would've noticed you if you'd ever been here before. Where're you from?"

"Uh, Connecticut."

"I mean in the company." He bent her memo toward him and then looked up at her. "Wakefield's new secretary, huh?"

"No, I'm just a temp."

"Floater program?"

"Well, yes," she said, and she lowered her voice. "But actually that was just a quick way to get work. My agency didn't have anything for me and a friend told me about the floater program, but I'm really not interested in staying too long."

"Why not? It's a great place to work. Great people, great vibes—"

"I can't tie myself down like that. I need to be free to go to auditions—something even my *agency* doesn't always understand—but that's just the way it's going to have to be."

"You're an actress?"

She smiled her shyest smile. "A hopeful actress is more like it. An aspiring actress, I guess you could say."

He stood up. "Hey, listen, you better get this memo to Whelan," he said, putting an arm around her shoulder. "His secretary's right down that hall, the first in the row —red hair, green eyes. And come back to my desk after, okay? We'll talk more about your acting."

"Okay. See you in a minute."

She walked down the corridor and handed the memo to Stu Whelan's secretary, a young woman who gave her a penetrating and hostile stare she didn't understand.

But she forgot about it a few moments later as she

walked back toward Jerry Manning and marveled at how smoothly things had begun to fall into place.

When she reached his desk, he stood up and began walking slowly toward the reception area. "So tell me," he said quietly. "What kind of jobs have you been getting? Acting jobs, I mean."

"None," she said glumly. "I had one call-back for a commercial, but that was eight months ago."

"You mean even with your knock-out looks you haven't been in anything?"

She smiled. "Thanks. And, no, I haven't." She looked at her watch. "But, listen, if I don't get back to my desk now, Mr. Wakefield's going to think I got totally lost. Nice meeting you."

"You don't even know my name."

"Oh, that's right. What *is* your name?" she asked innocently. *Careful,* she warned herself. *You almost blew it.*

"Jerry Manning. And I'll be seeing you again, Lisa."

"Laura."

"Ah. It said *lh* at the bottom of the memo. Lisa was my best shot. See you later, Laur," he called out, and sauntered back toward his desk.

Laura couldn't help watching—which she was sure he probably expected her to do anyway. His walk was a swagger, a predatory and proud gait that bragged to all the world of his prowess, and Laura smiled and shook her head. She had forced herself to act very young with Jerry Manning because that was the only way she could make herself believable. And it had worked.

At the end of the afternoon Laura looked up as she sensed someone approaching. As she had suspected, it was Jerry Manning—smiling and looking very pleased about something.

"Hey, Laur. Almost five o'clock. Which means it's almost happy hour down at Easton's."

"Where's that?"

"Over on Fifty-fifth. You'll like it. Theater types hang out there mostly. Agents, producers, you name it."

"Gee. That sounds interesting."

"So how about it?"

"Today, you mean?"

"Yeah, today. Why not today? No time like the present, I always say."

"Gee, I can't, Jerry. Sorry, though, because I'd like to go. Do you go there a lot?"

"Sure, sure. It's kind of a network hangout. You know."

She bit her lip. "I'd like to, but—"

He spread his hands. "Hey, what could be so great that you have to go somewhere else, huh? What is it? A boyfriend? Is that it?"

"No, just . . . something else." *Damn,* she thought. *I should have said I have a boyfriend.*

"So what is it? Another job?"

"No, I have to, uh, meet a girl friend of mine. She works over at Bloomingdale's. Selling gloves."

"So bring her along."

She smiled. "Another time maybe. Okay?"

"Yeah, sure," he said quickly. He gave a light tap to her desk with his fist, then turned and left without another word. And this time his walk was quick and strained.

A few minutes later Laura left the office, went to a large coffee shop in the lobby, redid her makeup and changed clothes in the cramped and dirty ladies' room, and headed back for the office. *You'd better speed up your progress with Jerry Manning,* she warned herself. The quick change in the bathroom was not a routine she wanted to repeat too many more times.

But the change of identities really was fun. Walking back into CTC headquarters, she felt like Laura Dawson once again, amazed that the character of Laura Hoover had actually taken over for the day.

When she had just finished Sandra Strachan's makeup, Gordon appeared at the edge of the studio, smiling and gazing at her with obvious appreciation. And as she approached him, he didn't take his eyes off her once.

"Every time I see you, you're prettier than the last time," he murmured, gazing into her eyes. "Why didn't you show me your Laura Hoover outfit?"

"Shhh."

"No one can hear," he said, taking her elbow and leading her into the shadows behind some large dusty backdrops. "Hmmm? Why didn't you come see me?" he asked, taking her in his arms. Fighting a smile, he traced feathery circles at the open neckline of her dress. "You look awfully kissable right now," he said hoarsely, his fingers making daring forays across her satiny skin.

"You're crazy," she whispered. "We're in the studio. Someone's going to see us."

"No, they won't. And if they do, so what?"

"Don't you care?"

The heat of his embrace, his thighs against hers, told her he had other things on his mind, and his voice was raspy as he said, "I don't care about anything but being with you—looking into your eyes, touching you, knowing you're close, hearing your voice. And see, you can't help smiling. I know you're trying not to."

"How do you know that?" she teased.

"Because that's the contrary and stubborn Laura Dawson I'm just beginning to understand."

She smiled. "Then how do you explain the smile?"

"Very simply. You're beginning to like me in spite of yourself. Against all your instincts and all your wishes, you just can't help it." She laughed. "Which is just fine with me because I'm going to keep trying and trying and trying until the only answer you'll have, to anything I might ask you, will be yes."

"Sounds interesting but unlikely."

"Oh, we'll see. We'll see. The best I can do is try. But one thing I came to tell you was that I couldn't see you tonight. I have a couple of meetings and I don't know how late they're going to run."

"Ah, the old late-meetings routine."

"If you want to have a late date . . ."

She smiled. "No, I'm just kidding. All this changing of personalities has actually been really tiring. I had *myself* believing I was an aspiring actress. And I acted a lot younger than I hope I usually act, and somehow that put a real strain on me."

"So you've met Manning already?"

"Met him! I practically ran off with him—or would have if he had gotten his way. It was incredibly easy."

"Too easy, do you mean?" Gordon asked with concern. "Do you think he suspected anything?"

She shook her head. "Absolutely not. He's so wrapped up in himself he wouldn't have noticed if I had come out and *told* him he was being investigated. He's completely unaware of anything but himself."

"Laura, you know I don't want to put you in any kind of jeopardy."

"Don't be silly. I told him I couldn't meet with him

this evening because I had to meet a girl friend, but I'm sure I can go out to lunch with him tomorrow."

"It's happening too quickly," Gordon said, concern lacing his voice. "I'd thought this would all take much longer. I didn't even think you'd get this far."

"Leave it to a pro and you get a professional job," she said with a smile.

"Laura, I'm serious," he said.

"So am I," she insisted. "Why did we start this if we're not going to go through with it? I thought you wanted to find out about this guy."

"I do—but not at your expense."

"I promise there's nothing to worry about. Just lighten up and don't worry. I'm enjoying it and it's a nice distraction from my other work."

"Well, we'll see," Gordon said, unconvinced. "There are other kinds of distractions, anyway. And other things you should be concentrating on. Which reminds me," he said, brightening. "I have what might be an interesting job for you." He reached into his pocket and took out his wallet, extracting an ivory-colored business card. "Here. Call this woman."

Laura took the card and read it. "Countess Luciana Rafaella di Lomazzo, 765 Park Avenue, New York, New York, (212) 555-9933." She looked up at Gordon. "Who is she?"

"A friend of mine. And a future customer of yours. Someone who can introduce you to literally dozens of other customers."

"Really! You've already told her about me, then?"

He smiled. "I had to be careful about what I was saying, actually. I was about to say that you could create miracles, that makeup was like magic in your hands, but

I realized just in time that she might not appreciate the suggestion she needs a miracle-worker."

Laura smiled. "Good point. *Does* she need a miracle-worker, though? How old is she?"

"No one knows. I've seen her look sixty and I've seen her look forty-five. I really have no idea. But call her."

"Thanks. I will."

Gordon raised a brow. "No arguments? No complaints? I thought I'd at least hear a diatribe about *something*. And I have a complaint of my own, actually."

"What's that?"

"I'm not going to be able to see you enough in the next few days. I have those meetings tonight and maybe tomorrow night, depending on how things go. We can try for tomorrow night if you're free, but I just don't know my schedule yet."

For a moment she said nothing as she looked into his eyes and thought about what he had just said. He seemed so intent on seeing a lot of her—as often as he could and as much as he could. She found it amazing that this handsome and attractive man seemed so intent on forging ahead.

"Then I'll see you tomorrow or maybe the next night," she said.

"Is something wrong?" he asked softly.

"No. Why?"

"You suddenly looked so worried."

She smiled. "If I did, it was nothing."

"Promise?"

"I promise."

He grinned. "You know what? Little by little I think I'm chipping away at your contrariness—an edge here, a corner there."

"What if I don't *want* to change?" she teased. "I *like* being contrary."

"I like you better when you're saying yes," he murmured, his gaze holding hers. "I just wish I didn't have to rush off. But I'll tell you what. At some point tomorrow, I'm going to stop by Wakefield's office and get a look at you. I want to see you as Laura Hoover."

She smiled. "Just don't look me in the eyes. I know I'd laugh."

"I love to hear you laugh," he said softly, gently stroking her hair. "But I understand. And now, you or I or both of us will be missed in a few minutes, so I'll say good-bye."

And he kissed her quickly, temptingly, on the lips and then left.

Laura sighed as she watched him slip out the studio door. It felt as if she had thrown away her resolve weeks ago, when in fact it had only been a few days. She had sworn she wouldn't get involved with anyone until her career was much more solidly launched; but Gordon had thus far been instrumental in getting her started. Yet, now that she was getting involved with him, she felt the other reasons more clearly. Gordon was so much like Matthew in so many ways. Wouldn't he in the end resemble him in bad ways as well as good? Matthew had seemed wonderful at first; the excitement over being together had hidden so much; but finally from beneath all his other feelings, the truth had come out: He didn't respect Laura, and that lack of respect was shared by most of his friends. And consciously or unconsciously, he had sabotaged her in all sorts of ways.

Would Gordon turn out to be the same?

"Makeup!" a voice called.

Laura walked back out onto the set as the broadcast broke for a commercial. She focused her thoughts back on her job: Sandra definitely needed more blusher and new lipstick, and Jocelyn needed blotting. And for the moment, that was all that mattered.

That night Laura got a call from Selena Johnson, her oldest friend in the city, and the two went out for dinner at an Indian restaurant around the corner from Laura's apartment.

Selena was amazed when Laura told her about Gordon. "Gordon Chase!" she gasped. "That's like going out with a star, Laura."

"He's not that famous," Laura objected. "I didn't even know who he was until Robert told me."

"That's just *you,*" Selena said. "The way you didn't know what a securities analyst was until you met Matthew."

Laura shrugged. "Why should I have? I'm not a stock-market follower. Something Matthew never failed to remind me of every day of the week."

"Oh, come on," Selena objected.

"I'm not kidding," Laura said. "He really felt I didn't know anything about 'the important things in life,' the important things for him being the stock market, racquetball, and who was giving the best parties at the newest clubs. Oh, and whatever was approved by *New York* magazine, the only thing he ever read except *The Wall Street Journal.*"

Selena laughed. "Ah, such fond memories you have."

"I wish they could just be memories," Laura said. "I can't help feeling Gordon's going to turn out to be the same type."

"Why? Just because he's successful?"

"It's hard to explain," Laura said. "Matthew always *said* he wanted me to have a career, but he was actually very ambivalent about it. He was definitely embarrassed that I hadn't gone to college, since everyone he knew—or almost everyone—had gone to Ivy League schools and then on to get their MBA's or law degrees. And because he was ashamed of what I did—he thought being a makeup artist was frivolous—he'd do all sorts of things to short-circuit me and basically sabotage me."

"Is Gordon like that?"

"Gordon seems to be the opposite. He's done nothing but help me since I met him. In fact, he's the most positive person I've ever met."

Selena raised a brow. "I really don't know what you're complaining about, Laura. He sounds great. And you've only known him a few days—so what are you worried about?"

Laura sighed. "I guess I'm just looking for problems," she said quietly. "Maybe that's the biggest problem of all." For she was indeed afraid—that things were moving too quickly with Gordon, that her fears and resolves just weren't strong enough to hold her back from being with him.

"Don't be such a pessimist," Selena said, interrupting her friend's thoughts. "You might just find he's as good as he seems."

Laura laughed. "Wouldn't that be a miracle." But deep down she was sure that could never be true.

CHAPTER FIVE

The next day Jerry Manning found Laura on the coffee line and followed her back toward her desk.

"So how was your girl friend?" he asked, swaggering along beside her as she carefully carried her own and Mr. Wakefield's coffee back toward the department.

"Oh, fine," she answered noncommittally, reminding herself that she was supposed to be nice to Jerry. "Except that she kind of depressed me."

"Oh, yeah? Why's that?" He sounded curious but also pleased.

"She just got a part in a commercial that's almost definitely going to go national."

He stopped. "I thought you said she was some kind of salesgirl. Shoes or something."

"She is," Laura said quickly. "Gloves. But she's like me. Her job's just something to pay the rent. And she's probably going to quit any day."

"So is she really beautiful, or what?" Jerry asked, rocking back and forth on his heels. "I mean, how'd she do it?"

Laura shrugged. "She went to about a thousand auditions, which is what I should be doing instead of carrying coffee."

He reached out and tapped her shoulder. "I gotta go.

But we'll talk at lunch. Twelve thirty, the lobby." He started to saunter off, thumbs hooked in his pockets.

"What?" Laura called.

He spun around. "Hey, you can't be meeting your girl friend *again,* right? I've got some advice for you, kid. Twelve thirty." And he walked off.

Laura shook her head. He certainly wasn't suffering from a lack of confidence. But it was making her work easier in so many ways that she couldn't complain. After all, she was pretending to be Laura Hoover when she was with him, and talking with him just plunged her more deeply into her role.

At twelve thirty Laura went downstairs and waited by the network reception area. The lobby was crowded, with employees, messengers, and visitors lining up for a tour of the network creating a crush of solid people. Suddenly, Laura saw a familiar face in the crowd; it was Gordon, walking with two men as they left the elevators that went straight to the executive suites. For a moment Gordon glanced at Laura, and she looked back with a smile, forgetting that she was made up and dressed as Laura Hoover. But just as she started to raise her hand in a wave, she remembered. And Gordon had already looked away.

She had been nothing to him. He hadn't even recognized her eyes.

It was a strange and unsettling—and disappointing—feeling, though she knew it wasn't rational. She *was* an excellent makeup artist—people called her a magician—and she wouldn't have expected Gordon to recognize her, especially in a crowded lobby when he wasn't looking for her or expecting to see her. But the incident had given her the sensation of being unseen, anonymous, a feeling she had always hated until she had made herself into the type of woman people *would* look twice at. Gordon was like many other men, someone who would look again at a woman only if she was very, very pretty. And there was nothing so terrible about that—she herself was more interested in good-looking men than in plain ones. But somehow, and for some reason, the incident was disturbing.

"Hey," said a soft male voice at her shoulder.

She turned. Jerry Manning flashed her a smile. "Ready?" he asked.

"Sure."

He gave her a wink. "I think you're going to find our lunch more than just enjoyable, Laura."

"Oh, really?"

"First of all, I'm taking you to Wesley's. Ever been?"

She shook her head. "Is that another place where all the network people hang out?"

"What? Oh, yeah. Yeah, sure," he said, leading her quickly through the lobby and out onto Sixth Avenue.

They turned south, and Laura noticed as she looked up at Jerry, his hair blowing in the springtime breeze, that he seemed to be genuinely enjoying himself. Other people she had met who were borderline con artists—employment agents and real-estate agents among them—had all been so worn-out and negative and obviously hard-bitten, completely cynical about their jobs and themselves. But Jerry Manning seemed so up and so positive that she found it slightly difficult to believe he was as terrible as Gordon had made him out to be. But then she reminded herself that he had apparently taken money—a lot of it—from a lot of people. Which meant that no matter what his manner was, if the accusations were true, he was someone she'd do well to help put out of his little business.

Wesley's was the kind of place Laura had been to dozens of times in dozens of parts of the city—plants hanging in the windows, a dark wood interior, a menu that specialized in quiche, burgers, and salads; and from what she could see, the lunchtime crowd looked as if it were more heavily represented by female shoppers lunching in midtown than "network types," as Jerry had put it. But as Laura Hoover, she reminded herself, what did she know?

"This place is great," Laura said, sliding into a booth. "Do you see anyone you know?"

Jerry glanced around the room and then looked at his watch. "Nah. But you know those network guys. They take their lunches later than this."

Laura shrugged. "I wouldn't know, but I believe you. I know when I worked in advertising for a while, half those guys went out to lunch for three or four hours a day. Only it wasn't always lunch."

Jerry laughed. "Yeah, those guys. What a life. So listen, Laura," he said, spreading his hands on the table. "I don't want to beat around the bush with you 'cause I want you to know where I'm coming from right up front."

"I don't understand."

"I like you," he said softly. "I like you a lot. And I'd like to see you go places. One, 'cause I think you deserve it, and two, 'cause it could help me."

"But what do you—"

"I'm an agent," he said quietly.

"I thought you—"

"I have a side business. Something I'd like to develop

before I go into it full-time. I've gotten eleven, twelve actresses on their way in the last year, but that isn't enough for me. Some people, let me tell you, would be happy with a lot less, but not me."

"But I still don't understand. Is this part of your job, or what?"

He leaned back against the banquette and looked directly into Laura's eyes. "I'm going to be frank with you, Laura, because like I said I like you." He shook his head. "The television industry is a lot more . . . complicated than some people think. It's more complicated than half the *network* guys think," he said, spreading his hands. "Half those guys don't see anything that isn't on a monitor or in a report; they could have an earthquake in that building and these guys wouldn't know. So, yeah, in the sense that they don't know zip, they don't all know about me. But that's the way I like it. Low profile." He turned angrily then, as if they had been talking about something entirely different, and snapped his fingers at a waitress who was setting down some drinks at the next table.

The waitress glanced at him with a look that said "drop dead" and turned away.

"Bitch," he muttered, then looked up and smiled at Laura. "She's new, that one. Doesn't know the regulars yet. But we're not in a hurry anyway."

"Well, I should be back by one thirty," Laura said.

He waved a hand. "Don't worry about it. I can fix it with Wakefield if you're late."

"Really?"

"Sure. No big deal. Hey, listen. I'm going to be looking out for you from now on, so get used to it."

"You mean by being my agent?"

"Agent, manager, protector, friend, you name it."

She looked down at her hands and then into his eyes. "Did you really help eleven women?"

"Twelve—twelve girls. And I could take you farther than any of them, I swear."

Laura smiled. "Tell me what kind of parts they got. Are they on TV? In the movies?"

"They're everywhere. All of them fantastic kids, all of them doing exactly what they want or on their way to doing what they want. That's the most important thing as far as I'm concerned, Laura. I never force a girl to do commercials if she doesn't want to do commercials. You know, that kind of thing. It's all up to the girl."

Laura frowned.

"What's the matter?" he asked softly.

"It all sounds too good to be true," she said. She had spoken gently and naively rather than accusingly, wanting to prod him rather than scare him. But as she studied his eyes, she didn't see any deception in them at all. As he reached out and took her hand in his, he seemed utterly sincere.

"I've had failures too, Laura, like anybody else. I didn't start out with twelve girls and take them all to the top. I had girls who went nowhere, too. I just don't mention them because it doesn't sound that great. And because they don't have anything to do with you. *You* I could make a star. I know that."

"What about guys? Don't you ever handle guys?"

He shook his head. "No way."

"Why not?"

"It doesn't work—not with me. I'm just the kind of guy that can't work with guys the way I work with girls. And don't get me wrong, Laura—I'm not saying we have strings attached, if you know what I mean. But I can't work with guys. And I can't work with girls who try to take everything over, either. You know, those strong types." He squeezed her hand. "But, hey, why talk about other girls when I've got *you* sitting here? I've got plans in my head that'll make you wish you had met me way before now, Laur."

"Well, I try not to look back and wish I had done things differently, Jerry. The important thing is that I did meet you. And that's really lucky because I'm only going to be at CTC maybe one or two more days."

"Oh, yeah? Why's that?"

"I think they must have hired someone to replace me permanently. I heard Mr. Wakefield say something about a Nancy starting in a couple of days."

Jerry shrugged. "All the better. No need for you to have a dead-end job when you have me."

"Well—"

"There's just one thing, though," he said softly.

"What's that?"

"We're going to need some up-front money."

"We?"

"*I* am, Laur."

"I don't understand," she said.

He reached out and put a finger on her forehead between her eyebrows. "Don't frown," he said. "You'll ruin your looks."

"I'm frowning because of the money," she answered. "I don't understand why you need it."

"For photo sessions, development, contacts—"

"But isn't that why you would get a percentage?" she asked. "I mean, I don't know too much about this, but I thought—"

He shook his head. "That's not the way it works in the

beginning," he cut in softly. "You see, Laur, you give me the start-up money and it guarantees *both* of us that you'll be serious about this." He sighed and spread his hands on the table. "See, you may not know this, but a lot of girls, they come into an agency like mine with the idea that I'm going to do all the work, that all they have to do is flash their pretty smiles and be stars. And that isn't the way it works."

"I know that. But still—"

"Wait. I haven't finished yet. See, you may think you're serious about our deal now, when we're in a nice restaurant having a nice leisurely lunch. But when I start asking you to pound the pavement, you may lose some of that interest. My arrangement makes sure that doesn't happen. You put something into this and you'll be damn sure it works. All good agents work that way. The new ones, anyway."

"How much money are you talking about?" she asked quietly.

"Don't frown."

She smiled. "Sorry. But how much?"

"Five hundred to start. That'll get the photography going—we'll need head shots, body shots, the works, for you."

"I already have some pictures—"

He shook his head. "Forget them. We start new and we start fresh."

"You have a photographer?"

"The best in the business."

"Really? What's his name?"

He smiled. "Jerry Manning. Yours truly. And the sooner we get started, the better. So how's tonight?"

Laura knew there was a chance—albeit a small one—

that she was going to see Gordon, and she didn't want to miss that chance if it came up. "I can't. How about the next night?"

He narrowed his eyes. "Do you have a boyfriend?"

"Why?"

"That answers my question," he said, leaning back angrily against the banquette.

"No, it doesn't," she insisted. "I was just curious about why you wanted to know."

"I was 'just curious,' to use your words."

"Oh."

"Well, *do* you?"

"No," she said truthfully, realizing that her relationship with Gordon was still unresolved. "But I have plans this week—dance classes and stuff. So let's make it tomorrow night."

He nodded. "Right. Sure. But let me warn you, Laura. When we get going with this, I'm the boss. I call and you come."

She looked into his eyes, trying to imagine what she would feel like if she were really putting herself into his hands. Five hundred dollars was a lot of money, and he had made a lot of not very specific promises. Anyone willing to part with that kind of money would expect and *want* their agent or manager to have a firm hand. But even so, she wondered just how far he went with his "clients" when he expected them to do what he wanted.

"Okay," she said quietly. "You're the boss."

That evening, at a softly lit corner table at Chez Antoine, Laura smiled into Gordon's eyes as she raised her glass to his. He had canceled his meeting and called her late that afternoon as she was making up the news team, and they had gone out to a late dinner near the station.

"I want you to tell me all the rest," he said softly. "Just hearing that you had lunch with Manning when I didn't get to see you at all today makes me crazy. But first"—he clinked his glass against hers—"to us, no matter how corny that may sound."

She smiled. "It may be corny, but it's nice."

"Just tell me you don't look into Jerry Manning's eyes the way you're looking into mine. And you're not supposed to grin when I say that."

She laughed. "Why not?"

"You're supposed to tell me you could never—ever—possibly look at anyone else that way," he said, battling a smile.

"You wanted me to play a part, remember?"

His scowl seemed genuine as he said, "Yes, I *do* remember. And I'm beginning to wish I hadn't involved you with this Manning character at all."

"Why?"

"Because he sees you more than I do, for one thing."

"You won't mind when I tell you what he said; he came right out and said he'd need money from me."

"He did? How much?"

"Five hundred. For now, he said. There might be more."

Gordon shook his head. "I should take you off this and put Legal on it."

"Why? What do we have yet? My statement about something some guy said over drinks. Why not see what he's really about, Gordon, as long as I've come this far? Why not see if he's using CTC connections the way the rumor said? Maybe there's some kind of corrupt little ring in your organization that you don't even know about, where it's not just Jerry Manning. We may be on to something bigger than we think, and if we stop now, we'll be losing out on that."

"But what about *you?* You've been working as a temp all day—not exactly what you dreamed of doing when you quit your job at the salon. This Manning thing is taking up all your time. Have you even called the countess?"

She swallowed. "Well, no, actually."

"Why not?"

"I . . . don't know," she answered honestly.

"You must have had *some* thoughts or feelings about it."

She sighed. "Well, I don't know, Gordon. In the back of my mind, every time I thought of calling the countess, I guess I thought it was one more thing I was doing through you rather than on my own."

"That's silly. All I did was give you her name."

"I know, I know," she said quickly. "I didn't say I was being rational about it."

"But I'm concerned, Laura—really concerned. When I met you, you were so fired up about starting your career. Now you're more involved with the Jerry Manning problem than with anything else in your life. When I give you a suggestion or tell you to call someone up, it's not that I'm trying to control you—I'm not interested in making you feel you owe me. I just want to help. But that damn streak of stubbornness is back stronger than ever."

She smiled. "I guess it never really left. I like to do things my way, on my own terms and at my own speed. Which usually is very fast; I don't wait around for things to happen. But with you trying to speed me up, I guess my only choice was to slow down. Which is silly, I know."

"So you'll call the countess?"

"Yes."

"And you'll let me help you some more without running in the opposite direction? I have some more names for you."

She smiled. "Okay."

"And you'll come home with me now."

She looked up at him.

"To talk, Laura," he said with a smile. "I just can't stand sitting here with twenty other people in the room when what I want more than anything in the world is to be alone with you. And anyway," he said softly, putting his hand on her knee and ever so gently massaging it, "I won't take no for an answer."

"Is that so?"

His fingers circled warmly, moving higher and higher along her thigh. "I have a limo with a driver who's paid rather handsomely because of his driving skills, Laura. I think it would be reasonably easy for me to follow you anywhere."

"You'd use your *driver* to follow me? That's not very romantic."

"It's practical," he said, the boldness of his touch deepening. "And you should know by now that I'll do anything I have to do to be near you."

She smiled. She liked the feeling of being pursued, and she liked his sureness. With someone else, that same sureness might very well have seemed more like conceit. But with Gordon, there was humor beneath the confidence; and she had also given him reason to feel confident.

"Tell me that smile means yes," he said softly.

"It means yes I'll come to your house. I'd like to see how the 'brash and outspoken president' of CTC lives."

"Like an American version of royalty, of course. What else would you expect of the head of such a vast empire?" He laughed. "Do you know that's what a reporter from *Personalities* actually said about me? Something about champagne having run through my faucets at one time in my life."

"Is that true?"

"Of course not," he said, signaling for the check. "It was white wine."

She smiled and shook her head. "You probably *told* someone that was true just to impress them; that's how rumors like that get started."

"Of course I did," he said with a wink. "A man needs *some* tricks these days. My problem with you is that I can't seem to figure out what will impress you. Sometimes I even think you'd like me better if I were poor."

They had been joking, but with his last words he had obviously been serious, and Laura knew it. And suddenly, more than anything else, she wanted to let him know how much she liked him. "I don't think you have anything to worry about," she said softly. "When it comes to impressing me, anyway."

"That's the best thing I've heard in weeks," he murmured.

Laura felt good when she'd let her guard down for those few moments, and as she looked into Gordon's beautiful brown eyes and saw so much pleasure in them, she knew that some sort of bridge had been crossed between them.

They laughed and talked easily on the limo ride up Park Avenue, joking about a terrible CTC show the night before, a show that Gordon was embarrassed Laura had seen.

And then they arrived at Gordon's apartment, a magnificent sixteenth-floor aerie at 67th and Park. Laura had been prepared for something fairly impressive, but she hadn't been prepared for such vast spaces. The apartment seemed to extend endlessly in all directions, with a sunken living room whose windows revealed a magnificent view of Central Park and the West Side; long, low furniture that seemed almost an extension of space; and large paintings everywhere, bright splashes of color that caught one's gaze and held it with surprising power.

"I can't believe this apartment," Laura said. "I didn't know anyone could have this much space. It's enormous."

"If you had called the countess, you would have seen an apartment that makes this place look tiny," he said, pouring out two snifters of brandy at a bar set into an oak-paneled wall. He picked up the glasses and carried them over to the couch, and Laura came and sat down beside him. "But I didn't want to bring you here to talk about the countess," he said softly, handing her her brandy. "All day, Laura, all day today and yesterday, every day and every night since I first met you, I haven't been able to think about anything or anyone but you." He took a sip of brandy and shook his head. "Even to my own ears, that sounds like a line," he said softly. "But I don't know what else to say when that's the truth. And I don't want to push you, to be like some kind of steamroller that just keeps moving forward on automatic. It's just that I'm so sure." He smiled, his handsome brown eyes sparkling. "Another line." He leaned back into the couch and threw up his hands. "I give up. For some reason, every word out of my mouth sounds like an attempt to try to talk you into something."

"No, it doesn't," she said softly. "I can distinguish a Jason Higgins from a Gordon Chase any day of the week."

He smiled. "How can you tell?" he asked, trailing an index finger along her inner arm, delicately teasing her satin skin.

"Oh, there are ways," Laura said vaguely, never having put into words the way she could in fact tell. "A man like Jason Higgins doesn't even seem to be looking at you when he talks. Or if he is, the gaze is studied, as if he wants to hypnotize you," she said, laughing. "But when I look into *your* eyes . . ." At that moment his eyes looked more beautiful than she had ever seen, and the deep, smoldering feeling that drew them together suddenly burst into flame as he lowered his lips to hers.

The kiss was one of desperate hunger, the first time Laura realized she did want Gordon fully, that making love was only the natural progression, a fulfillment of the connection she had been fighting since she had first seen him across the room.

She had fantasized about him countless times since then, in fantasies that flowed with passion she knew might even be surpassed. In her dreams, Gordon had kissed just as he was kissing her, but the kisses had been only a prelude to wild lovemaking in which his passion had been fully unleashed, masculine flesh awakening the heat deep inside her and swelling her pleasure until it rippled and burst in ecstasy. In fantasy he had been gentle and forceful, bold and provocative, at times daring her to take possession of him and take the lead, at others persuading her to give herself entirely over to receiving pleasure. She had imagined him in all his masculine beauty—tall and lean, dark swirls of hair covering muscled flesh, virile strength ready to arouse and play havoc with her every need until together they went over the edge. She knew the hardness of his body, his virile strength, the scent of desire that was so primitively arousing. And she wanted him.

As he nuzzled her lips and ran his fingers through her hair, over her shoulders, over her breasts, the heat of his touch showed he had gotten the message from her, without words, that this time she really did want him fully, deeply, completely. Breathless hunger had taken the place of protestations, and her racing heart told him the fire in her veins was ready to flame. As he trailed his lips downward, unbuttoning the front of her dress with deft fingers as he seared her with lips and tongue, he was amazed at her loveliness, at the silk of her skin, the beauty of her breasts, the pleasure she so obviously was taking in his touch. When he had parted the fabric of her dress to fully reveal her breasts, he moaned with pleasure as he took a nipple in his mouth, and she echoed him fully, from deep inside, clutching at his hair with urgent fingers. He teased each nipple to a tingling peak, circling with his tongue till they were erect with pleasure, and then he moved on, unbuttoning the rest of her dress with a hunger that was growing by the moment. He wanted to please her as she had never been pleased, to make her melt with a pleasure she would want again and again, but as he got a glimpse at the rest of her beauty, at cream-smooth thighs and the wisp of fabric that hid her warm sweetness, he was aroused with a desire that wouldn't wait long.

When she saw the pleasure in his eyes as he slipped off

her dress, she knew that instinct was all that mattered, that there was a rightness in being with Gordon that just couldn't be ignored any longer. Every touch of his so far —every gaze, every breath—had fired the heat that flowed through her. And as he lifted her into his arms and carried her toward the bedroom, all she wanted was to let him know the moment was right, to let the delicate rhythm continue unbroken. As he laid her down on the bed, she gazed up at him with wonder and pleasure, and he inhaled deeply, fiercely wanting to possess her but wanting to hold back as well. He undressed quickly and she watched with pleasure as he revealed himself as he had in her fantasies so many times—lean, strong, potent. He lowered himself beside her and in one quick move slid down her bikini panties, and that first touch of flesh against flesh was like fire for Laura. She embraced him with hunger, reveling in the warmth of his skin, crisp curls of hair against her soft skin, the hardness of his thrusting desire against the heat between her thighs, feeding the flames of her need with held-back strength just waiting to bring her pleasure.

"I've wanted you," he murmured against her neck. "I've wanted you and needed you and made love to you in my dreams, Laura, but I never knew I'd want you quite this much, that everything about you would be so lovely." His fingers coaxed and melted her with thrilling persuasion, his masculine flesh demanding against her thighs, and she moaned, sinking her teeth into his shoulders, his neck, merging in a wet kiss that joined their moans of desire.

And he could wait no more. He drew back and gazed down at her and saw fire in her eyes, heard need in her voice as she whispered, "Take me." And with a cry of pleasure, he made them one as he thrust inside her. And from that moment on she was his, felt as if she would be his forever as his rhythm united them quickly, filling her with his wanting, branding her with growing, smoldering pleasure that she thought could burn no hotter.

"Yes, darling," he rasped as she wrapped her legs around him, "yes," he moaned as she clutched at him, "yes," he whispered as she sank her lips against his neck, and he quickened and quickened, as her heat grew and burst into ripples of pleasure, ripples that grew to waves and then pure ecstasy, blissful happiness that united her with him forever. And he let himself go in an explosion of pleasure deep inside her, crying out with satisfaction. And then they slowly, very slowly, came back, sated, wet, skin against skin in an intimate closeness that could never be forgotten.

As he tenderly rubbed his cheek against hers and kissed her gently on the lips, looked down at her with gentle brown eyes and stroked her damp forehead, she knew only one thing—that the future could bring anything, that there was no certainty, but that she was glad they had made love, that there had been a rightness to it she'd never forget.

"Are you okay?" he asked softly.

She smiled. "Wonderful."

He smiled then too. "You *are* wonderful. Absolutely magnificent. Not to be forgotten and not to be given up."

She wondered. But she wasn't going to think or worry or do anything but enjoy his company, a nearness and closeness and tenderness she hadn't ever experienced in quite this way before.

"Can you stay the night?" he asked quietly.

"Sure." She grinned. "I don't think I'm going to get

out of this bed for anything. I am supremely, perfectly, blissfully comfortable right now."

"That makes two of us," he whispered, kissing her on her forehead, her eyes, the tip of her nose, her lips. "I'm just so glad," he murmured. "So glad."

CHAPTER SIX

The first thing Laura was aware of when she awakened the next morning was a wonderful familiar scent—the scent of Gordon's chest, then the warmth of his skin, the wonderful feel of his arm around her, the slow steady rise and fall of his chest beneath her cheek.

She had known and sensed deep inside that making love with Gordon would be as wonderful as it had been, but knowing and imagining weren't the same as actually experiencing. And she was immensely glad she had let down her guard.

And what amazed her more than any other aspect of making love with Gordon was the fact that it had been the best she'd ever experienced in her life. With men she had known better than Gordon, she had never felt quite as wonderful—and afterward, with them, she had never been aware of the warmth, the obvious caring and pleasure and appreciation, that Gordon showed.

She knew that in one sense her initial fears *had* been well-grounded. Gordon would be a distraction, an element in her life that could and probably would take up time and certainly emotional energy. But wasn't that good on some level? Even if she did find that seeing Gordon took her away from work to a certain extent, perhaps it would be beneficial, as Gordon had suggested.

She felt so good and relaxed and happy that she was sure he was right. She was ready to face the world and make her way in it.

And she knew too that Gordon would be behind her all the way, ready to help her whenever she needed his help.

Gordon awakened slowly, feeling as if he were half in a dream as he inhaled the soft scents of Laura beside him, as he realized with growing pleasure she was finally really there and not just in dream after dream.

He smiled as he reached out and brushed her hair back from her face and she looked up at him.

"You look so beautiful right now," he said softly.

She smiled, then stretched out and sank back onto the pillows. "What time is it? I feel as if I've been asleep for days."

He glanced at his watch. "It's early."

"How early?" she asked.

He grinned. "Early enough that we have time to make love," he said huskily, swinging himself on top of her. He looked down at her with a hungry gaze. "If that's all right with you, that is."

"Gee, I don't know," she teased. She reached up and grasped his hard thighs, taut and lean and scratchy. "Maybe that's not a good idea." Her fingers trailed upward, teasing a warm path designed to provoke and arouse.

"Laura," he warned hoarsely.

"Mmmm?" she asked playfully, boldly taking his rigid flesh between her fingers.

"God, what you're doing to me." She abandoned his virile strength in favor of his chest, taking his male nipples between her fingers and bringing them to immediate hardness.

"You're playing with fire," he rasped.

"Am I?" she whispered.

"Touch me again and you'll see. Or maybe I'll show you," he murmured, and he suddenly moved back and commenced his own form of teasing, coaxing her with magnificent fingers that swelled her with desire, filled her with desperate hunger.

"Gordon," she whispered.

"Tell me to stop," he dared as he leaned down and curled his tongue around a tingling nipple.

"Gordon, I want you," she whispered as he moved between her thighs, his hard thighs vigorously parting her legs.

"I'm yours," he moaned huskily. And he brought them together with a thrilling bold stroke that rocked her to the core, unleashing her pleasure with blazing heat that swept them both along like wildfire. And as they brought each other closer and closer to the edge, with whispered love words and moans and kisses rained on wet flesh, they quickened and came together in a fiery burst of searing ecstasy, muffled shouts and passion cries taking them one step further into shattering pleasure.

And afterward they settled into each other's arms, whispered and smiled and gathered strength to move, until he finally raised his head and looked down at her with a smile.

"I don't know what I'm going to do about you," he said softly as he nuzzled her hair.

"What? What do you mean?" she asked, shifting so she could look into his eyes.

"If spending the night with you is always going to be

as wonderful as it was, and if spending the morning with you is going to be even better, how are we ever going to leave this apartment? I've worked all these years to get where I am and I'm on the verge of throwing it all away for a few hours of pleasure with a beautiful woman."

She laughed. "Sure, sure, Gordon. I can just see the chaos down at CTC when you don't show up at eight thirty as usual. Somehow I think you'll make it down there today and every day, pleasure or no pleasure."

"Hey, I can dream, can't I?" he asked, reaching out and caressing the back of her neck. "I know we both have the kinds of careers that can't exactly be put on hold whenever we feel like it, but I can pretend, even if it's only for a few minutes. And *you're* the one I'm worried about. Today you have to call the countess even if you do nothing else. And I'll give you some other names also before we leave."

"Okay. But I *am* doing something else, you know, aside from the news team and the calls. I'm going to Jerry Manning's studio."

Gordon swore under his breath. "I forgot all about that bastard," he said, shaking his head. "You know, it makes me wonder about the young women who've believed him. How naive they are."

"I wouldn't be too critical," Laura said quickly. "I really wouldn't, Gordon. Because even if some of what Jerry says is obviously untrue on the surface—*to us*—it's easy to see how someone who wants to believe him could believe him. I can really see how if you've been pounding the pavement for days or weeks or months, meeting with agents and sending your picture out and never getting a response to anything, and then if this good-looking guy who works at a network starts taking an interest in you, how much are you really going to question it?"

"Five hundred dollars would make me question a lot of things," Gordon said quietly.

"Well, I'm sure there were a few who walked away," she conceded. "But you don't know what it is to be desperate. You've never had to try that hard against those odds."

He shook his head. "I guess you're right. But it makes me want to catch that bastard more than ever."

"Oh, we will," she promised.

"That's why I really love you," he said softly. "You never give up."

The radio by the bed suddenly blared on, and Gordon reached over and quickly shut it off. "Now it really *is* time to get up."

She looked at him with narrowed eyes and tried to hide her smile. "When did you have time to set that thing last night?"

"Oh, there are some things I can do in my sleep," he said easily, "or nearly in my sleep."

Like talking, she almost said, though she stopped herself. In the middle of the night, when Laura had awakened after a deep and very peaceful sleep, she hadn't known where she was at first. The room was completely dark, with only the sound of breathing and nothing else. And just at the moment when she realized where she was and whom she was with, Gordon spoke.

"What about Christine?" he murmured, and then hugged Laura close.

Laura couldn't believe how classic the words were, how much of a cliché it was to have a man talk in his sleep about another woman. But cliché or not, it had never happened to her before, and she felt unsettled by the incident. Of course, it probably didn't mean a thing: she, too, talked in her sleep, and from what friends always told her the next morning, she knew the words were often near-nonsense.

But still, Gordon's words pointed out something she had avoided thinking about because it had been unimportant until now. She had no idea of how deeply Gordon wanted to get involved, or even whether he was involved with someone else at the moment. She seriously doubted it, since he was a busy man and seemed interested in seeing her as much as he could, and since everything he had ever said had pointed to the contrary. But still, she realized she would rather know than assume.

And now, as Gordon rose out of bed and stretched his wonderful body, she was afraid to ask, for fear she'd hear an answer she didn't want to hear.

That afternoon Laura called Jerry Manning and got the address of the studio. Then she called the countess, who was strangely hesitant about making an appointment for the next day. But the two women whose names and numbers Gordon had given her that morning were both enthusiastic about setting up appointments, and she had a good feeling that she was moving ahead, that her career was progressing, and that the stubbornness that had held her back was finally giving way.

And when she finished the makeup for the news team, she changed her hair and makeup in the ladies' room and then left for Jerry Manning's studio in the East 20s, with the sinking feeling the "studio" might be nothing more than an apartment.

But when she arrived at the studio, she was relieved—

and surprised—to find that it was indeed a real studio, with backdrops and tripods and photographs, a small office area partitioned off from the rest of the loft, a darkroom, and a bathroom. And Jerry seemed thoroughly professional as he welcomed her.

"You're early," he said as she followed him toward the brightly lit center of the studio. It was a small but very professional-looking loft, with the main area apparently set up for actual picture-taking: spotlights were directed toward one wall, which had lavender photographic paper hung from the ceiling down to the floor. Potted palms and some scattered pieces of furniture hung back along the edges of the area, and Laura saw Jerry had excellent taste in everything he had chosen in the way of props.

"This is quite a place," Laura said. "Have you had it for a long time?"

"Uh, yeah, yeah. A friend and I share it, actually." He shrugged. "I let him use it during the days when I'm at the network. No sense wasting it and I like to help the guy out. But, yeah, I've had it for six, seven months. And rents aren't cheap, you know."

"I know," Laura said.

"I guess I don't have to tell *you,*" he called out over his shoulder as he sauntered over to a small bar area at the edge of the studio, "being that you live in New York and all, but some of the girls think this all comes cheap, just because the building's plain-looking. No frills."

"Oh, I understand," Laura said. She watched as he poured out some white wine for each of them. "Uh, none for me, thanks," she called out.

He picked up both glasses and brought them over to the circle of light Laura was standing in. "Don't be silly," he said softly. "You need to look relaxed in these pictures, Laura—relaxed and inviting and intriguing. Wine is just what you need." He raised her glass and she took it. "There. That's better. You just remember who's directing you today. Yours truly, Jerry Manning."

The wine was sweeter than Laura generally liked, but she drank it anyway, almost as a reflex in the face of Jerry Manning's jittery energy. Just being near him made her nervous and jumpy, and she found she had drunk half a glass within a few seconds. "Well, okay," she said quietly. "Where do we start?"

He looked her up and down, his dark green eyes intense as they scrutinized her. "I think we should start with some head shots. But your makeup looks like hell, Laura."

She smiled inwardly. He was right; not in the sense that she looked dreadful, but in the sense that she looked less pretty than she could. "Well, what should I do?"

He spread his hands and smiled. "Leave it all to Jerry. When I told you I was in charge of everything, I wasn't kidding. Right in there, right through there, there's a bathroom with all the makeup you could ever need. Go in, scrub your face down, then call me."

"I can do my own makeup," she said quickly. "And I think I know what you mean. Remember, I came in here from a job; I know I have to look more—"

"Dramatic," he supplied. "You could be an unbelievable knockout if you made your eyes up right."

"Okay, I'll see what I can do," she said. She finished her wine and went into the bathroom, where there was indeed an extensive makeup collection. But when she'd finished washing her face and stood studying herself in the mirror, she was faced with a question she couldn't answer: Had Jerry seen her down on the news sound stage? Or, if not, had he seen her in the building as Laura Dawson? She thought of Jerry as she had just left him—filled with a nervous energy that was almost explosive, a hyperactivity she felt could turn malevolent. Yet he had been nothing but generous lately. Did she have good reason to fear being discovered, or not?

Damn. She looked in the mirror and decided that all she could do was her best. Since the news sound stage was a closed set, it was extremely unlikely Jerry had seen her down there. She would do her makeup as well as she could, trying to minimize her chances of being recognized, and if he did recognize her, she'd just have to play it by ear.

She put on what she always recommended for clients who were having their pictures taken: foundation, powder, blusher, concealer under the eyes, two shades of shadow, eyeliner, two coats of mascara, lipstick with a fine brush.

Then she walked out and stood, waiting for his reaction, as he fiddled with some spotlights a few feet away.

"I'm ready," she said, her voice bouncing back from the walls with an echo.

He turned, and he looked so startled that her heart raced. "I don't believe it," he murmured.

Oh, God. "What's the matter?"

"I don't believe it," he said again, his voice barely there.

"Jerry, what is it? What's wrong?"

"Wrong! Nothing's wrong. I just can't believe what kind of winner I've got on my hands. You're going to be a star or my name just isn't Jerry Manning."

She smiled, enormously relieved that his surprise had

come from appreciation rather than discovery. "Well, I'm glad you like it," she said.

He unscrewed a lens cap from the camera and then came over to where Laura stood. "You bet I like it." He put his hands on her upper arms and held her in a surprisingly tight grip. "If I'd've known you were that much of a knockout, Laura, I wouldn't've let even this many days go by."

She had to use some strength in order to move out of his grasp. "Let's just get to work," she said quietly.

"Hey, I said no strings. And I meant that, Laura. I'm a man of my word and you can ask anyone." He strode over to the stereo and pushed a button, and suddenly the room was pulsating with a heavy rock beat.

We'll see if there are no strings, she said to herself. *We'll see.*

He snapped dozens of pictures of her—head shots only—against the lavender backdrop, and as the shooting went on, she felt more and more self-conscious. But she didn't know whether this was because she was naturally self-conscious in front of a camera or because Jerry seemed to be stretching his "no strings" promise. Every few minutes he'd put down the camera and come over to touch her in some way—brushing her hair back, angling her face, positioning her shoulders. And while the touches themselves weren't that sexual, Jerry's words certainly were: "You look just beautiful, Laur—incredible. Make those lips fuller, though—pout. That's right. And think about the best sex, the hottest sex you've ever had. Let your thoughts just flow, Laura. And pulse with the beat. Get into it. Just get into it."

At one point, when Jerry was laying on the "that's

great, baby" routine a little too thickly, Laura reminded him they weren't shooting pinup shots—just head shots.

"You let me be the judge of what's right, Laura. And what's sexy." He rose from the crouch he had been in behind the camera and came up to where Laura was sitting on a stool. "And I can tell you right now that sexy's better than unsexy any day of the week." He reached out and ran a finger along her neck and the edge of her collarbone. "And you've got what it takes to turn any man on."

"Jerry," she warned.

With exaggerated acquiescence he raised his hands over his shoulders. "Hey, I said no strings, Laura. I meant it."

She looked him in the eye. "Then continue to mean it or I'm walking."

He shook his head. "Sorry. They say old habits die hard and they're right. Let's take a break, okay?"

"Sure," she said, glad for the chance to unwind a bit.

He pulled up a chair and straddled it backward, then poured more wine into each glass and handed Laura hers. "Where're you from, anyway?" he asked. "You don't really act like you're from the city."

"I'm not," she answered. "I'm from a town called Allenville in Connecticut that practically no one's ever heard of."

"Hey, I'm from a small town too—up near Buffalo." He smiled. "I've been here for fifteen years but it seems more like fifty, sixty years. I'm thirty-three going on a hundred."

"I know what you mean. I've been here for eight years and sometimes it feels much longer."

He nodded. "Like that feeling that people who were

born here have such a head start, you know? I had to bust my—my brains to get where I am today. And then I look at some young kid, maybe twenty-two, twenty-three, and he's a hundred times further along than I am."

"I know what you mean," Laura said, surprised by Jerry's frankness. He was so different from the Jerry of the wild promises and the false confidence.

"And you know what?" he asked. "Sometimes I wonder if the world is divided into two groups—the people who were born with everything and who'll always have it, and the people who were born with nothing and no matter how hard they try, they'll never make it. The haves and the have-nots, I guess." He shook his head. "And the haves make you *think* you can make it, because that way you'll work hard and they'll get a lot out of you. Like a boss who promises you a promotion so you work and work and work only nothing happens in the end. You're born an underdog and you die an underdog, you know?"

"Well, I know what you're talking about, but for both of our sakes, I hope it isn't true."

"Yeah, well, just be glad you're only going to be working at CTC for a couple more days. It's the kind of place I'm talking about when I talk about the haves and the have-nots. People like Gordon Chase and his cronies running the show and they don't want anyone else to have a piece of the action."

"I don't know if I agree with you there," Laura said. "My boss, Mr. Wakefield, seems really nice."

"Hey, he isn't that high up," Jerry said. "It's the real higher-ups I'm talking about. They're the ones who make it hard for people like me. And *they're* the ones, along with people from my hometown, I want to make squirm when I ride by in a limousine someday. Which is why this side business is a lifesaver for me. This is my ticket out. And believe me, the *only* reason I keep my job at CTC is to be on the inside—at a network. I'm not *quite* at the point where I'm ready to quit. But, believe me, when I'm ready, I'm walking. And then they'll be sorry." He sipped his wine and then stood up. "Hey, I don't know what the hell we're doing talking like this when we've got work to do. Go into the bathroom and pick out one of those bathing suits."

"What?"

"You're a what? Size four? Six? I've got 'em all, basic black, all new. Look in the drawers in the bathroom. Just put one on and relax. And don't look at me like I'm going to attack you or something. I'm a professional guy trying to do a professional job, okay? And I'll tell you what I tell all the girls, Laur."

"What's that?"

"Pretend you're on a beach if you're uptight. What am I going to see in here that I can't see on the beach? Less, probably. Or what if I was a doctor?"

She took a sip of wine and thought about it. Technically, he was right. And all the models and actresses she knew had bathing-suit shots in their portfolios. But she still felt there was something seamy or just too suggestive about the idea. On the other hand, though, she did want to go through with the whole plan, and she also felt she knew Jerry a lot better now that he had talked a little about his background. All his talk about being an underdog had struck a chord with her; what if he *was* just an employee trying to better himself during his hours away from work? He hadn't even mentioned CTC except in the context of disliking it, and he hadn't made her any promises he couldn't keep. In fact, so far he hadn't done anything wrong that she could see. She was investigating him because of Gordon's suspicions, but when she thought about it, what made Gordon so right? What business was it of his if someone relatively low on the ladder tried to better himself outside work?

What if Jerry was sincere and on the level?

As Laura looked around the small dressing room/bathroom, her feelings about Jerry were reinforced by what she saw. Not only was there all the makeup she had seen before, but inside the bureau, there were indeed new bathing suits of all sizes. He had clearly gone to some expense. Was that the work of a fraud, or of someone who really wanted to make a go of his business? Weren't both *possibilities,* at the very least?

Laura found a size six black maillot and pulled it on, and she had a moment's hesitation as she looked in the mirror. Though it was a one-piece and not a bikini, it was very revealing, with high-cut legs and a plunging neckline that showed off her figure in a way she wasn't sure she wanted to show off.

And a few moments later, as Laura walked out into the studio, she felt uncomfortably self-conscious as Jerry looked her up and down and gave a low whistle.

"Hey, I knew I could pick out bathing suits that would look good on almost anyone, but you wouldn't have needed any help at all. You are in some kind of shape, Laura."

He had removed everything from the shooting area except the backdrop, and he looked at it and then at Laura with concern. "But we're going to need something," he mused. "Something to make the most of this." He brought out a small wooden platform with steps and motioned for Laura to stand on top of it. "That'll look super," he said as she went up the steps. "Now just drape yourself—you know, sit like you're on the beach or something. I want a profile first."

She sat as he had told her to, and followed his directions as he told her to move her arms this way or that, to throw her head back and then forward, to let her hair cover her face and then tumble down as she held it above her head. He turned on a fan and turned up the music, and Laura began to feel less self-conscious and more relaxed, even though Jerry was continuing with his silly "that's beautiful, baby" comments.

She knew that chances were he was a fraud, she knew she was on an investigation, she knew that the whole situation was unreal. But something had made those facts unimportant, almost nonexistent: for the fact was that Jerry Manning, with his oohing and aahing and silly compliments, was making her feel good. For years, in the back of her mind and then more consciously, she had wanted to be a model, and she had always known it was impossible. Now Jerry Manning was making her feel glamorous and beautiful and very much as if she could really make it. And she realized how easily his "girls" had been fooled now that she saw how seductive his whole approach was, crude or not.

Unless he was for real. It was a thought that kept coming back, that simply wouldn't go away.

For what he had said had reached her in an emotional way.

She wondered how she would be able to explain her new thinking to Gordon. She certainly didn't want to put it on an emotional level. But wasn't there more to it than that? Today, Jerry had been nothing less than professional. He had made no impossible promises, had made no unreasonable demands, and he'd seemed to be nothing more than an unhappy employee who was trying to improve his lot. And while it was true that he had probably exaggerated his level of success in the agency business, that was certainly no crime; in every area of business, every day of the week, perfectly legitimate businessmen and women did the same thing. Exaggerating wasn't a crime.

But Laura couldn't see Gordon agreeing with her; she simply couldn't imagine anything but anger on his part when she thought about what she might say to him.

When Jerry was finished with the bathing-suit shots, he told Laura she should get dressed and that they'd talk afterward.

She dressed quickly and came back out into the studio, where she found Jerry over in the office behind the partition, looking through an appointment book that was filled with names and dates, checking his Rolodex and then rechecking the date book.

"I want to fit you in as quickly as I can," he said, flipping through the pages of the book. "I can develop our film tonight, but I've got something on for tomorrow. . . ."

"Well, whenever you th—"

"Hey, hey, don't worry," he cut in. "I'll cancel someone else if I have to—just so we can get going."

She smiled. "Okay. Whatever you say."

He studied the calendar. "What about tomorrow night at seven? I can move my other appointment up. How's that?"

She shrugged. "Fine. But what are we meeting about?"

"You," he said with a smile as he leaned back in his

chair and put his feet up on the desk. "You and your career," he added softly. "And me. We're both going to go places fast. And I don't even care whether you believe me or not, Laura; *I* know it's true." He swung his feet back down and leaned forward.

"There's just one thing," he said gently.

"What's that?"

"The check."

Of course. She had completely forgotten about the money. "Oh, right," she said, a natural hesitation creeping into her voice. She had taken out five hundred dollars in cash from her savings account today, and she'd been nervous all day about being mugged. And she hoped he wouldn't question the fact that she was giving him cash instead of a check; but she couldn't give him a check with the name "Laura Dawson" on it, and getting a money order would have meant giving her name as well.

"Hey, I don't like that look in your eyes. I thought we went through why I needed it."

"We did," she agreed. "I just . . . five hundred dollars is a lot of money."

He spread his arms. "Hey, if I thought we could make it by changing the rules, I'd change them in a second. But let me tell you: this is tried and true. I don't like to change a sure thing when I don't have to."

She sighed and went over to her purse and took out the five crisp hundred-dollar bills. When she looked up, Jerry was frowning.

"Cash?" he asked.

She feigned surprise. "Isn't that all right?"

"Yeah, yeah, sure. I'm just surprised you'd want to walk around with all that money."

She shrugged. "Well, I really didn't want to, but then

you hadn't said whether you wanted a check or cash, so I thought I'd be safe."

"Hey, what do you think? I'm not legit? I take checks."

"Well, okay. Now I know," she said, handing him the cash.

He nodded. "Okay, no hard feelings. And we're on for tomorrow night, right?"

"Right," she said.

"Good. Then get out of here so I can get going with the developing. I think we're really going to have something great here."

"Okay, see you tomorrow," she said, and she picked up her purse and left.

Strange, she said to herself as she went down in the elevator. It was just so strange that he suddenly seemed legitimate, or at least well-meaning.

She had arranged to meet Gordon at his apartment when she finished up, and she walked over to Third Avenue so she could find a taxi heading uptown. She found one miraculously easily and took some pleasure in that, but the closer she got to Park and 67th, the less sure she was of anything. Last night and this morning seemed more like dreams than anything else—wonderful dreams in which reality had been replaced by fantasy, uncertainty replaced by pleasure.

Was that what the relationship was really all about? she wondered. Did its intensity come from the fact that it was ninety percent physical, or was there more to it than that?

She had discovered the hard way, with Matthew, that a relationship could be very one-sided, with each person feeling very differently about what it meant. And while it was true that Gordon had been very persistent and seemed very interested, did she really know where his interests lay?

When she arrived at Gordon's, he was so happy to see her that she forgot her uncertainty—at least while he held her in his arms and looked down at her with his wonderful brown eyes.

"You look lovely," he said softly. "Don't tell me you're just coming from Jerry Manning's."

"Yes, I am. Why?"

His grip on her loosened slightly. "And you look like that? What happened to Laura Hoover?"

She shrugged. "I changed my makeup. It's actually a good sign that Jerry asked me to. It means that—"

"What do you mean 'a good sign'?" Gordon cut in.

"Well, he was really serious about the pictures. I went in there looking all wrong—looking like Laura Hoover, young temp—and I came out looking good because he insisted I change my makeup."

Gordon studied her. "And? I'm still wondering what you mean by 'good sign.' "

"I think he might be for real," she said. "Not a fraud, I mean."

"What? What are you talking about, Laura?"

She slipped out of his arms and stepped down into the living room, then walked over to the windows and looked out at the night sky. "Why are you so angry? I thought you might even be pleased to find you were wrong about Jerry."

"Just tell me what happened," he said, coming in after her. "Although I can't imagine what Manning could have done, short of handing you a contract with a producer, that could have turned you around like that. Although I notice he did give you something to drink."

Her eyes widened. "I don't believe what I'm hearing. Is it so terrible that I had a drink? I really don't understand why you're so upset."

"You come in here looking absolutely incredible," he said quietly. "More beautiful than I've ever seen you. And then I learn you've been drinking with Manning—'Jerry' to you—and that he's convinced you he's for real. All I'd like to know is how and why."

"I was going to tell you," she bit out, "until you started talking about the drinking. Which consisted of a glass and a half of white wine, if that's all right with you. And it was nothing specific that convinced me, Gordon—no single thing he did or said. I don't even know if I *am* convinced; but I'm *not* convinced he's a con artist. What if he's someone who's really trying to make a go of something in a way you just don't happen to understand?"

He frowned. "What's that supposed to mean?"

"Well, I started thinking about it when he was talking to me this evening. If he's abusing his position at CTC in some way, then obviously you have the right to look into it and to stop it. But he never once mentioned CTC to me tonight in any suspicious way, Gordon. All he talked about was how hard it is to get ahead at a big company like that. And if he's trying to advance himself on his own time, I don't see that that's any of your or anyone else's business." She suddenly stopped, aware that she sounded overly emotional, that indeed her emotions were running her thoughts more than logic was. "I'm sorry," she said softly. "I do understand why we're looking into the situation. It's just that Jerry didn't say anything that pointed in the direction of guilt tonight. And I just wish you could have a slightly more open mind."

Gordon's eyes were dark with annoyance. "Did he ask you for the money?"

"Yes. And I gave him cash."

"How did he react to that?"

She shrugged. "He was surprised. Maybe even a little offended; he said I could have written a check."

"But he wasn't suspicious."

"No, not at all."

Gordon reached into his pocket and pulled out his checkbook.

"What are you doing?" she asked.

"Paying you back."

"You don't have to do that this *second.*"

He gave her a look she didn't understand. "Just take this," he said, writing quickly. Then he handed her the check, that mysterious look still in his eyes.

"I really don't know what you're so riled up about," she said.

"I'm not riled up," he said testily, going over to the bar. He poured two glasses of Scotch in silence.

When he turned to hand Laura her glass, she raised a brow and said, "Plying me with liquor?"

"What?"

"Plying me with liquor?"

"Of course not," he said as he sat down. "I assumed you wanted a drink."

"Well, I do. But that's what Jerry did, too. He *can* be polite. So don't assume that everything he does is some dark and terrible deed."

"I worry about you, all right? At this point, that's my main concern." He put down his drink and took Laura into his arms. "I missed you," he said softly. "And I worried." As he looked into her eyes, he wondered what she was thinking, wondered whether she could possibly feel as he did. When they were making love, he didn't question anything: she was there for him in every way, as caught up as he was in the pleasure of the moment.

But what about when that moment was over?

"Tell me something," he said quietly.

She looked up at him. "What is it?"

"I've never asked you about anyone else," he began, his voice velvety soft. "At first it didn't seem to matter. Then it mattered too much and I didn't want to ask. But now I have to—because sharing you with someone else wouldn't be my idea of a relationship." She smiled crookedly, and he looked at her with pleasure. "That's the smile I love," he said. "The lopsided one. I think that's your real one."

"Well, in this case it means I love what you're saying, Gordon."

"Then you're not seeing anyone else."

She shook her head. "And you're not."

"I don't know how anyone could see you and possibly want to have anything to do with anyone else," he said huskily, reaching out for her. The touch of his hand at the back of her neck was like fire, and her breath caught as she saw the lust in his dark eyes. "I want you, Laura. And I don't intend to let you get away."

Her eyes dared him as she let her hand trail down his stomach to the waistband of his pants. "Do I look like I'm running?" she asked softly.

CHAPTER SEVEN

Her eyes never left his as she unfastened his pants, as she slowly unzipped them and let daring fingers find their way inside.

His eyes darkened as she grew bolder, a hand teasing his masculine flesh.

"Laura," he whispered.

"Let me show you I'm yours," she said softly. She undressed him slowly, pulling away his shirt and tie to reveal curls of hair she trailed her wet lips through, stopping at each nipple with a moan of pleasure. She deftly made each one hard with flicks of her tongue and teasing bites, all the while making provocative strokes to his virile strength. Then she trailed her mouth downward, along the flat of his stomach, and she eased off his pants with tantalizing delays, kissing and nipping at each inch of flesh she exposed.

"Laura," he murmured, his fingers roving through her hair as she brought him to a pitch of arousal that sent fire through his veins.

With a groan made up of pleasure and pain, he moved away from her teasing touch. "I want to please you," he rasped, sliding urgent hands up her thighs as he gazed into her eyes. "I want to make you see something, to show you something you'll never forget," he said hoarsely, his voice ragged with desire.

With lightning fingers he freed her from her clothes, and then he held her shoulders between warm, strong hands. "I've been looking for someone like you my whole life," he murmured. "In all the wrong places, at all the wrong people, and now that I've found you . . ." His voice trailed off as he lowered his lips to hers and he gently laid her back on the couch. "I want you to look at me," he said softly, and she gazed into dark brown eyes she loved. "See these eyes and know they're for you." He took her hand and placed it over his heart. "This heart beats for you." He brought her hand lower. "And I've never wanted a woman as much as I want you." She took hold of him and his eyes closed under the pleasure of her touch. "Oh, God," he whispered. "What you do to me."

He took firm hold of her and brought her hard against him. "I just want to give you more pleasure than you've ever dreamed," he whispered as his eager hands roved over her buttocks, awakening her flesh with his sensuous touch, his hard strength demanding against her thighs. He seared the core of her need with deep confidence, a touch that said he knew her desires, her pleasures, her most intimate secrets, and then he was inside her, filling her throbbing inner sweetness with hot strength, vigorous strokes, shattering pleasure that was almost instantaneous, that threw them together in an eruption of molten sensation. His cries mixed with hers as their sweat mixed and ran down their bodies, as their hearts had united in that place where thought was impossible. And it was some time—though neither knew how long—before either one spoke.

Slowly, with a smile, Gordon raised his head. "You're

too wonderful for words," he said softly, gently caressing her hips.

"No, *you* are," she murmured. "Or if I am, Gordon, it's because I'm with you." *Because I've never felt this way before,* she added to herself.

"You know, I mean what I said," he said quietly, idle fingers stroking the silk of her stomach. "About wanting you . . . not letting you run." He paused. "Have you had many serious relationships? Lasting, I mean?"

She shrugged. "Not that many."

"How many is not that many?" he asked.

"Well, I don't count the relationships I had in high school because I was so young. Since then, I guess two."

"With whom? What were they like?"

"Um, one was with a guy from my hometown who kind of followed me down here," she said. "I mean, he didn't live here, but he came down every weekend, and we saw each other for about a year."

"Then what happened?"

She shrugged. "He wanted different things. Very different things. He wanted me to move back to Allenville and marry him and have four or five or six kids at home while he supported us all—kind of like my father's attitude about my mother. I didn't want that."

"And he didn't want to move here? Even for you?"

"Are you kidding? He didn't even like to come down here on weekends. The idea of living here, with me or without me, just wasn't even something he could consider."

"So you broke up."

"We had to. And it was the right thing to do, too. I knew I'd never be ready for the kind of life he had always planned to have. Not for going back in that way, anyway. So to continue would have been a waste."

"What about the other relationship?"

She shook her head. "The less said, the better."

He stroked her hair. "Tell me," he said softly. "But wait. I'll get us something to drink. I'm dying of thirst." He rose from the couch and walked out to the kitchen, and Laura sighed. She really didn't want to talk about Matthew; but if she didn't, she knew it would only pique Gordon's curiosity all the more, and that he'd keep pressing the issue. And more importantly, she felt it was a sign of weakness to be so hesitant. It was all in the past; there was no rational reason that talking about it should cause any pain; and if it was all really over, she would have no problem discussing it.

But as Gordon came back in with two glasses of Perrier, she realized she *would* have difficulty talking about Matthew—not because any good feelings still lived inside her, but because on the outside many similarities bound Matthew and Gordon together. And it was these similarities that had driven Matthew and Laura apart.

"I don't mean to push you," he said gently as he gave her the Perrier. "But I want to know everything about you. Especially the things and people who have meant something to you."

"Well, the other serious relationship . . ." She hesitated for a moment. "I was going to marry him. But he doesn't mean anything to me anymore. He was the wrong kind of person at the wrong time for me. And I was so caught up in the romance of the relationship at the beginning that I didn't even know how wrong he was for me." She sipped her Perrier and Gordon reached out and covered her other hand with a warm hand of his own.

"Tell me who he was."

"His name was Matthew," she said, aware as if from far away that her voice was listless, lifeless, flat. "He was a securities analyst, and I met him at a party. This was three years ago, when I was twenty-five, and even though I had been in New York for a few years, I didn't know what a securities analyst was."

"So what?" Gordon asked.

She shrugged. "I don't know. It illustrates . . . Well, anyway, we began going out together, and I really liked him, and it was obvious that he liked me. But there was one thing that always nagged at me."

"What was that?"

Laura hesitated and then finally spoke. "It wasn't something I could put my finger on at first—just an uneasiness I felt at certain times. An uncertainty I just couldn't place. But when I finally realized where it came from, I could look back at all the times I had felt strange, and I knew why." She shook her head as if to shake off the memory. "It had to do with the differences in our background, in our upbringing, I guess. I remember once we were at his office and four of his friends were going off to play racquetball at some fancy athletic club, and they asked if Matthew and I wanted to go along. I said I didn't know how to play, and Matthew looked at me as if he wanted me to disappear. At the time, I thought I was just being oversensitive and reading into his words and expressions."

"Maybe you were," Gordon suggested.

She shook her head. "No, no. That day told me something and I should have paid attention to it. But I didn't, and it just got worse and worse." She sighed and sipped her Perrier, and then said, "He didn't like who I was. He didn't like the fact that I hadn't gone to prep school, that I hadn't gone to college, that I didn't dress the way he and all his friends did, that I was just too different. And he didn't like what I did for a living."

"I don't understand," Gordon said.

"He was embarrassed. All the women he had gone to college with were lawyers or doctors. Then here I was, a makeup artist. He thought it was frivolous and he thought I was uneducated and he couldn't hide his feelings. I remember there were a few times when he actually changed the subject when he thought someone was going to ask me what I did."

"Why did you put up with it?" Gordon asked gently.

"Looking back on it now, it's hard to understand. But at the time, before I saw that side of him, I really liked him. And when I realized how he really felt, I did break the relationship off."

"He sounds like a real prince," Gordon said disdainfully. "What a fool."

"He isn't that rare a species," Laura observed.

"Why do you say that?"

"I think it's true in a lot of cities and particularly places like New York and Washington, where a lot of women come from other places hoping to find a boyfriend or husband or whatever. I've certainly seen it with friends of mine, women who've become secretaries or assistants or paralegals; they're trying to go out with the bankers and doctors and lawyers they work for, and it doesn't often work out that way. But the men get the very clear—and accurate—idea that they can be as rotten as they want because if one woman leaves them, there'll be another waiting in the wings." She shrugged. "And I decided I just didn't want to buy into that game."

"I think you were absolutely right," Gordon said, stroking her knee. "But what about now?"

"What do you mean?"

"You know that I'm different, Laura. Just now I heard such passion in your voice that I couldn't help wondering whether you still . . ." His voice trailed off for a moment. "Whether you think *every* relationship is a game you don't want to buy into."

She shook her head. "Not at all. But I don't ever want to come into contact with that kind of value system again. I care about my career as much as anyone has ever cared about theirs; but there are things to me that are more important than status and getting ahead. And I don't want to share my time with people who look down on other people the way Matthew did—people who think their kind is the only kind, or that this city is the only place in the world that matters. You know, I don't think he even knew the names of half the secretaries in his department. He—"

"Come here," Gordon said softly. He tilted her chin up and then kissed her gently, tenderly on the lips.

She smiled. "What was that for?"

"You. Us. Me, so I can see your eyes when I tell you I'm falling in love with you."

"Oh, Gordon," she whispered. And he drew her into his arms and held her close, and she wondered if he could mean what he said, if being with him could ever be as right as making love with him was.

Laura spent the night at Gordon's, and in the morning, woke up to what sounded like the whispering of her name.

When she opened her eyes, Gordon was smiling down at her.

She sleepily stretched and then asked, "Did you say something just now?"

He slowly shook his head, still smiling. "Nope. We're just on the same wavelength. I willed you to wake up, and you did."

"Liar," she teased, pulling at a lock of hair that had fallen across his forehead.

He laughed and looked at her in mock astonishment. "You're just looking for a fight, aren't you?"

"Fight! I was asleep! You woke me up and now you say it was wavelengths!" She laughed.

A warm hand under the covers suddenly tickled her ribs.

"Stop," she said, laughing.

He raised a brow. "Didn't have that in mind, huh? What about this?"

His touch became suddenly delicate as his fingers trailed a sensuous path across her stomach; then with deep-velvet tenderness he found the honeyed softness between her legs and began to melt her with his intimate strokes. She whispered his name and reached for him, moaned beneath his bold touch as she felt him swell with arousal, his hard flesh making her warm with the memory of his scorching strokes deep inside her. And moments later it was more than memory as he brought them together and seared her once again, his forceful thrusts taking hold of her and filling her with pleasure. Their heat burned with a glow that joined them together as if forever uniting them in unforgettable passion. "Darling," he whispered hoarsely as she cried out with bliss that was about to take her over the edge, "darling, yes, give yourself to me," he said, urging her with vigor deep inside her, and then she was his, engulfed in the heat he had created, wave after wave after wave of pleasure washing over her. And with a wild urgency he followed, in a release that shook them both to the core.

As Laura slid in and out of the sleepy haze she was in, she fought a feeling she didn't want to face. Gordon had told her he was falling in love with her. She hadn't been able to find words for him, hadn't been able to offer anything more than a smile and a look of affection. But when she made love with him, she felt she loved him, even though that was something she didn't want to face. Love created problems as far as she was concerned—problems she didn't have time for at the moment. But she couldn't deny there was a very special feeling that came with their lovemaking, that came stronger each time. She had *never* felt like this; she'd never experienced this closeness, this overwhelming affection that seemed to swell and overflow every time she made love with Gordon.

She didn't have to think about it; but that didn't mean it didn't exist.

He sighed happily into her shoulder and wrapped his arms around her. "What are your plans for today?" he asked softly.

"Well, I have the countess at two, and those two other friends of yours, Mrs. Althorp and Mrs. Simon, then the news team, then Jerry Manning at seven."

Gordon raised himself and looked into her eyes. "I want this to be the last time."

"We'll see."

He stared at her. "Are you doing this just to drive me crazy? Because if you are, Laura, it's working."

"Don't be silly. Come on, Gordon. This doesn't even

sound like you. Until last night you never struck me as the type of man who'd be even remotely jealous."

"I don't like to think of you with him, Laura. It's that simple. And it shouldn't be that hard to understand."

"Well, it is. I don't think he's as sleazy as we thought. I told you that, and I mean it. And as long as I've started this, I intend to finish it. I just wish I had your support—since I did start it for your sake."

He knew she was right. She *was* doing it for him, whether he liked what she was doing or not. But it infuriated him that she had changed her approach, that now she even seemed to believe the bastard. He *knew* she was wrong on that count; but how many times could he tell her?

"Anyway, I have an idea," she suddenly said. "And I'm sure you'll like it because it will speed things up."

He raised a brow. "I have my doubts, because I don't like any of this, but tell me the idea."

"Well, it could really clarify a lot for us," she said. "I know he has a Rolodex in his office—at his desk at the studio, I mean—and it's right next to the phone. *If* I get the chance—and by that I mean *if* he's not around and I know I won't be caught—I could get a few names and we could call *those* women to see what he's been telling them. I know he does have other clients."

"That's an excellent idea," he said. "If you really wait until it's safe."

"Of course. Obviously. Listen—just because I may have my doubts about your theory doesn't mean I'm crazy or interested in getting hurt."

"I know, I know. But I worry. I don't seem to be able to convey to you that what he's doing is wrong. If he's using CTC—"

"He hasn't even mentioned CTC, Gordon, except to say he's having a hard time."

"But according to the note to Stu Whelan, Manning did promise some people CTC-connected acting jobs. And that's against the policy of the network. That's not to say there aren't a lot of people who have a say in casting; we're not against hiring friends or relatives or favorites of our employees. It happens all the time in any business in the world. But I'm talking about top people, Laura—top management—"

"And you won't even give the lower echelons a chance."

"That isn't fair," he argued.

"Why not? You and your friends at the top already have everything you need; why should you give anyone else a chance?"

"We're not talking about giving someone else a chance here. We're talking about a guy who's charging money for something he shouldn't be doing to begin with. And I'd like to know why you feel it's necessary to leap to his defense."

"Maybe because no one else is willing to do that, or even to give him a chance, Gordon." When she spoke and heard the stridency in her voice, she wondered what she was so upset about and why she was going out on a limb to defend Jerry Manning, someone she didn't even really like. Last night Gordon had told her he was falling in love with her. Wasn't that what she should be thinking about?

But maybe that was part of the problem. . . .

Just a day before, she had worried that her feelings would run deeper than Gordon's, that she would be hurt. Now he had told her he was falling in love with her. But somehow that only made her nervous. Memories of Matthew hurting her came back, memories she really hadn't touched on with Gordon.

It was easy for Gordon to say that Matthew sounded like a fool; but he hadn't known Matthew. She had fallen in love with him and been hurt by him, and though she hated to admit she was afraid of anything, she had to admit that being hurt emotionally was her sorest point. She had always been able to do anything on a dare from the time she'd been a kid, and she wasn't the slightest bit afraid of confronting people in work-type situations. But when it came to that part of her heart that she saved for love and hope and dreams, she was deeply afraid of being hurt.

"Laura," Gordon murmured, interrupting her thoughts.

She turned and looked into his eyes. "What?"

"I'm not going to let someone like Jerry Manning come between us."

"I don't see why he should," she said.

"Anything can come between two people if they let it."

"You're the one who's making an issue out of it," she said quietly, "by refusing to even consider the remote possibility that I could be right."

He sighed impatiently. "I'm taking a shower," he said as he got out of bed. "Do you want to join me?"

"No. I have a lot to do today," she said coolly. "As you know. I'm going to go home and get ready from there." She rose out of bed, conscious of his eyes on her, and turned to get dressed.

"All right, then," he said quietly. "Maybe I'll talk to you later this evening. Will you be home?"

"You know I have the meeting with Jerry Manning."

"I meant afterward," he said testily.

She shrugged. "Sure. I'm not spending the night with him."

He gave her a black look and stalked off to the bathroom, and she sighed as she pulled on her shirt. Her last remark hadn't deserved a response. But she had felt provoked. It was easy for Gordon to say that she was "letting" the question of Jerry Manning's guilt come between them. But just because Gordon said it, didn't mean it was true. For she *was* bothered by the fact that he couldn't, even for one minute, consider the possibility that she could be right. And that was damn annoying. They could get along magnificently in bed—no small matter as far as she was concerned. And at those times her affection for him seemed so deep that nothing could ever interfere. But all that wonderfulness could somehow be wiped out over one small argument. And that gave her real doubts about the future of the relationship.

She couldn't stop thinking about Gordon even as she was on her way to the countess's. This would be an important appointment for her: according to what Gordon had once said, the Countess di Lomazzo was a woman who could introduce her to dozens of possible customers if she liked her work. So it was important that she concentrate. The only problem was that that was easier said than done.

But the moment she was shown into the countess's apartment, she forgot all about Gordon. Never in her life had she seen such opulence. As she stood in the parquet-paneled foyer and waited for the butler to summon the countess, she could see the living room on the right, a graceful sweep of stairs leading to the second and third floors of the triplex directly ahead, and a music room to her left. The colors were dreamlike—white and gilt walls, peach furniture, pale beige rugs, fine carved woods so rich they glowed as if alive, paintings that belonged in a museum.

"The countess will see you shortly," the butler said, showing Laura into the living room. "Please have a seat."

"Thank you," Laura replied, and she sank onto the softest, downiest sofa she had ever felt in her life. The room was amazingly peaceful, the light coming in through the French doors as lovely as dawn, and Laura thought, *This is how different the same city can be when you have money.* Up here on the fifteenth floor there was no morning gear-grinding from garbage trucks, no brakes screeching or horns honking—just tranquillity and beauty everywhere.

But the quiet was broken when Laura heard an angry "Where!" from another room.

"She was to sit in the *foyer,* Andrew," said a female voice without a trace of an accent. "Honestly. Would you have invited the *butcher* into the living room? What do they teach at the agencies these days?"

"I'm sorry, madame," came the butler's apology. "I didn't think—"

"No, you didn't," she cut in. "And your time here will come to no more than a week if you don't *significantly* improve your performance. But it's too late now. Just be *certain* it doesn't happen again."

The flush of anger was burning Laura's cheeks and ears, and she took a slow, deep breath to try to calm her racing heart. The countess's tone had been even worse than her words. She had acted as if the butler had done something unspeakable.

The clacking of the countess's heels across the parquet floor made Laura turn and then stand. She knew her face still had to be red, that there was a good chance she looked shocked and furious. But she didn't really care.

"Laura Dawson?" the countess asked imperiously.

"Yes. Pleased to meet you," Laura lied, extending a hand.

The countess's handshake was cold, weak, and reluctant, and Laura was unpleasantly aware of being scrutinized from head to toe.

"There's no reason for us to dawdle in here," the countess snapped. "Gor—Mr. Chase told me you had done a rather nice job down at his network. So let us proceed to the dressing room."

"Fine," Laura replied, telling herself that she owed it to herself and to Gordon to remain polite.

As she followed the countess through a maze of lovely rooms, all decorated in various shades of beige, peach, and gold, she thought about what she might do in the way of making the countess up. Gordon had been right when he said the woman was one of those ageless types. She was probably in her late fifties, but she could have been much older and simply well preserved. And she clearly did know how to make the most of her appearance: her makeup was slightly heavy-handed, but the subtle shades she used were fine, and her hair was lovely —a rich dark auburn swept up into a chignon. And her clothes—a velvety-looking black suede suit and beige silk blouse—seemed to be well chosen and very well made.

They walked into a room that was larger than Laura's living room, and the countess showed Laura to a dressing table that ran the length of one wall. It was draped with beautiful white linens and lace and covered with more cosmetics than Laura had in her entire collection.

"We can sit here," the countess said, pulling out a white and gilt chair. "And we can talk. After we talk, I shall decide whether I'd like you to work with me."

Laura pulled out a chair and tried to compose herself. Gordon hadn't said anything about auditioning for this woman! "Uh, Countess di Lomazzo," she began, looking into the countess's gray eyes. "I wasn't aware that our appointment was anything other than definite."

"It *is* definite, Miss Dawson. The question is whether you will proceed past our little discussion."

"Well, that's fine," Laura said. "Only I want you to understand that whether or not I proceed, you will be billed for the visit."

"My dear, do you honestly think that is a concern of mine?" the countess asked with astonishment.

"I really wouldn't know," Laura answered simply. "I just like to be sure both parties agree before—"

" 'Parties'?" the countess interrupted, apparently even more astonished than before. "We are not entering into a legal contract, Miss Dawson. In fact, you would not be here at all were it not for the rather eloquent powers of persuasion of your employer, Mr. Chase."

"All right. As long as you understand," Laura said as calmly as she could, silently cursing Gordon at the same time. She was used to a certain arrogance in many of the women she worked on; they sometimes acted in a way she never had—and never would. But the countess seemed not only arrogant but hostile; and that was the kind of customer Laura had learned she'd do well to live without.

"Well, we might as well begin," Laura said. "Please

face me so I can look at you. And I'll just turn this light on over here," she added, reaching up and flicking on a small spotlight as the countess turned.

In the bright light Laura saw that the countess was older than she had thought at first. "Hmmm," Laura began. "The first thing I see is that we're going to have to plan your makeup very carefully in terms of the light you'll be in. I'd say that this lighting is standard office lighting. And it's—"

"I have no plans to take a job," the countess said crisply, "if that's what you're thinking."

"I wasn't finished," Laura said evenly. "I was *going* to say that if you were going to spend a lot of time in offices *or* department stores, which have similar lighting, we could plan a color scheme that would look really great in daylight *and* the places I mentioned. What I like to do with regular clients, you see, is to set up a variety of routines for different situations—nighttime, work, though in your case we could leave that out, and—"

"I really don't think I have any interest in pursuing what sounds like an elaborate course of study, Miss Dawson. I've used the same makeup for fifteen years and I haven't been remotely dissatisfied with it."

Laura sighed. "Countess di Lomazzo. I didn't ask to come here; you *did* invite me. I don't mean or want to be rude, but I seem to have missed something: I thought you wanted to be made up."

"Perhaps it's my fault," the countess said, surprising Laura. "You see, your employer, Mr. Chase, mentioned your name and before I knew it, I had agreed I'd see you. But now that you're here . . . Frankly, I don't like anything you've told me—about yourself *or* your ideas."

Laura blinked. "I don't understand."

"Your preoccupation with money, for example. I have the uncanny and unpleasant feeling that I'm the sole guest at one of those little parties I've read about from time to time—in which women of little means go to each other's houses and spend more money than they should on those little cooking receptacles."

"You mean Tupperware?"

"I really wouldn't know the name, Miss Dawson. But you seem to harbor the idea that you're going to sell me an elaborate array of cosmetics I have no need for—as you can see," she added, gesturing with a sweep of her hand at the dressing table.

"I didn't intend to sell you anything, Countess di Lomazzo, other than knowledge, which you could accept or reject."

"I am sorry," the countess said, standing. "My mind is made up."

Laura stood. "Well, I'm sorry too, because you might have learned something."

"Perhaps," the countess conceded reluctantly. "But I have decided. I shouldn't have agreed when Mr. Chase asked. But I don't want you to be concerned, Miss Dawson. I shall tell your employer you did a fine job."

"Please don't bother," Laura said, picking up her makeup case. "I'll tell him at dinner tonight."

And she turned and walked out. As she made her way through what seemed like endless rooms of beige and pink, she wondered if she'd be able to leave gracefully or whether she'd end up lost in the huge apartment. But anger led her right to the door, which she yanked open before the startled butler could come to her aid.

When she got out onto the street, the first thing she felt like doing was calling Gordon to yell at him. Though the countess was clearly an unpleasant and difficult woman to begin with, it was equally clear that Gordon had twisted her arm to hire Laura, and that she had agreed to do so only very grudgingly. And Laura didn't need that kind of help.

But there was something about the idea that bothered her, and as she walked down Park Avenue to try to calm down, she had a sense she knew the reason.

This morning, she and Gordon had argued over Jerry Manning. She had felt slightly irrational during the discussion, as if she were taking a more extreme position than her real one just because she was so annoyed over what Gordon thought. And she hadn't really known why that was happening.

But it was clear to her now that at least *part* of the reason she tended to fly off the handle with Gordon was that he saw things—people, issues, even jobs—totally differently from the way she did. In Jerry Manning he saw a nervy upstart who deserved to be fired. Gordon had never been under suspicion for anything and probably had never been fired from a job. As with the makeup artist Victor Marcel, Gordon seemed to consider his effect on people's lives only minimally if at all; he always saw things from the perspective of a man who thought any failure was the fault of that person, that any obstacle could be overcome. But what obstacles had he ever had to overcome?

And with Countess di Lomazzo he had seen a wealthy woman who could "help" Laura with her career, when in fact the woman had been almost totally uninterested in the idea of hiring Laura. Worse still, Gordon probably had no idea of the arrogance and unpleasantness that ran so deep in the countess, because the woman had never shown that side of herself to him. And why *should* she have? Laura wondered angrily. Gordon was someone who attended dinner parties at her house. He wasn't an employee or someone who was supposed to enter only certain quarters of her apartment.

And Laura realized then that she was angriest at herself. When she had heard the countess telling the butler he had made a mistake, shouldn't she have left right then and there?

She knew there were no easy answers. She *was* in a position of subservience, by definition. She was an employee of each person who hired her, and with that came a difference in status—something Gordon had probably never thought of.

Damn. Was her career always going to be so fraught with difficulty? And would she be able to get past her resentment of Gordon? Did she even want to? When she thought of some of his values—the way he wouldn't be able to understand what had gone wrong with the countess, for instance, and why Laura had felt so angry over the countess's attitudes—she wasn't even sure she wanted to make up with him.

But then she thought of the good times they had had—Gordon's obviously genuine affection for her, his laughter, his passionate lovemaking—and she wondered how one man could have so many different facets.

And she wondered if she'd ever have a chance to discover whether one Gordon was more "real" than the other.

CHAPTER EIGHT

The rest of Laura's appointments that day went as well as the one with the countess had gone badly. Mrs. Charles Althorp, her second client of the day, couldn't have been nicer—chatting with Laura over tea before they got down to business, laughing over the makeup she had worn in the past, treating Laura as a respected aide rather than as an unwelcome intruder. And Laura's third client of the day, another friend of Gordon's, was friendly and gracious. And since both women were friends of Gordon's, Laura felt slightly less alienated from him than before.

But still, even though the appointments and her makeup session with the news team had gone beautifully, Laura had once again felt the sharp contrast between the lives of her customers and her own life. And they were Gordon's friends. Which meant that if Laura did get seriously involved with Gordon, the situation would perhaps be painfully reminiscent of those times with Matthew.

Damn it, she was proud of her background. She loved her hometown, she loved her family, and she loved her friends back home. Most of them had stayed there after high school. They'd gotten married and had kids, some of them had gotten divorced, none had made a tremendous amount of money.

Laura had set out to do something slightly different

with her life. But she didn't judge those friends of hers who had traveled the more traditional routes; she had just wanted something different, and she was doing the best she could to achieve her goals as quickly as she could. But she wondered if the route was going to be even one tenth as smooth as she had thought at first.

As Laura walked into Jerry Manning's studio, she was thinking more about Gordon and her annoyance at him than about Jerry. Had her feelings about Jerry been colored by her resentment of Gordon? she wondered. Had they been created as a backlash?

Jerry was all friendly smiles as he greeted Laura, and he held out a sheaf of pictures to her even before she sat down.

"We did it!" he said enthusiastically. "We really did it, Laur. Now I go to work, and you're on your way."

"That's great! Do you mean it?"

"Hey, what do you think? I'm just *saying* that? Look at the pictures and then tell me you think I'm lying."

Her surprise grew as she worked her way through the stack of pictures. She almost always hated the way she looked in photographs, but she had to admit that the pictures were damn good. And it wasn't just a matter of her looking prettier than she usually did in photographs; they looked very professional as well, much like pictures she had seen of her clients after photo sessions.

"These are really good," she said when she had finished. "I mean it."

"Hey, I know you mean it. This is some of my best work. So what do you say we get going?"

She shrugged. "Sure, I guess. Depending on what that means."

"I'll get us some wine—that's what we need. Then we'll talk."

"Okay," she said as he crossed the studio toward what seemed to be his never-ending wine supply. Every time she said "okay" to him, she used a certain voice—what she thought of as her submissive, Laura Hoover voice. And it reminded her that she was on a mission, a mission she had begun with as much suspicion as Gordon still harbored.

She watched Jerry pouring out the wine and realized that her best bet in terms of getting a look at his Rolodex would be while he was pouring, since the wine was at one end of the studio and his office area was at the other. Still, it was a nerve-racking idea, one that made her heart pound just thinking about it.

"Now we've really got something to celebrate!" he called as he came back with the wine.

"Something more than the pictures, you mean?"

His face fell. "Hey, give me some time, Laura. Success doesn't happen overnight anymore. There's too much competition. You've got hundreds—thousands—of girls out there as pretty as you who are trying to make it just like you are. So it doesn't come easy. It doesn't come easy at all."

"Then what are we celebrating?" she asked.

"Hey, you could have some faith, you know what I'm saying? It would make my job a hell of a lot easier. We're celebrating the pictures, okay? That should be enough right there for a start, okay? Some girls, I find they come out like dogs in their pictures, and what can I do? I can tell them, 'Nice knowing you'—that's what. So we're celebrating that that didn't happen and we can continue our association."

"Okay," she said, raising her glass and sipping, feeling like Laura Hoover again. At times like this she once again felt Gordon could be right. But just because Jerry could sometimes be a little cheap-sounding didn't mean he was a criminal. With Gordon's prep school, Ivy League education, of course he'd find Jerry less than perfect. But she had a different perspective.

Damn. Now she didn't know *what* to think!

"You look pretty as hell tonight," Jerry said. "Really, Laur."

She smiled. "Thanks. I look better in the pictures, though; they really are great."

"Hey—you come to a professional, you get professional work. I've got big plans for us. *Big* plans."

"Well, what next, then? Do I go out on auditions through you? Will you start setting them up? I just don't know how—"

He held up his hands. "You leave everything to me and you do everything through me, you understand? You can buy the trades like *Backstage* and *Show Business,* you can talk to your friends, anything. But when it comes to work or any ideas you have, you come to me first, understand?"

"Sure. But where *do* we go from here?"

"We put together your portfolio, I start making calls, sending some eight-by-tens out, feeling out the market. It's a tough time to break in right now, though—a hell of a time."

"But you think I'll be able to do it?"

"Hey, there are no guarantees, you know what I mean? I'll do my best. That's all I can promise you."

"But I thought you said I was going to make it."

He sighed. "Look. There are no guarantees, like I said.

If anyone can make it, you've got a hell of a chance. A *hell* of a chance. The best chance going of any of my clients."

Which reminded Laura that she wanted to look up the names, if she could, of some of Jerry's other "clients."

She glanced over at the partition that screened the office area from the rest of the loft. "Uh, would you mind if I used your phone, Jerry? I have to call a friend."

"Sure, sure. Go ahead. Right over there on the desk."

"Great. And it's a little, um, private, so do you think . . ." Her voice trailed off. She was hoping he'd suggest something that would ensure his staying at his end of the loft.

"Hey, look—I have to do some work in the darkroom anyway. So use the phone, talk as long as you want, and then give me a knock when you're done and we can talk some more. Just don't open that door—that's all I ask."

She smiled. "I understand. And thanks."

"Hey, listen. If things go our way we'll each be able to afford ten phones and ten secretaries, you know what I mean? So relax."

"Okay. See you in a few minutes."

She watched as he went into the darkroom and closed the door, and then she walked quickly to the other end of the studio.

She knew it would be safer and easier to talk to someone real than to pretend, so she called her friend Selena at home.

"Laura! I was just thinking about you. How's everything going?"

"Oh, okay," Laura answered quietly.

"Just okay? I thought by this time you'd be rich and famous and engaged!"

Laura laughed. "Is that the big three? I'm none of those things and not even close."

"Well, you're not the only one," Selena said. "But then you never cared about the third thing. I've been talking to Claudia so much I've gotten brainwashed into thinking *everyone*'s obsessed with getting married, just because she is."

"How is she, by the way? Still working temp?"

"Mmmm. Ask me in ten years and I'm sure the answer will still be yes. Always looking for the perfect company to work at."

"Well, I give her credit anyway. She supports herself and she meets a lot of interesting people. . . ." Laura hesitated as she began to look through the Rolodex. There weren't many names, luckily, but as she flipped through the cards, she realized she had no idea if the people Jerry had listed were clients or just friends or business contacts. Sometimes it was obvious, as was the case with a messenger service and a pizza parlor, but Laura had no idea if the other names—ninety-nine percent women's—were clients.

"Laura? Are you there?" came Selena's voice.

"Yes. Sorry. I'm just . . . in the middle of something." She realized she hadn't even brought a piece of paper with her, so she ripped one off Jerry's note pad and began writing. Sheila Cassidy, 555-1376. Janis Leeds . . . Claire Isaacs . . . She flipped the Rolodex back and forth, picking names at random, until she had hurriedly written the names and numbers of six women.

"Laura, why don't you call me back?" Selena asked. "You're obviously busy."

"I can't," Laura said. "I need to be talking to someone."

"What?"

"I'll explain later," Laura said quietly. "But I do have to keep talking, so just talk." And she kept writing, barely able to concentrate.

"What about?" Selena asked, obviously mystified. "Laura, I—"

"How's Charlie?" Laura asked. "Or Chuck. What's his name?"

"Chuck," Selena answered. "That's over. I wish you would tell me what you're doing."

"What are you doing?" Jerry Manning demanded.

Laura nearly jumped out of her skin. She turned and found Jerry standing about six feet away, hands on his hips, looking not at Laura but at the Rolodex she had been flipping through only moments earlier.

"What are you doing?" he repeated, his voice so sharp she felt as if she had been slapped.

"Laura?" Selena called into the phone. "Laura? Are you all right?"

"Uh, yes, Selena. I . . . I should get off now," she said abstractedly, unable to think about anything but the stormy menace in Jerry Manning's eyes.

"Laura?"

"I'll call you back," she murmured, and clumsily hung up the receiver.

"I asked you a question," Jerry Manning warned, stepping forward.

"I was on the phone."

"I could see that. And you know damn well what I'm asking. Why were you going through my Rolodex?"

She swallowed as she tried to picture where the slip of paper she had been writing on was in relation to her hands. She couldn't exactly reach backward and crumple it in her fist. But what if he found it?

"Well?" he demanded.

She had no idea what the right approach was or even if there *was* a right approach, but she decided she'd better plunge ahead. "I just wanted to see something," she said weakly.

"See what?"

She shrugged and told herself to play Laura Hoover, not Laura Dawson. "You're going to think I'm silly," she said quietly, looking down at the floor. "Or maybe you'll be angry. I guess you *are* angry, huh?"

"What do you think? Damn it, I deserve an explanation."

She sighed. "Okay. Here goes. Don't get mad, though. It's just that . . . today I kind of felt that you didn't have as much experience as you said. I don't know why I felt that—just that I had some doubts. You said some things you had never said before."

"Yeah? And?"

"So I wanted to see if this was a real business—whether you had names of important people in your files. I mean, I wouldn't have even thought of it if I hadn't had to make a call and I saw the Rolodex right there."

"And what did you find?"

She forced herself to smile. "I found out that I wouldn't know if you were successful or not. I just don't know enough about the business."

He reached forward and grabbed her wrist. "Come here."

"What?"

"I'm not attacking you. Just come with me." His grip was strong, and for a moment a shock of fear shot through her. But he simply led her across the studio to the area where they usually drank wine. "Now sit," he said firmly.

"Jerry, I—"

"Just sit down."

She sat down and he straddled a chair across from her, and he looked her straight in the eye. "Now I'm going to say this once, and once should be enough. I don't like girls who sneak around my back, Laura. I mean in my personal life and in my business. You want to know something, you ask me. I'll tell you anything you want to know, as long as I think you should know it. There's a lot in this business you don't understand—steps I'm going to take that you might not understand. That's why you hired me, okay?"

She looked into his eyes and just managed to say yes. There was a new threat in his voice, a warning that chilled the blood in her veins. And all she wanted to do was leave as soon as she could.

But then she remembered the piece of paper she had written the names on. She couldn't leave it on the desk. If Jerry found it, he'd know she had lied. And then . . . it was hard to say what he'd do. All she knew was that she didn't trust him anymore.

"Um, Jerry, I understand what you're saying. I really do. I wish you wouldn't make such a big deal out—"

"A big deal!" he roared. "Hey, listen. Have you ever found someone going through your things? Have you?"

She shrugged. "I don't know. I can't think. I guess so. I don't—"

"Yeah, well, let me tell you—you may like it, but I don't."

"Okay," she insisted. "I really do understand. And I apologize."

"Look—I know there are some people, they want to share everything and be like a family. But I'm not like that. I'll work my ass off for you, Laura, but we're not family."

"I understand." She looked at her watch. It was eight fifteen; suddenly she wanted to leave more than anything in the world. But she had to get the piece of paper.

"Why are you looking at your watch?"

"I told my friend I'd meet her. I should actually get going."

"Should you?" he asked, his voice flat and dry.

She couldn't read his expression at all. "What do you mean? I thought we were finished."

"Are we?"

She stood up and tried to decide whether to go get the piece of paper or just leave. She didn't like the strangeness of Jerry's voice or his replies.

"Where are you going?"

"I have to make another call," she said impulsively.

He gave her another warning look and she turned away, and as she walked back across the loft toward the phone, she could feel his eyes on her.

The second she got to the desk, she pocketed the notepaper and then picked up the phone and dialed the first seven numbers that came into her head. She had no intention of talking to anyone at that moment; all she wanted to do was get out. And a moment later she hung up and came back out into the main part of the loft.

"Well, it was busy," she said as casually as she could.

"Stay and try again."

"No, I have to get home."

He looked up sharply. "I thought you said you were meeting a girl friend."

"I am. I'm meeting her at my house," she improvised.

"When?"

"Jerry, I really don't—"

"You don't what?" he asked, standing up.

She grabbed her purse and started walking to the door.

" 'You don't understand,' " he said in a high voice that mimicked hers. "Is that what you were going to say?"

"Yes. Why are you so suspicious?"

"Why would you make a date with someone else when you knew we had a meeting? You knew we had a meeting tonight, but you—"

"Jerry, I didn't. I told my friend I'd call her, which I did—from here. I don't know what you're getting so upset about."

"I'm not upset. Just surprised you would walk out when I was about to tell you some interesting news."

"What interesting news?"

"Hey, look—you have a date. We'll talk another time."

"Jerry, why can't you just tell me? What's the interesting news?"

"Oh, I had some interest from a producer, that's all."

"About me?"

"No, about Marilyn Monroe. Of course about you."

"Who? What producer? How could they have seen the pictures yet?"

He looked her in the eyes. "You really *don't* believe me, do you?"

"I do. But I just thought it seemed strange that—"

"Yeah, yeah," he said, reaching past her and yanking open the door. "I believe you like you believe me, Laura. Call me when you change your mind."

She stepped out of the loft with relief, even though she was still curious. "I'll talk to you tomorrow, Jerry."

"Whenever." And he slammed the door.

Laura felt a physical relief as soon as the door had closed, and she decided to take the stairs rather than to wait for the slow-moving elevator. She didn't want to be standing in the hall if Jerry opened the door again. And it wasn't so much his reaction over the Rolodex that bothered her; she too would have been very annoyed if she had found someone looking through her files. No, what disturbed her most was afterward, when he had been so hostile and suspicious when she'd wanted to leave. His hostility at that point had reached her in an almost physical way, and she was immensely glad to be out of there.

She ran down the stairs, purse swinging against the banister, and out into the night air, and hailed a cab for home. This was no time to think about expense, she decided. All she wanted to do was get home and sink into a warm bubble bath and forget about Jerry and his reactions.

And the fight she had had with Gordon.

Damn it, he had—in a way—been right. But that wasn't the point, she felt. He had *happened* to be right; he hadn't been right because of any deep thought processes or any great understanding.

But she missed him. She had seen him every night lately, and when she put aside all the feelings she had had at the countess's, and all the anger that had plagued her this morning, a glimmer of love shone through, a glow of warmth that made her miss him enormously.

She didn't understand how it would all end. She *wanted* to be able to put aside her feelings; the memory of

Gordon saying, "I think I'm falling in love with you," brought tears to her eyes.

Maybe Gordon had been right when he'd said anything could break two people apart. She was so sure there were so many reasons they couldn't be together; but maybe that didn't have to be true—unless she made it true.

As the cab pulled into her street, Laura thought about the first time Gordon had come over and tried to compliment her on the building. And she had snapped at him.

"Six twenty," the cab driver said, and Laura paid, gave a generous tip she could ill afford, and got out.

She got her mail—all bills—and climbed what seemed like a million flights of stairs to her apartment.

And there stood Gordon in front of her door.

CHAPTER NINE

"Gordon!"

He didn't quite smile. "Are you busy?"

"No, no. I was going to call you." She glanced up at him and then opened the door. "Come on in."

He followed her and shut the door. "I want to say something before you say anything," he said quietly.

She turned and looked up at him, and suddenly she was frightened. She had just about made up with him in her mind; now was he going to say something negative? She had completely put *his* feelings out of her mind. "What's the matter?" she asked.

"I shouldn't have let you go this morning," he said softly. "Laura, all day I wanted to call you, to tell you I was sorry, to tell you I'd listen to what you had to say." He came forward and put his hands on her shoulders and looked down at her with dark, loving eyes. "I let my jealousy get in the way."

"Jealousy? You mean of Jerry Manning?"

"Tell me I was wrong."

"Of course you were wrong."

He let his hands travel downward to her waist, where the familiar pressure of his persuasive fingers brought back a flood of memories. "It's a side of myself I've tried to hide from you."

"You mean being jealous? I think it's kind of nice."

"Oh, it's anything but nice when it breaks up a relationship." He thought back to last year, to Christine, the only woman who had meant anything to him up to now.

"Has it happened a lot?" Laura asked.

Gordon shook his head. "Until recently, I didn't think I was the jealous type, because I was never involved enough with anyone. But with the woman I was involved with last year, it did become a problem."

"Who was she?" Laura asked.

He took her face in his hands and looked deeply into her eyes. "You don't really want to talk about someone else, do you?"

"Yes, I do," she insisted. "I want to know everything about you, Gordon, everything I can. And I think I'd feel better about a lot of things if I knew more about you. We have this fantastic relationship in bed, but I don't feel I even know you that well in other areas. I mean, I don't even know who this other woman was."

He shrugged. "It isn't that interesting, but I'll tell you if you really want to know," he said, following her into the living room and onto the couch. "I was going out with a woman. I was suspicious of her when she began a project with a man. I could never drop my suspicions and it drove her crazy. So we broke up." He glanced at Laura. "End of story."

She sighed. "Okay, obviously you don't want to talk about it. I had just thought—"

"I'll talk if you want, Laura; I'll tell you anything you want to know. I just don't know what you want to know."

"Well, who was this woman who was so important to you? How long did you go out with her?"

"Oh, for about a year. A year and two months, actually. Her name was Christine Kelly."

Christine, Laura thought. So that was who the Christine of his dreams was. "When did it end?"

"Oh, six months ago," he said quietly.

She wondered whether the wistfulness in his voice was in her imagination or not. "Was it difficult to get over?"

He shifted onto one elbow and looked into Laura's eyes. "In a sense," he said carefully. "But not in the sense I would have expected. What was different—and best—about Christine was the fact that she was always there for me, something I had only come to want very recently. It was nice to have someone after all those years of being alone."

"Did you live together?" Laura asked softly.

"No, but we just shared a lot, especially at the beginning. She went to a lot of parties with me, a lot of network functions, all the things I had once gone to alone. And when the jealousy began, it just didn't quit."

"It's strange that you were never like that until then," Laura pointed out.

"Well, there *were* some good reasons to be jealous. Christine was working on a very complicated project; she had to spend a lot of time with this man, and I knew what would happen." He shrugged. "And it did."

Laura frowned. "But that means jealousy *didn't* break the two of you up."

He shook his head. "No, it did," he insisted. "I really believe that if you look at a relationship closely enough, you should be able to figure out—logically—why it's gone wrong, or why it's not going right."

She smiled. "I can't believe what you're saying! You're talking about emotions, Gordon—not logic. Most of the time people have no idea why they do things, why they feel certain things."

"Well, I've always believed you ought to *try* to treat relationships the way you treat anything else. With you, for instance," he continued, his voice suddenly gentle. "From the moment I saw you—the very first moment—I knew I had to know you, that I had to figure out a way to get to know you. And that I wasn't going to let you go once I did. Now, I can't explain why I felt that way about you, but I treated it as I would treat anything else—something I could go after. And I know that isn't completely logical—and I know it sounds unappealing. But it's the way I've lived my life; it's the only way I know how to be. When I want something, I plan for it, I try for it, I do whatever I have to do to get it. And then when something goes wrong . . . well, maybe I don't handle it that well." He looked into her eyes. "And you're so lovely," he said softly, "that I can't help worrying when I hear you change your mind about someone like Jerry Manning. I *do* get jealous, Laura."

"Well, I promise you it's unjustified," she said. "And anyway, I hate to admit it, but I think I might have been wrong about him."

Suddenly she remembered that she'd left Selena in the dark about what was going on, and that Selena was probably worried. "Oh, my God," she said, jumping off the couch.

"What's the matter?" Gordon asked.

"I have to call Selena!" She ran to the phone and quickly dialed her friend's number.

Selena answered on the first ring.

"Selena, it's Laura."

"Finally! What's going on?"

"I'm really sorry," Laura said. "I completely forgot I was talking to you when I was caught." Out of the corner of her eye she saw Gordon look up sharply.

"Caught?" Selena asked. "What's going on?"

"I'll have to tell you later or tomorrow," Laura said. "I don't want to stay on, because Gordon's here right now."

"But everything's okay?"

"Yes. Definitely."

"All right, I'm glad. But you'd better either tell me what you're involved in or leave me out of it completely, Laura, because I was a nervous wreck wondering what had happened to you."

"I know. I'm sorry. Can you meet me in a few days? Maybe Monday? I can tell you about it then."

"Sure. How about for lunch?"

They arranged to meet at a convenient place near Selena's job, and Laura was about to hang up when Selena interrupted her good-bye. "Just tell me one thing, Laura."

"Shoot."

"Does Gordon know what you're involved in?"

"Sure. I'm doing it for him. Indirectly, at least."

"Now I'm totally mystified." Selena laughed. "But that makes me feel better. And I'll see you Monday."

"Okay. Bye." When Laura hung up, she was aware that Gordon was staring at her, that he had in fact been staring at her during the entire conversation. She sat back down, and when she looked at him, she saw he was angry.

"I'm not usually rude enough to listen to other people's calls," Gordon said, "but I obviously couldn't help it. Tell me what's going on."

Laura sighed. "Okay. I sort of told you before. I believe you about Jerry Manning now."

"How were you 'caught,' as you said?"

"I wasn't caught in the scheme," Laura explained. "I mean, he doesn't know who I am or anything like that. But he found me looking through his Rolodex."

"Oh, God," Gordon murmured.

"No, it was okay. I think I covered it. I said I had had some suspicions but that I realized I was being silly. Basically, I just played up the naive Laura Hoover and hoped that he believed me. The scary part, though, was that I left the piece of paper with several women's names and numbers from his Rolodex on his desk."

"Oh, no."

"Well, I got them back," Laura said, "but it was pretty scary because after he found me with the Rolodex, he was acting very strange. I think he's a little paranoid."

"I wouldn't be surprised," Gordon said flatly. "And that's it for you and meeting with him in person, Laura. It's too risky."

"You won't get any arguments from me there," Laura said quickly. "All I wanted to do was leave."

"Thank God you got out of there," Gordon murmured, his eyes darkening with emotion.

"Well, I don't think anything *really* terrible would have happened; I mean, I don't want to exaggerate. But it was a little frightening. And if we call the other women, I'll be really interested to hear what they have to say."

"I'll call them," Gordon insisted. "I want you to stay behind the scenes from now on. It's clear we're dealing with a con artist, and perhaps a sick con artist at that."

Laura shook her head. "I still can't tell about his connections," she mused.

"I thought you said you agreed with me," Gordon said with surprise and a hint of annoyance.

"I do, basically. But at the end . . ." She hesitated. "I don't know. I guess it was fake—just a move of desperation on his part."

"What was?"

"As I was leaving, he said that a producer was interested in me." She shrugged. "Of course, it seemed strange since I don't know how anyone could have seen my pictures yet. But I was thinking about it on the way home, and I thought that maybe he *had* been planning to tell me about the lead at the beginning, when I first arrived, and he wanted to build up the suspense—you know, saying how tough the times are, and how hard it is to get started. That way, whatever little morsel of possible future success he held out would seem that much greater." She sighed. "I know it's silly that I keep going back and forth on this. I *know* I wouldn't want to be alone with him again. But . . . I guess it has to do with vanity. And I guess that's the reason there are a thousand new Jerry Mannings operating every year—people *want* to believe them, and so they do. It felt good to have my picture taken, and to be told that I was beautiful and promising and—"

"I could have told you all that," Gordon said softly, reaching out and stroking her cheek. "And I'd tell you that every moment I was with you if I thought that was what you wanted to hear."

She smiled. There was so much love in his eyes; how could she have been so angry at him just this morning?

"Knowing you, though," Gordon continued, "with your stubbornness and contrariness, you'd have run as fast as you could in the opposite direction."

"Do I look like I'm running?" she asked with a wink, rubbing her hand across his chest.

Just as Laura was leaning down to kiss Gordon's chest, the phone rang.

"Do you want me to go into the bedroom?" Gordon asked.

"No, that's okay." She answered just as she glanced at the clock: ten twenty-five.

And she couldn't believe it when she heard her mother's voice on the phone. Her parents were usually asleep by nine.

"Mama, is everything okay?"

"Yes, hon, everything's fine. But I was worried about you."

"Worried? Why?"

"I had a funny feeling around eight tonight. I told your papa and he said to call you and I called and got your answering service, so I just hung up and worried."

"But what were you worried about?"

"Just a funny feeling, that's all." There was a silence then, and Laura wondered if her mother wasn't holding something back. "Mama, is something else wrong?"

"No, hon. I promise." She paused. "Just as long as you're okay."

"I'm fine. Really. And I've been meaning to call. And I've been meaning to come up."

"You know we'd love to see you, Laura. And you could get some nice color in your cheeks. Try selling *that* to your customers and you'd be rich as a king."

Laura smiled. "I know. Everyone's skin is gray here, including mine. Well, look—I'll call you and let you know if I can get a train that fits in with my schedule, and then you or Papa can pick me up."

"We'll be waiting."

"Love to Papa."

"I'll tell him, dear." And as usual, her mother hung up without saying good-bye, a habit Laura couldn't get her to break no matter how hard she tried.

When Laura hung up, she shook her head and smiled. "That woman is lucky she doesn't have to make business calls. Her reputation would be mud if she did that."

"She hangs up without saying good-bye?" Gordon asked with a smile.

"Mmmm. She insists it's 'obvious' the conversation is over. Anyway, I think I'll go up there tomorrow. She sounded a little funny, and I'd like to get out in the fresh air anyway."

"How about company?"

"What?"

"You heard me. How about some company?"

"Well, I don't know." Laura hesitated.

She avoided his eyes as he scrutinized her. Finally he said, "All right," in a voice that showed he was hurt.

And she realized he couldn't possibly know why she had said no. She wasn't even sure herself. Her parents were, as she had told Gordon on their first meeting, as poor as church mice, two people who just hadn't been able to make it no matter how hard they'd tried. Her father, a skilled electrician, got fired from job after job because of his bad temper, but no matter what straits they were in, he wouldn't let his "woman" work outside of the house. Laura certainly wasn't ashamed of them, or of the tiny house they lived in in the woods. But she did have some hesitation about letting Gordon in on it. He was from such a different world. Today she had been angry at him for some of those differences, until she'd realized how much she cared for him. And for a while, at least, she wanted to keep the waters smooth and not stir things up.

But as she watched Gordon stand up and walk slowly —glumly—over to the living room window, she knew she had to say something to make the situation better. For he seemed to think she didn't want him to come because she wanted some distance.

"Gordon, maybe we can talk about it. I don't know—"

"Forget it," he said quietly, his back to her.

"But I don't think you understand." She didn't intend to explain her real reasons, but she did think she could make the situation better.

He turned to face her. "I understand that I'm trying to move forward, Laura. I've met a woman I think there are real possibilities with. Real possibilities. To me, the natural next step is to bring each other into our lives more fully. *My* parents are dead; but I thought I could meet yours." He shrugged. "If you don't want to do that, fine. I've obviously been on the wrong track."

Laura walked up behind Gordon and wrapped her arms around his chest. "Come with me tomorrow," she said softly.

"Not if you don't want me to, Laura. I've never pushed myself on anyone."

"Damn it, you're not pushing yourself!" she insisted, and he turned around. "Don't you think I might have had other reasons, reasons I've changed my mind about?"

"What reasons?"

She thought quickly. "Oh, I was thinking of visiting some friends in town and I thought I'd want to be alone." She shrugged to help cover the small white lie. "But actually I just remembered they're away anyway. And it was a silly thought because if they were here, you could certainly come along. So let's go up. It's supposed to be a beautiful day tomorrow."

"Well, you know I'd love to," he said softly, and he saw a flash of apprehension in her lovely eyes. Damn it, he was pretty sure he knew what she was nervous about, and he wanted to take her in his arms and tell her he loved her, tell her she never had *any*thing to fear when she was with him. But he knew that if she wanted that kind of comfort, she'd ask for it. Though she had bragged that she "moved fast," he had come to realize that she was a deeply cautious person, especially with her feelings. When she was ready to talk about something or to do something, she'd do it—but if you pushed her, she'd run.

And all he wanted was to be with her, to let her see for herself why her worries were so unnecessary.

CHAPTER TEN

The next morning, Saturday, Laura called her mother and told her she was driving up with a friend and would be there around noon. Her mother was wildly curious about who the "friend" was, and Laura laughed and said they'd find out soon enough, but after she hung up, her doubts from the night before came back with full force.

It was only when she had grown up and left town that she realized her shame over being poor was silly; yet the childhood feelings often came back—especially when she went back home—and she wondered how she'd feel with Gordon.

When Gordon arrived at her apartment, though, some of her fears dissipated. He seemed happy to be getting out of the city, and Laura was vastly relieved to see he hadn't brought his limousine but was driving a dark green Triumph instead. And in the back luggage area was a picnic basket he said was filled with fruit, cheese, and other lunch food—something Laura in her nervousness had totally forgotten to discuss. For she was certain her mother would have cooked a large hot lunch—something she always did even at the height of summer, because Laura's father, Clyde, insisted on it.

The drive up was beautiful—springy and fragrant and just sunny enough to make the budding leaves and flowers bright against the blue sky, and Laura began to relax as they sped along the road.

"I haven't been for a drive in the country in ages," Gordon said with a smile. "And I've never been to Allenville. What's it like?"

"It's beautiful," Laura said. "Really kind of like a classic New England town except that it's so close to New York. And you know, friends of mine from the city have always been amazed when I tell them most of my friends from home stayed in Allenville, but the fact is that it's so pretty that most people can't imagine moving, unless they're really interested in a career that's very city-oriented." She hesitated for a moment, and then went on. "And one other nice thing about the country is that if you don't have much money, the place you live in will almost inevitably be a lot nicer than you'd get in a place like New York."

"I can imagine," Gordon said quietly, feeling for Laura because he was sure she was trying to "prepare" him in some way for meeting her parents. He wanted to tell her it was all unnecessary; but he knew she had to do things her way.

They turned off the highway and progressed onto a series of smaller and smaller roads, and as Laura directed Gordon, he could sense a growing pleasure on her part, an excitement over coming home that he was glad he could share.

"This is Allenville proper in both senses of the word," Laura said as they pulled into a picturesque little town. "And we live in North Allenville, so just keep on this road till the drugstore and then make a right."

"This is lovely," Gordon said. "Let's stop here later."

Laura shrugged. "Okay."

"You don't look too enthusiastic."

"My friends are all in North Allenville," she said as he turned at the drugstore. "And I kind of still have some bad feelings about the main part of town."

"Why? What about?"

She shrugged. "I know it's silly," she began. "And I'm probably too old to still feel this way. But when I was going to school—make a right at that red oak—"

"Where?"

"The red oak. That big tree right here." She grinned. "Don't you know a red oak when you see one?"

"Hey, I just run a network. You were saying, though . . ."

Laura's smile faded. "Mmmm. When I was going to school, there was a definite division between the kids from Allenville and the kids from North Allenville. There weren't even that many of us from North Allenville, either. As you can see, it's pretty remote."

"Beautiful," Gordon said as they reached the crest of a hill. Beyond were pastures dotted with cows, sheep huddled near a pond, new spring wildflowers swaying in the breeze. And the air smelled of honey and flowers and sunshine.

"Anyway, my best friend in school for years was a girl who lived on Main Street, in one of those big white houses we passed in the town square."

"Those are amazing."

"Well, some have actually been divided since then. But at the time, my friend Lizzie's family had this giant white house that was just picture perfect in every way. Inside and out, it looked like the houses on television where perfect families lived those really perfect lives, and I was so jealous I would just wish—even though Lizzie was my friend—that somehow it could all be taken away, because while Lizzie lived in that huge white house with an Irish setter and two brothers and perfect parents and all the money they would ever need, my parents and I lived in the woods in a broken-down house, with rabbits and a couple of chickens and a pig we never had the heart to slaughter. Anyway, at first Lizzie and I were such great friends that the differences didn't matter that much. But eventually, especially in high school, the envy over what Lizzie had and I didn't just ate away at me."

"That must have been tough."

"Well, it really got worse. Naturally, when you grow up, clothes and possessions just become *more* important —what you wear to school, what you wear on dates, if you have a car, which of course I didn't." She sighed. "And what bothers me now—turn right at that sign—is that I was so wrong."

"What do you mean?" Gordon asked, steering onto a narrow one-lane near-dirt road.

"I had everything that was important," Laura said quietly. "In everything that counted, I had a thousand times more than Lizzie had. My parents loved me, they loved each other and still do, and they did their best for me in every way they could. And I didn't realize it until long after I had moved away."

"You mean after you moved to New York."

She nodded. "Turn left at that sign."

Gordon smiled and turned at a worn-out sign that was completely illegible, its lettering obscured by weather or perhaps design. "I like that sign. Not too many people would even notice this road."

"That's the way they want it. Papa kept taking the old sign down and telling the town he didn't know what had happened to it, and the town kept putting newer and shinier signs up—which is silly because this is a dead-end road and our house is the only house left. So Papa finally put out one of the old signs, sanded it down till you could hardly read it, and the town let it stay. They figured it made more sense than spending the money every year to put up a new sign. Watch right up here, Gordon, on the right there's a giant ditch in the road."

He steered away just in time. "You really know this road."

"I could walk any of these woods around here with my eyes closed and find my way back to the house or any spot you named."

"You really love it here."

She nodded. "And the only thing I really care about in terms of making money is someday buying a house of my own. All the rest I could do without."

"That sounds like you," Gordon said with a smile. "Is that the house up there?"

"Mmmm," Laura said, brightening at the mere sight of it. She had had so much anxiety about this moment—Gordon seeing the tiny house with its peeling gray paint and the broken attic windows, the old porch sagging at one corner and the broken-down car and truck parts in the yard. But she loved the house, and at that moment it might as well have been a castle.

Gordon didn't say anything as they turned in to what was a kind of makeshift half-grass, half-gravel driveway. He was afraid of saying anything that Laura could interpret as condescending, as she had when he'd complimented her on her apartment in the city. And he was also genuinely surprised at the house. Laura had talked about being less well off than her friends in Allenville, but he hadn't been sure she wasn't exaggerating. Now, though, he saw that her parents lived in greater poverty than he'd imagined. There was definitely a natural beauty to the place—almost a magical loveliness that came from the lush green trees, the sound of the birds, the gentle sunshine that drenched everything in its amber glow. But Gordon hadn't expected the half-demolished cars heaped in a pile, the cracked paint and broken attic window the sense of neglect that contrasted so strongly with the trees and grass.

There didn't seem to be anyone around, but Gordon and Laura got out of the car and began walking toward the house.

"Aren't they home?" he asked, taking Laura's arm as they approached the porch.

"They must have the radio on," Laura said. "When it's going they can never hear a thing."

But at that moment the screen door swung open, and a woman Gordon thought looked amazingly like an older version of Laura came down the wooden steps, wiping her hands with a dishcloth.

"I *thought* I heard something," she cried with a smile as Laura fell into her arms. The two hugged, and then Laura looked up at Gordon and introduced him to her mother.

"Mama, this is Gordon Chase. Gordon, this is my mother, Louisa Dawson. Oh, and there's my father," she cried with a wave as a man in overalls came out from behind the house.

Clyde Dawson, walking with a slight stoop, made his way over to his daughter for a kiss and then shook hands with Gordon.

After all the introductions, Laura and Gordon followed Mrs. Dawson back into the house and Mr. Dawson went back to whatever he had been doing.

Since Gordon had never seen the house before, he couldn't be certain of his impressions, but from the general look of things, it looked as if Mrs. Dawson had done some considerable preparing for the visit. Fresh-cut flowers graced the small wooden table at the center, everything from the wooden counters to the windows to the tiny stove absolutely sparkled, and some sort of stew or soup that was cooking filled the room with a wonderful aroma.

"Lunch will be ready in about half an hour," Mrs. Dawson said. "But if you folks are hungry now—"

Gordon shook his head. "I'm fine, thanks."

"Me too," Laura said. "And actually, Mama, we brought a picnic. I didn't really think—"

"Don't be silly," Mrs. Dawson said. "That's no way to treat a guest, making him bring his own food. What's the matter with you, Laura?" Mrs. Dawson turned to Gordon. "Please sit down, sir—"

"Gordon, please."

"Gordon. Sit. And I hope Laura doesn't treat you this badly *all* the time."

"Mama . . ."

Gordon smiled. "Your daughter has been the perfect hostess at all times," he said with a wink. "Until today, of course."

"Gordon!" Laura protested. "But speaking of hosts, Mama, what's Papa doing that he's not in here?"

Mrs. Dawson shrugged. "Pick an idea out of the air and you'll have as good a chance of being right as I do. His back's so bad he shouldn't be doing *any*thing, but who knows? Him and the wind."

"Do you think he'd mind if I went and found out?" Gordon asked. "I'd like to have a look around."

"Be my guest," Mrs. Dawson offered. "But don't go getting involved in something that's going to take more than half an hour. And don't listen to him if he tells you it doesn't matter."

Gordon smiled. "Don't worry about that. I'll drag him back in if I have to."

The moment Gordon was out the door, Mrs. Dawson changed seats and moved closer to Laura. "I like your man. How come you've never told me anything about him?"

"I haven't known him that long," Laura said.

"I like him a lot."

"Mama, you just met him."

"And you know I'm the best judge of people you've ever met, Laura. Who was it told you that that Matthew fellow was no good?"

Laura felt ill at the memory. She had brought Matthew up at the very beginning of the relationship, and the visit had been a disaster.

"And who was it told you that your so-called friend Colleen was out to stab you in the back?"

"That doesn't make you a hundred percent right," Laura argued.

"Tell me when I've been wrong. Name me once."

"That isn't the point, Mama. Anyway, I don't want to argue. I like Gordon a lot. I'm glad you like him."

"What line of work's he in?"

"Television," Laura said, running her finger along a crack in the table.

"He's an actor?" her mother asked with alarm.

Laura smiled. "No, Mama. He's an executive. He's president of CTC-TV."

Her mother stared, and Laura's smile grew; she didn't know when the last time was that she had seen her mother speechless.

"Mama, say something or I'm going to think there's something wrong with you."

"That's a big job," she finally said.

"I know. Which is something that bothers me, actually."

Her mother narrowed her eyes. "Why? What's wrong with having a big job, Laura?"

"It's not the job," Laura insisted. "It's . . . it's the values I see in so many people—this drive to get ahead."

"Honey, you have the same drive. Money can buy things, and you know that as well as anybody."

Laura sighed. "I know. And I *want* to be financially independent; I want to be a success; but I wouldn't want those things if I thought I'd lose my morals in the process."

"Are you telling me this Gordon Chase is an immoral man?"

"Not at all, Mama, but—"

"Because from what I can see he's a decent man, Laura. A decent man."

"After thirty seconds," Laura pointed out. "I don't know—it's hard to explain. It's not that I would be more interested in someone who was a failure. I'm impressed with Gordon's success. But I don't feel he's had to work for it. And because of that, I don't think he has a good understanding of the way people on the other side of the fence live."

Mrs. Dawson sighed and looked into her daughter's

lovely eyes. They had always been wise, those eyes, and filled with pain at much too tender an age. Laura had been hurt by their circumstances; she had held her anger and pain and resentment inside for years, and they had only begun to talk about it after she left home.

Now, she wanted to point out to Laura how her thinking had gone wrong somewhere. "Laura, honey," she began. "Oh, wait a minute. I can't sit here and talk and do nothing. Help me make the salad?"

"Sure, Mama."

A few minutes later the two women stood by the sink, rinsing and drying lettuce and radishes and tomatoes. "I don't want you getting mad over what I'm going to say, Laura."

Laura put down the tomato she had been slicing. "What?" she asked warily.

Her mother sighed. "Just that it's as easy to fall in love with a rich man as a poor one. As long as he's a good man. That's what counts."

"I know that," Laura said with a trace of indignation. "I'm not *looking* for a poor man. I don't *want* to repeat—" She shook her head, trying to find different words. "I don't want to be poor. I don't know who would. But I'm never going to depend on a man to support me anyway, so that isn't the point. Right now I'm struggling to make something of myself—to be something on my own, independent of everyone else in my life. But if I *were* to get seriously involved with someone, I would just want to be sure . . ." For a moment her voice was lost in confusion. "I just want to be sure . . ."

Her mother reached out and covered her hand. "You want to be sure he's the right man. I understand that. But you've got to look past your blind spots, honey."

"What blind spots?"

"Just what we've been talking about. I may joke about my sixth sense about people and how I'm never wrong; but inside, I know I couldn't judge anybody after just meeting him. But you know Gordon, honey; don't mess things up because of some crazy idea you have."

Laura sighed. She knew her mother was right in a theoretical way. But her mother didn't know Gordon. Of course he had his wonderful sides; if he didn't, Laura wouldn't have been with him in the first place. But was there another part of him she didn't know? She kept getting glimpses of it. Was she being unfair, unjustly critical, or would she be painfully surprised at some point in the future when she discovered that her least favorite side of Gordon was his true self?

"I suppose it was all our talk when your papa lost his jobs." Her mother sighed. "Talking against Jake Chalmers, talking against Ken Marshall, talking against Tom Johnson."

"Papa sure lost a lot of jobs."

"That he did, Laura. He's a stubborn man and I'm not sure those men were one hundred percent wrong."

"Mama!"

Her mother shrugged, avoiding Laura's eyes. "How could they all be wrong, honey? They all found it in their hearts to hire him, so they couldn't be all bad."

"They didn't 'find it in their hearts,' Mama. You know Papa charged less than anyone else in town. I really can't believe you're not on his side."

"I've just been thinking, that's all." Her mother sighed.

"That's a fine way to think—against your own husband," Laura said accusingly. "Papa's just had a lot of bad breaks."

"And I don't want to see you come back here and live the way we did. I know how much you love it here, and you can always come back, but you were meant for another kind of life. I don't want to see you throw it away."

At her mother's last words Laura suddenly realized something: her mother was connecting her future success with the man she was with rather than her work; she hadn't mentioned anything about her career—since to her, what was important was the man's earning power. "Mama, you haven't even asked me about my job," Laura said.

"Well, honey, when you bring a good-looking man like Gordon Chase in, you can't expect me to think of *everything*." Mrs. Dawson smiled. "I just wonder what Lizzie Stapleton would say if she saw you now. With Gordon, I mean. You know, I heard she was coming back from Canada with that new husband of hers. Maybe to live."

"In *Allenville?*"

Mrs. Dawson shrugged. "That's what I heard, though how they'd live I don't know, since he's a bigtime city-type lawyer. If she comes, though, you can be sure I'll tell her about you and your new beau."

Laura smiled at her mother and said nothing. Clearly she *was* more impressed with Gordon than with Laura's new career risk, and there wasn't much—if anything—that Laura could do about it.

And Laura heard her father and Gordon scraping their shoes on the front porch anyway.

Gordon came in first, and he looked exhilarated and absolutely wonderful, tousled hair falling over glowing cheeks.

"You look happy," Laura commented with a smile. "What have you guys been doing?"

"Chopping wood," he said breathlessly.

Laura's father rubbed his back and limped over to his wife, who took over the back-rubbing without a word. "For someone who never chopped wood before, I'd say you were damn good, Gordon. Damn good."

Gordon smiled. "Then next fall I'll be up here as soon as you need me and you'll have all the wood you want."

Clyde Dawson shook his head. "Come up any time and we'll give you a good meal and plenty of work, Gordon. What I can't understand is why you'd want to stay down there anyway. But I guess you don't have any choice, from what you were telling me outside. You sure can't move your office out of the city." He looked around at his wife, who was still rubbing his back. "Honey, did you know Gordon's head of that CTC network down in New York?"

Louisa Dawson beamed. "I sure do."

"Well, I enjoy my work enormously," Gordon said, pulling out a chair and sitting down. "And as long as I enjoy it, I'll give it everything I've got. But the minute I lose interest, I'll be out. I guarantee you that."

"It's a big job," Louisa Dawson said with admiration. She patted her husband's back and then began setting things out for lunch. "You must have worked hard to get where you are, Gordon," she said, glancing at her daughter.

"Well, it was a combination of hard work and luck, really," Gordon said. "You know—being in the right place at the right time never hurts. Do you watch much, by the way?"

"Nah," Laura's father grumbled, seating himself at the

head of the table. "Nothing to watch, if you ask me." He paused, and Laura was certain her father had momentarily forgotten Gordon's role. "No offense, Mr. Chase."

"Gordon."

"Gordon. I'm sure you do a fine job."

Gordon raised a brow. "Not if there's nothing you like. What kind of changes would you like to see?"

"Something I can watch—that's what I'd like to see."

"Oh, don't listen to him," Mrs. Dawson called as she gave a last stir to the stew. "He doesn't sit still long enough to watch anything anyway."

"What about you?" Gordon asked.

"Oh, I don't have much time," Mrs. Dawson said vaguely.

"Mama, you watch *The Sinners,*" Laura said. *"That's* on Gordon's station. And so is *Coronado."*

"Oh, I watch them if I remember to," Mrs. Dawson murmured.

"If she remembers!" her husband cried, slapping the table. "She won't even talk on the telephone when those shows come on. Those nights are sacred in this house and don't you believe anything different—no matter what she tells you."

Gordon smiled. "I'm glad you like the shows, Louisa. They're two of my favorites. And if it weren't for people like you, I'd be out of a job."

Laura was amazed at how well they were all getting along. Her father was usually uncommunicative and unimpressed when she brought men home. But as lunch progressed, he and Gordon did more talking than either of the women.

After lunch, Clyde, Laura, and Gordon went for a walk in the woods, and the afternoon flew by.

By the time Laura and Gordon were getting ready to leave, Laura felt as if Gordon had known her family for years. He hugged Louisa as they said good-bye and brought a blush to her cheeks as he gave her a kiss, and he and Clyde shook hands heartily and with genuine affection.

"Don't forget your promise," Clyde warned Gordon.

Gordon laughed. "Don't *you* forget. One sunny Saturday morning in September I'll be here with an ax and an appetite."

"Don't wait that long," Louisa said with a smile.

Moments later, as Gordon turned the car around and pulled out onto the road, he shook his head and said, "They are really great people. I had the best time I've had in—in I don't know how long."

She gave him a sidelong glance. "Thanks a lot."

He smiled and hugged her with one arm. "Not counting the times I've been with you, silly. Your parents really are wonderful."

"I'm glad you had a good time. They were obviously crazy about you. I don't even know which one liked you more. My mother kept kind of glowing whenever she smiled, and my father didn't stop talking. You don't know how unusual that is."

"And what about you? Did you have a good time?"

"I did," she said, leaning back against the headrest and smiling. And to herself, she added that it had been more than a good time. She had been so worried about the "core" of Gordon's spirit, about his values and his outlook. But today, at his most relaxed, he'd been more wonderful than ever. Now thoughts of their different backgrounds, of people like the countess and comparisons with Matthew, seemed irrelevant.

She loved Gordon. And now that she realized it, she saw she had loved him since that first night they'd made love.

Suddenly, Laura said, "Wait a minute. Pull over here for a second."

Gordon pulled the car over onto a strip of grass that had been worn down and crushed from years of parking. "Do you want to get out?" he asked.

She thought for a moment. "Sure. Why not? I can show you where I spent years swimming and fishing. Come here."

They both got out of the car and she led him through brambles and bushes, beneath low-hanging boughs and through tangled vines, until they came to a brook, sandy-banked and flowing full with spring rains. The sun was just setting over the mountain, and the dusky glow bathed everything in its purple rays.

"This is lovely," Gordon said.

"Isn't it? Down there, along this path, there's a swimming hole, and up there in those woods, my father once built me a tree house."

"This is your land?"

"Nope. It's leased to hunters now. It wasn't our land back then, either, but my father built the house for the kids who used the swimming hole. Sort of an adjunct to the tire swing and other things we had rigged up."

"Your father seems like a great guy."

"You're great," she murmured, wrapping her arms around him. "You really are, Gordon. There was something about today . . . about seeing you in a different atmosphere. . . . I'm so sorry for some of the things I've said."

"I don't understand," he said softly.

Suddenly she realized that much of what she was apologizing for had never been said. She had had lots of negative thoughts about Gordon that she'd never expressed, and *these* were the ideas she was now discarding. "Oh, it's not important," she said quietly, gazing up into his wonderful brown eyes. "What is important is that I love you. I just wanted to tell you that."

The look in his eyes made it all worthwhile. He looked as if she had just given him the most precious gift in the world, and he wrapped his arms tightly around her and held her close, her head against his chest, his hands gently stroking her back. "Darling," he whispered. "If you knew what those words mean to me—how I've hoped you felt the way I do."

He drew back and gazed down at her, and as she looked up at him, dark against the glow of the sunset, she thought he had never looked handsomer.

"I love you," he said—not softly, not loudly, but strongly and surely, as if he'd love her forever and nothing could stop him.

And she wished, as he brought his lips down to hers, that the moment could last forever.

CHAPTER ELEVEN

On the drive back, about halfway down, Gordon flicked on the radio and turned to an all-news station to get the traffic report.

"Coming into the city at this time is murder," Gordon muttered. "I just want to see if there are any big jam-ups."

The news droned on and on and finally got to the traffic report, which revealed what Laura and Gordon had expected: traffic into the city was heavy, with delays on all bridges and tunnels. No surprise.

"Well, enough of that," Laura said, reaching forward and turning the dial until she found a country-music station. "Ah. Now, *this* is a lot nicer. Do you like country music?"

Gordon shrugged. "I've never listened to it much." He smiled. "You know, I was about to say it was because I'd never had the time. Which is true: one reason I have a chauffeur is that I like to work on my way to and from the office, and I couldn't work—obviously—if I were driving. But that means no music in the limo, and the rest of the time, until recently, has always been—well, just taken. Today was the first day I've taken off and completely relaxed in a long, long time. I literally forgot about the network, which has *never* happened before."

Laura shook her head. "I don't know how you can live like that."

He shrugged. "It's part of my job. And I love my work, Laura; I don't see it as a sacrifice. What I do see as a sacrifice is the fact that we won't be able to see each other quite as much from now on."

"Why not?"

"I've been letting things slide," he said with a sigh. "Putting things on hold and delegating things I really would rather have handled myself, just so I could see you. But there is one plus side."

"What's that?"

"Part of what I've let slide is the social side of things—the parties, the fund raisers, the charity events. I've said no to too many of them lately because there was nothing more important than seeing you. But I'd like you to come to as many as you can—now that you've gotten a bit of a start with your own plans."

"That sounds nice," Laura said.

"Good. The first one I should take care of is the countess's annual spring charity ball. Can you come to that with me? It isn't for a while now—about two months—but I'd like to let her know."

"The countess?" Laura asked.

"Yes. Why? Didn't everything go all right the other day?"

Laura laughed. How ridiculous. The countess! "No," she said. "It didn't go all right, as a matter of fact. It didn't go well at all."

He frowned. "Why didn't you tell me? What happened? I just assumed—"

She shook her head. "It's really not worth going into in detail, Gordon. The countess was rude to me, she didn't want me there in the first place, and I think the biggest mistake was that she agreed to something she wasn't interested in just because she wanted to please you."

"She was rude? How was she rude? I've never seen Luciana act rudely in all the time I've known her. Except . . ." He stopped.

"Except what?"

He hesitated.

"Gordon, what?"

"Well, I *can* think of a few incidents," he said quietly. "Damn it, don't tell me she was rude because she thought of you as a—as some kind of underling."

Laura raised a brow. "I can't say she didn't, Gordon. That's what she did from the moment I met her—even *before* I met her. She actually scolded the butler for having 'let' me sit in the living room."

Gordon swore. "I'm going to call that woman," he warned. "I'm going to call her and give her a damn good piece of my mind."

"Oh, what's the use?" Laura asked. "Really, Gordon. I was upset, but I'm not anymore. It's *her* loss that she's such a damn snob. Nothing you say can change her."

"I don't know how you can be so calm about it. And damn it, why didn't you tell me, Laura?" He suddenly looked her straight in the eye. "Would you ever have told me if I hadn't brought the subject up?"

"Keep your eyes on the road."

"I'm asking you a question."

"It's a silly question," she argued. "*I* don't know if I would have brought it up. But what does it even matter?"

"It matters because I don't think you trust me," he said. "We have something wonderful together; I know it. But if you keep things like that from me, it can do nothing but hurt the relationship. And it implies . . . it just implies a lack of trust. Don't you see I want to share? If you're hurt, I want to know it; if you're hurt, I want to do something about it. And that goes for any situation, Laura—but especially one that I got you into in the first place."

She sighed. It was wonderful to hear him talk about trust and how much he valued the relationship. But she really wanted just to drop the subject. She had been angry with Gordon after the incident with the countess, almost holding him responsible for the countess's outrageous behavior. But he hadn't been responsible for the countess; and she didn't feel she needed him to defend her at this point. "I *was* angry then, Gordon. Before. And I was angry at you because I thought you should have known, or that you had forced the countess just for my sake, so it was your fault. But I don't feel that way anymore."

He glanced at her. "And that's it? Don't you want to do something about it? Get even, maybe?"

"How could I do that?"

"Well, for one thing, if what you said is true—and now that you've said it, I don't know why I didn't anticipate it —nothing would stun her more than if you showed up at the ball."

Laura shook her head. "I really can't believe anyone could be such a snob. I mean, I realize I'm not a bank president or chairman of the board of some huge company, but what I do for a living is respected by a lot of people."

"You don't understand," Gordon said. "If I brought you to the ball and she had never met you before, she'd think your work sounded fascinating. She wouldn't invite you over for tea the next day, but she wouldn't make a great fuss over your being there. We would be doing this to embarrass her—don't you see? Now that she *has* shown such poor manners. It's not your work that would make you persona non grata: it's the fact that she was extremely rude to you, and you'd be coming in on my arm."

"I don't know," Laura said uncertainly. "You should know I'm not chicken about it; I'd love to go and stir things up. It's just that I don't know if I have any desire to see her again. Maybe she'd think I cared about what she did."

"Well, it's up to you. But think about it."

"I will," Laura said. "I will."

"Tell me something, though."

"What?"

"What about the other two names I gave you? Grace Simon and Evelyn Althorp?"

"They were great."

"Thank God. Otherwise you might have thought all my friends were like the countess. I want you to understand, Laura, when we start going to some of these parties—half these people are *not* my friends. It's just part of my work; you get to know who's who and who's on a new project, who's financing a new movie or play or whatever."

"Are the people that bad that you need to make a disclaimer?"

"Some are and some aren't. But it'll be good for you; Luciana notwithstanding, you can probably pick up more work."

"Mmmm," Laura said absently. Something in what Gordon had said had reminded her about Jerry Manning.

She had an uneasy feeling, based not on facts but on an inner instinct she had come to know and trust. It was just a sense—and an unpleasant one—that something bad was going to happen. And that same sense told her not to bring it up with Gordon. She wanted the time they were sharing to stay good for now—undisturbed by any more complications. And anyway, it was just a feeling she had. . . .

When they got back to Gordon's apartment, they shared the picnic he had packed, and Laura spent the night—a night she'd always remember because "I love you" was whispered and murmured and moaned so many times.

And the next morning Gordon announced that he was going back on his pronouncement of the day before about work. "I said this man-of-leisure routine had to end, but I forgot it would be Sunday," he said, holding her in his arms as they lay in bed. "And as far as I'm concerned, *this* Sunday is going to be a day of rest, and love, and more rest"—he smiled—"and more love, and more rest—"

She laughed. "And a *lot* more rest, I think. Last night wasn't exactly without its interesting activities."

"Mmmm," he murmured, nuzzling her neck. "We could pick up where we left off."

And so they spent the day in and out of bed, making love and eating English muffins and jam, making love and reading the paper, laughing and talking until the sun went down and it was finally, sadly, Sunday night.

Laura had hated Sunday nights from the time she had begun going to school; she had always found that no matter how good a time she was having, that awful Sunday-night feeling would inevitably cast a pall over whatever she was doing.

For years she'd tried to get rid of the feeling, but it seemed there was always something to dread on Monday: working temp at a new and unfriendly office, reporting for work at yet another coffee shop or restaurant, and, more recently, showing up Monday after Monday after Monday at the salon. When she'd finally quit that job, she'd thought she'd be free of the feeling. But she still had it.

And that night, at Gordon's, one of the unpleasant feelings that floated in on the tails of dread had to do with Jerry Manning. Every time she thought of him, she had an unpleasant, uncomfortable feeling. And the more she tried to put Jerry out of her mind, the more she ended up thinking about him.

As if reading her thoughts, Gordon reached out across the kitchen table, where they had been drinking tea in bathrobes, and tipped Laura's chin up with a gentle hand. "What's bothering you?" he asked softly.

"I was thinking about Jerry Manning."

"You are *not* going over there again," he warned.

"I know. You don't have to tell me that. But I've just had this unpleasant feeling"—she shivered—"I'm sure it's nothing, but I can't get rid of it."

"What is it about? Just a feeling, or do you know something you haven't told me?"

"It's just a feeling." She shrugged. "And I'm sure it's nothing. But don't forget I have to give you those names and numbers from the Rolodex."

"And then *I'm* doing the calling, Laura."

"Right."

The feeling passed, but late that night, when she had

returned to her apartment, it came back stronger than ever.

And then, at 1:00 A.M., just when she had drifted off to sleep, the phone rang.

Instantly awake, Laura reached for the phone on her bedside table. "Hello?"

Nothing.

"Hello?"

She slammed the phone down. And the more she wished she could get the thought out of her mind, and the more she told herself she was paranoid, the surer she was that it had been Jerry Manning.

The next day at lunch Laura told Selena the whole story about Jerry Manning, after swearing Selena to secrecy. Then she told her about the phone call and asked if she was reading too much into the situation.

"Who knows?" Selena said with a shrug. "I've known you to be pretty psychic or at least sensitive in the past. Like that time you thought Matthew was around and he walked into the restaurant. But that doesn't mean you're always right. I've seen you be wrong, too. But in your situation, Laura, I might have come to the same conclusion."

"Why?"

"Because Jerry Manning sounds like a pretty unbalanced guy—someone who got more unbalanced when he felt he had lost your confidence. I can't believe you looked through that Rolodex. Although if anyone had to do it, I suppose you would have been the one."

"Mmmm. I'm getting kind of sick of this fearlessness I used to be so proud of. I think it's okay if you live in a place like Allenville, but in New York it's more of a liability than an asset."

"Well, you'll just have to see," Selena said. "And, obviously, don't go to his studio anymore. What's Gordon doing about him?"

"Firing him, eventually. But he wants to keep him on until we've—or *he's*—looked into it some more. We both figure that as long as we've gone this far, we might as well keep him where we can catch him."

"So you're sure he's a con artist now."

Laura shook her head. "I'm still not sure about that part, Selena. I just really can't tell. You know, there are a lot of people around who seem like con artists just because they happen to be failures. And that's what always makes me hesitate about acting quickly against someone like Jerry. I understand a lot more how Gordon feels than I ever did before. Naturally, Gordon doesn't want to have someone like that connected with CTC or representing CTC. And what I *do* know is that Jerry is either paranoid or—or something. But I really can't say he's totally dishonest."

"I think you're too generous," Selena said. "But you could be right. Remember that creepy guy, that real jerk, who told Alison he'd sell her paintings?"

"Oh, God, I forgot about that."

"Remember how we were going to call all the art magazines and newspapers, even the district attorney?" Selena laughed. "Thank God we were so incompetent and disorganized that we didn't get around to doing it."

"Mmmm. I wish I had bought one of Alison's paintings *then.*"

"Me too," Selena said. "And I see your point about this Manning guy. Alison's dealer was a real nut case, and an incredible jerk, *and* someone who seemed totally fake at the time. So you never know, I guess. Wasn't he operating out of a phone booth for a while?"

Laura laughed. "For about three months. Alison almost died worrying about her paintings. But he came through for her eventually. And I guess we'll just have to see about Jerry when Gordon gets going. I'm definitely going to try not to have anything more to do with him."

Gordon hung up the phone and consulted the list one more time. Lisa Hardy's number had been permanently disconnected. There had been no answer at Stacy Tompkins's number. Was it worth going on before his two o'clock meeting? He had spent the morning talking with CTC's senior attorney, Clay Brinkley, and he was tired of talking, tired of arguing.

One of the most frustrating parts of Gordon's morning meeting with Clay was that he had learned he should have acted much more quickly against Manning. According to Clay, under state law it was illegal for anybody acting as any kind of agent to take money up front for their services. Which meant that as soon as Manning had accepted the five hundred dollars from Laura, he had committed a crime. And Gordon was annoyed at himself for not having known the law, and for having let the situation continue.

He sighed and looked back at the phone. Damn it, it was important to make *some* contact with at least a few of the names.

And so, with an angry sigh, he dialed another number, this one belonging to a Claire Isaacs, and waited.

It rang only once, and then a pleasant female voice answered.

"Is this Claire Isaacs?" Gordon asked.

There was a cautious pause. "Who's calling?"

"My name is Gordon Chase. Of CTC Television. I—"

"I don't believe it!" she cried. "Sorry. Sorry. I didn't mean to interrupt. Please go on. I'm sorry."

"That's quite all right," Gordon said easily. "You sound . . . almost as if you were expecting my call."

"I wasn't ever expecting to hear from you personally, sir. And I had really quit hoping."

"Uh, Miss Isaacs, this is rather difficult for me. I was wondering if it would be possible for us to meet somewhere—either here or near you. If you wanted to come here, I'd send a car for you. I—I don't know how to say this to you gently, so I'll just come out and say it. It's come to our attention that an employee of ours by the name of Jerry Manning has been making what could only be termed unauthorized promises. From your response to my name, I assume you know him."

"Well, yes."

He could hear the disappointment setting in, and his heart went out to her. If only there were an easier way. "Miss Isaacs, all I can say at this point, while emphasizing that Mr. Manning had absolutely no right to make any promises to you on behalf of CTC, is that I would like to talk to you, to offer our apologies and to find out what we can about what Jerry Manning has been promising. And while I can't promise you anything specific, I can guarantee you a friendly ear and perhaps a helping hand."

There was a silence. Then: "Are you saying it was all a lie?"

"I don't know what Mr. Manning told you."

"He told me he'd get me a part—maybe in a series."

Gordon sighed. "When can you come in?"

"I can be there in five minutes," she said. "Believe me, I don't have anything else to do. I just quit a job I couldn't stand anymore, so—"

"What about tomorrow morning at nine?" Gordon asked.

"That would be fine."

"All right, give me your address and I'll have a car pick you up at eight thirty."

A few moments later, after he had hung up, Gordon called Clay. "I think we're going to have a bit more trouble than we'd anticipated. Can you meet me in five minutes?"

"Of course, Gord. Anyone else going to be there?"

"I'm calling Jerry Manning in. This has all gone far enough." He slammed down the phone and dialed Manning's supervisor's office.

"Mr. Whelan's office," came his secretary's singsong voice. "May I help you?"

"This is Gordon Chase. Get me Stu."

"I'm sorry, Mr. Chase, he's out of the office at the moment. Could I—"

"Then get me Jerry Manning. Transfer me to his line."

"Uh, I would do that, Mr. Chase, but I'm afraid Jer—Mr. Manning is out of the office as well. He hasn't come in today."

"Is he ill?"

There was a silence.

"Is he ill? What's his reason?" Gordon demanded.

"Uh, as far as I know, he hasn't called in," the secretary said quietly.

"Aren't you responsible for attendance as Stu's secretary?"

"Uh, yes, I am. And as far as I know, Jerry hasn't called in. But it's very possible that he reached Mr. Whelan when I was away from my desk. I was down at Duplicating.

Gordon warned himself to try to hold his temper in check. "I see. When will Stu be back?"

"Any minute now, I'm sure. Would you like me to have him call you?"

"The *minute* he gets back. And the same goes for Manning if he decides to come in."

"Oh." The secretary sounded surprised. "All right. Sure, Mr. Chase. Good-bye."

Gordon angrily hung up and jumped out of his chair. Where the hell was everybody? Why did it take ten minutes to get the very simplest facts out of people? Why, when he had finally decided to take action, was the rest of the world moving like molasses?

There was a knock at the door, and he yelled, "Come in," surprising even himself at the anger in his voice.

Clay Brinkley walked in and looked around. "Where's Manning?"

"Not in today. I don't even know if that's unusual or not. Damn it, I've got a network to run and I . . ." He shook his head. "I don't have time for this sort of nonsense."

"Look, Gordon," Clay said, sitting down in one of the comfortable leather easy chairs near the window. "I can handle any of this you need me to. Just give me the word."

Gordon shook his head. "I want the law from you, Clay—what our liabilities are and what our best approach is. And whatever that turns out to be, I have to sit down and think about the ethics of this whole damn thing." He sat down across from Clay and folded his hands. "So what do you have?"

"It's fairly simple," Clay said, tamping his pipe with tobacco and then lighting it with that pleasant air of relaxation Gordon heartily appreciated at times like this. He had hired Clay because the man could reduce the most complicated issues to simple ones, and forced his staff—after much grumbling—to do the same. "Jerry Manning is or was a sales assistant at CTC. He was not authorized to make any promises to any outside parties or deal with the public in any way as a representative of CTC, other than in sales of commercial time, and to the extent that he went beyond his obligations, he did so without your knowledge. Just as you—meaning CTC—wouldn't be held liable if Manning committed murder, you're not liable in this instance. You didn't know about it, and it's as simple as that. And you *know* that what I object to, Gordon, in all of this, is this feeling I get that you're going to go out on a limb to help these girls. That's going to give a lot of them the idea that we owe them."

Gordon sighed. "Look—part of this *is* my fault, Clay—and Stu Whelan's fault. We heard a rumor. We didn't act on it as we should have. We should have fired Manning right then and there, and we didn't."

"Why didn't you?"

"I wanted to be sure it was justified," Gordon said. "I had no way of knowing whether the rumor was true or not."

Clay shrugged. "Sounds reasonable to me. So where does your guilt come in?"

"We let him continue."

"Did you? You've told me about asking your friend to

pose as a hopeful actress so you could gather evidence. That, too, sounds entirely justified to me."

Gordon shook his head. "But who knows how many women were duped out of money while we were fooling around with the investigation? Damn it, I didn't think."

The intercom buzzed, and a few moments later Gordon hung up with the news—from Stu Whelan—that Jerry Manning had *not* called in, that this was indeed unusual, and that Whelan would get back to Gordon after trying to track Manning down.

"What I want to know from you, Clay," Gordon said, sitting down again, "is whether we're admitting any kind of liability or opening up any nasty legal cans of worms by doing what we can for Manning's victims."

Clay shrugged. "Look, Gordon. You know as well as I do that anyone can sue anyone for anything, at any time. The suit may get thrown out of court, but that doesn't mean too much when you get socked with the kinds of legal costs we've got. You know as well as I do that networks have always gotten hit with nuisance suits, and that we always will—and don't get excited; I'm not saying these would be nuisance suits. But if you're asking whether it would increase our actual liability, I have to warn you to be careful. You could change the situation by the very words you used with any of these young women. How many of them are you planning to contact, by the way?"

"I don't know. I've talked to one of them," Gordon said. "But we really don't even have any idea how extensive Manning's reach was. Laura said there were a lot more names than she could have copied down."

Clay nodded. "All right. I'd like to be present when you meet with any of them."

"Fine," Gordon said. "One is coming in tomorrow morning, but I'm going to call some more this afternoon when I get a chance."

"Are you sure you don't want me or one of my staff to handle this, Gord? I'd be more comfortable about it, and you're certainly busy enough."

Gordon shook his head. "These women have lost money and hope, Clay. I'd like to make it easier for them, and I don't want them scared off by a call from an attorney. Aside from the fact that I think it's my duty. Delegation is half the reason things like this happen. There isn't enough communication when companies get this damn big."

"I'll agree with you there," Clay said, rising. "By the way, I'm just curious. Where did the rumor about Manning come from?"

"It was anonymous," Gordon said. "Stu Whelan found a note in his office one day. But it sounded real enough that he brought it to my attention, and I took it from there."

"Hmmm. Any idea where the note came from?"

"It could have been anyone," Gordon said. "Anyone."

Laura, meanwhile, was in the offices of the editor in chief of *Beauty Life-styles* magazine. Jasmine Cole was absolutely beautiful, with the kind of fine bone structure and lovely grace all of her readers tried to emulate. She had an unusual column, one in which she herself posed each month instead of models, and each month her column would illustrate new ideas and concepts in makeup and beauty. Laura had met her only once, two years earlier, when the magazine was doing a shooting at the salon. But Jasmine was a friend of Selena's, and Laura had called Jasmine the week before, reminding her of the connection and suggesting they get together. And though Jasmine had a reputation in the industry as being a bit off-putting, she was very friendly to Laura.

"I think you *might* be making a mistake, Laura," Jasmine said gently. "The kind of women you want to develop as a clientele might not be overly impressed if they see your work in a magazine. They like the idea of using someone private. Private and expensive."

Laura looked around Jasmine's office—at the layouts of forthcoming issues on the walls, the splashy photographs of Jasmine framed and unframed, dressed and nearly nude, laughing and serious. It was a bit odd, this woman who surrounded herself with pictures of her own image, but she was very, very successful, one of the top editors in her field. And Laura had to take what she said fairly seriously. Yet Laura was determined to act on her own from now on. She had been taking advice from everybody she knew; it was time she made her own decisions. And she knew she'd have to make this clear to Jasmine.

"If you have enough makeup artists free-lancing for you, Jasmine, I really will understand. I know you use Caila Creeley, and I've seen Felicia Peterson's name in the magazine a lot. But if you *want* to try someone else, I'd love to do some work for the magazine—number one, because I like what you're doing with your monthly feature, and number two, because I want to develop experience in as many areas as I can—print work, private work, television, everything."

Jasmine leveled her gray eyes at Laura. "You'll be working with one of the most uncooperative and impatient models in the world," she said, almost smiling. "Do you think you can handle that?"

"Oh, I think so. You don't look that tough. And if you'd seen some of my clients at Gleason and Gibbs, you'd know I'm ready for just about anything."

Jasmine nodded. "All right. I do like your work. And I do need someone for our September issue, which we'll be shooting in a couple of weeks. Do you want work right away?"

"Absolutely," Laura said. "And I appreciate your fitting me in that soon."

"Don't worry about it," Jasmine said. "We should have the idea for the theme of the layout by the end of next week, so I'll give you a call then."

"Great."

Jasmine looked at her watch. "Well, I *do* have another appointment in a few minutes, Laura, so—"

"Sure," Laura said, standing. "I'll be expecting your call, then. Let me just give you my card."

As Laura was looking through her wallet for what seemed to be the last of her new business cards, Jasmine stood up. "I hear you've been seeing Gordon Chase," she said suddenly.

Laura looked up. There was an odd glint in Jasmine's eyes. "Yes, we've been seeing each other for a while now."

"Hmmm. A good friend of mine used to see him—Christine Kelly."

"Really?" She suddenly felt she had to say something more, as if her calm had somehow been challenged. "When was that?" she asked, wishing immediately she had simply said "that's nice" or something equally neutral.

"Oh, pretty recently," Jasmine said. "I met him a long time ago at one of their parties. They used to give them all the time, of course. Which was one of the factors that drove Christine away from him."

"I don't understand," Laura said, wishing more than ever that she had ended the conversation. But she was rooted to the spot.

"Christine said that Gordon Chase wanted a hostess more than a woman, someone who could perform the thousand and one social functions those corporate wives perform—without the benefits of marriage, of course. Anyway, it wasn't for Christine; her career was too important."

"Well, Gordon knows I have a career," Laura said, snapping her wallet shut. "So I don't expect we'll have that problem." She extended her hand. "Thanks again for your time, Jasmine. I'll be looking forward to getting together with you."

Jasmine smiled. "So will I, Laura. Good-bye."

As Laura left the office, she silently cursed herself. Why had she let herself get sucked into that conversation with Jasmine? She had known the minute Jasmine brought Gordon up that she wasn't going to like what she heard. Not because she knew Jasmine to be bitchy, but because there'd been something in Jasmine's tone: a challenge, almost. Selena had said that Jasmine ran hot and cold, that she was a friend but a friend not to be trusted too much. And Laura saw that Selena was right.

But Jasmine didn't concern her. What concerned her was her reaction to what Jasmine had said. Obviously, Jasmine had had some reason for telling her about Christine. Perhaps she had meant it as a challenge; perhaps as a friendly warning. But something in Jasmine's words had hit Laura hard, and Laura knew this was because they had brought up concerns she had forced herself to bury. Gordon, too, had said Christine had played an important social role in his life. And Laura knew what that kind of role was like. Many of her clients at Gleason and Gibbs had been traditional corporate wives, women whose time was completely taken up by social functions connected with their husbands.

And Laura didn't want to overreact; Gordon hadn't asked her to do anything more than attend a few parties, something that sounded like a lot of fun. But it reminded her of that long-ago resolve, the one she'd made before she ever met Gordon: that now was the time to devote herself to work. And she had let it slide completely ever since.

Was now the time to draw the line? She had to face the fact that her career wasn't going nearly as well as she had hoped. Today, in seeing Jasmine and plotting out a new course, she had taken a first step. But was that enough? Or was her affair with Gordon distracting her in a way she just didn't want to admit?

Damn. She felt caught in a situation she couldn't win. Gordon wasn't someone she could just put aside. But if she kept seeing him, would her career dwindle until there was nothing left? Would it become a mere hobby, like the hobbies of those corporate wives?

Laura had to face the fact that she hadn't been trying hard enough. She'd have to turn over a new leaf, devote at least a few hours each day toward making new contacts and reviving old ones, and concentrate.

And if that meant seeing a bit less of Gordon, well, that wouldn't be the end of the world.

Spending all that time on the Jerry Manning matter

had been a diversion; she had been nervous about starting out on her own, and she'd jumped at the chance for a distraction. But Gordon was handling the matter now. She wouldn't have anything more to do with it.

Laura stepped into a coffee shop on Third Avenue and called her answering service to see if she had gotten any calls.

There were three calls, the woman said. All were from Gordon Chase, and all were urgent.

CHAPTER TWELVE

Laura's stomach lurched as she hung up the phone.

Urgent. Lord, what could it be about?

She dialed Gordon's office number and was put through right away.

"Laura?"

"Yes. What's the matter?"

"Where are you?"

"I'm in a coffee shop on Third in—I don't know, in the Forties. Why?"

"I need to talk to you. Do you have any afternoon appointments?"

"No, nothing."

"Then get in a taxi and come up to my office."

"Can't you tell me—"

"I'm in the middle of ten phone calls, Laura. Just come." And he hung up.

Mystified, she walked out of the coffee shop and out onto Third. She had gone in not only to call her service but because she was hungry, and she felt slightly faint as she stepped out into the street. Not that there was any question of getting food now, of course. Whatever Gordon had to tell her was obviously urgent.

Twenty minutes later, when she got out at CTC headquarters, she felt even fainter, but she walked through the lobby without stopping and went straight up to Gordon's office.

When she walked in, she was surprised to see another man there, someone Gordon introduced as Clay Brinkley, the station's senior attorney.

"Laura, why don't you sit down?" Gordon said, gently guiding her to one of the leather chairs.

She looked up at him with concern. "I wish you would tell me what this is about."

"We will. I will," Gordon said, sitting down next to her. He steepled his fingers between his knees and looked down at the floor, and then finally spoke. "You know that I was going to call at least some of the women on your list."

She nodded.

"I reached a few, and the first one I reached is coming in tomorrow morning. I didn't get any specific information from her, but it was clear that Manning had made exactly the kind of promises we had assumed he was making." He sighed. "Anyway, the next woman I reached—Lisa Crane—seemed almost frightened to hear who I was. It turned out she *was* frightened, and confused."

"Why?"

"She didn't think I could really be part of CTC. She thought it was a trick, that Manning had put me up to calling her. The way I convinced her I was really from CTC was by saying we were investigating some complaints about Jerry Manning. I had to convince her on that score, and then she told me he had threatened her with violence only two days ago, and that she had every reason to believe he'd go through with his threats."

Laura swallowed as she was hit by a wave of dizziness. "What kind of threats?" she asked dully.

Gordon shook his head. "I don't know exactly. I asked her why she hadn't gone to the police, and she said she was embarrassed and afraid to, that she's only been living in the city for six months and that something—fear—just stopped her." Gordon sighed and looked into Laura's eyes. "I wanted to tell you right away, Laura. I don't want you seeing that man, I don't want you talking to that man—"

"I won't," she cut in. "I've already decided I wouldn't. He's here at the network anyway, isn't he?"

Gordon shook his head. "He didn't show up today. I had Stu Whelan call him at home, but there was no answer."

"Did you try the studio? The number I gave you?"

Gordon nodded. "No answer. No nothing."

"Do you think he's gone?"

Gordon and the lawyer looked at each other.

"We think he might be," Clay Brinkley said, leaning forward, "though there's no sure way of telling. We've sent a man over to his apartment and the studio address you gave Gordon, but so far we've had no word. Of course, if we don't find Manning today, that won't necessarily mean anything. He could have gone away for a few days and he could be back at his desk tomorrow morning."

"But you don't think he will be," Laura put in.

Clay shook his head. "Many, many years ago, my first year out of law school, as a matter of fact, I was an assistant district attorney in the D.A.'s office. I saw a good many cases with unfortunate similarities to this one, and the same thing always happened. Just when the victims were starting to get suspicious, just when the one victim who was in a position to do something realized what was going on, the man would skip town. It happened nine times out of ten then, and I'm sure it hasn't changed." Clay shrugged. "It's a sixth sense these con men have. Almost never—when we caught them—did it turn out they were operating on anything other than instinct. In almost all cases it was a matter of getting nervous, getting jittery. Restless."

"So then how would you ever catch them?"

"When they had pulled the same scam hundreds more times." Clay sighed. "You see, one of the reasons our record was so poor was that people rarely came forward. That's certainly less true now than it used to be, but it's still a big problem. Think of this young woman Gordon was talking to this afternoon, the one Manning threatened."

"Is she coming in?" Laura asked.

"She's thinking about it," Gordon said. "She's still pretty shaken up about the whole thing. She—" He shook his head and said nothing.

"What?" Laura prodded.

"She was *so* nervous," Gordon said musingly. "It made me wonder whether there was more she wasn't telling me."

"Great." Laura sighed.

"You don't seem all that apprehensive," Gordon said. "I'd thought you'd be much more upset."

"I'm upset thinking *back* on it—thinking about what might have happened, especially when he found me looking through the Rolodex."

"We think that might have been what tipped him off,"

Clay said. "It may have set his instincts on end. Thinking about it afterward, perhaps."

"Which is why I'm so damn worried about you," Gordon said.

"Look—I'm not going to his studio again. That's obvious. But I'm not going to spend every minute looking over my shoulder, either."

Clay leaned back and crossed his legs. "I don't think there's any need for inordinate concern, Gord. Jerry Manning is a con man with a bad temper. We don't know the whole story on Lisa Crane, but I suspect—and I know you suspect—that she hasn't told us everything. For all we know, they could have had a lovers' quarrel. Which doesn't make Manning a better person, but it does clarify the situation. If Manning were the type to go after someone like you, Laura, he would have done it when he discovered you with the Rolodex—as you suggested."

Suddenly Laura remembered the phone call she had gotten in the middle of the night. But that was just her intuition telling her it'd been Jerry. She had gotten dozens if not hundreds of calls like that since she had first moved to the city, and had never given them any thought. For her to do so now was silly.

"Laura?" Gordon said gently. "What are you thinking? You look a little pale, you know."

She shook her head and brushed her hair back from her face. "I'm fine. I've just hardly eaten anything today and I'm really hungry."

Gordon looked at his watch. "I'll have Vera send out for something."

Laura smiled. "Don't you have a, uh, network to run?"

"I've canceled two meetings for the afternoon so I can finish these calls."

"Then what?"

"We find out what we can, we bring it to the attention of the district attorney's office, and we do what we can for the women who've been victimized."

Clay sighed. "I've pointed out to Gordon that he's got to be very careful with these women, Laura. As it stands now, the network has no liability in this matter. No liability whatsoever. Jerry Manning was acting on his own, without authorization and without the knowledge of the network. But if Gordon decides to play Robin Hood to these young women, some of them may feel they've found a gold mine. We may even find ourselves with a few lawsuits on our hands."

"Well, I think it would be very nice if Gordon did as much as he could." She smiled into Gordon's eyes. "I'm glad to hear your plans," she said softly.

Gordon looked at Clay. "Isn't there something we can do about putting Laura under some sort of protection?"

Laura's smile grew. "Gordon, I don't need protection," she said, standing up and swaying slightly. "I need food. I can take care of myself. I promise."

"I could use your help this afternoon," Gordon said. "Talking to some of the women on the list."

"Now I *know* you're just looking for busywork to keep me here," Laura said. "You already said you didn't want me involved anymore."

"I've changed my mind."

She picked up her purse. "I have lots to do, Gordon."

Gordon stood up. "I'll walk you to the elevator, then."

Laura said good-bye to Clay and left with Gordon, and he walked her, arm in arm, slowly down the carpeted corridors. "I don't want you to leave," he said softly.

"Gordon, I promise you. I promise I'll be all right. I

really think you're overreacting. And that's nice—I like your caring—but it's unnecessary." She smiled. "And you do have a network to run."

When they reached the elevators, he took Laura's hands in his. "The thought of something happening to you," he murmured. "It's just so difficult for me to see you walk out of here."

"I'll see you later if you're free."

He nodded. "Around eight or nine, yes. I have late meetings. But I wanted to ask you something."

"What's that?"

"I'd like you to stay with me until . . . until this Manning business blows over."

"It might never blow over."

He tilted his head. "So much the better." He reached into his jacket pocket and pulled out a set of keys. "Here. I had these made for you. Take them."

"Gordon, I really don't think—"

"Just take them. We can talk later." His brown eyes implored her. "Just take them and be there when I get home. As a favor to me."

"Okay," she agreed. "But I really have to go. If I don't get something to eat, I'm going to faint."

"All right," he said as the elevator doors opened. "But you'll be there."

She nodded. "See you later."

When she reached the lobby, she walked straight to the newsstand and bought a Milky Way and a copy of the *Post.* As she was paying, she was conscious of someone standing beside her, staring, and for a moment she froze. What if it was Jerry Manning?

She turned, slowly, and looked. But it was only a

young woman, someone who looked vaguely familiar. Red hair, green eyes . . .

The woman turned quickly and headed in the direction Laura had just come from, and suddenly Laura remembered who she was. Stu Whelan's secretary. The secretary to Jerry Manning's boss.

She didn't like the way the young woman had been staring.

But then again, she reminded herself as she tore open the Milky Way and took a big bite, she was tired and tense and hungry and not thinking straight.

And as she walked out of the lobby and was caressed by an amazingly fresh spring breeze, she smiled as she thought about Gordon and his concern.

She knew she couldn't take him up on his offer. It had been made for the wrong reasons, for one thing, and for another, it was exactly the wrong time in her life to move in with somebody else. But it pleased her that he had made the gesture.

She went home and called her service, ate a giant sandwich and made a few calls, then sat down and tried to regain some of the momentum she had felt earlier in the day. She *had* to start doing better; she had to establish more contacts. Jasmine Cole was a start. But she had to go further.

For the rest of the afternoon she held a brainstorming session with herself, writing down the names of everyone she knew—in any field and in almost any way. And then she wrote letters to some and made notes to call others, making it clear in the letter that she wasn't selling any products; she was simply a makeup consultant.

That done, she packed up and took the bus to the station to make up the news team, then left for Gordon's, and arrived at his apartment building at seven, just when the crush of people returning home from work had subsided. Laura liked the feeling of coming into Gordon's building as if she lived there, entering his apartment as if it were hers, basking in the pleasure of things as simple as walking barefoot on his thick carpeting. Everything in his apartment was beautiful—from the leather-bound books in his wood-paneled study to the lovely abstract paintings on the living room walls, and Laura wondered how it was, with Gordon so wonderful and attractive and—she had to face it—such a catch, that he had stayed single so long?

Jasmine had mentioned Christine and the role Gordon had expected her to play in his life that she had ultimately turned down. Of course, it was hard to assess the truthfulness of such a spare story, one whose details she *knew* had been left out. And now that she thought about it, she realized Jasmine had left out the not insignificant detail of the other man. Maybe Gordon *hadn't* expected too much from Christine; maybe Christine had never even told Jasmine about seeing another man.

Which wasn't the point, Laura knew. *These other women shouldn't even concern you,* she told herself. *Deal with Gordon on your own terms. Forget about everyone else.*

But since she was surrounded by so much luxury, by so much that reminded her of what she wasn't, she couldn't help thinking. Was she making a mistake getting more deeply involved with Gordon at this point in her life?

Laura helped herself to a few things in the refrigerator—some cold wine, Brie, French bread—and then took a long, hot bath. The apartment was quiet, peaceful, as calm as the streets below were raucous, and Laura was finally beginning to unwind. As she lay in the warm water and thought about Gordon, she wondered how she could have been so tense only minutes earlier. There was no need to make any decisions; problems could work themselves out on their own. And the Jerry Manning business seemed far away, as if it had happened to other people in another time, another place.

When she got out of the tub, she wrapped herself in one of Gordon's shirts and went back out into the living room. *The Sinners,* her mother's favorite nighttime soap opera, was on, and though she watched it only occasionally, her mother had piqued her interest enough on Saturday that she was eager to watch. A third of one of the walls in Gordon's living room was taken up with television sets built in behind oak panels that slid closed. Laura knew that if she wanted to, she could watch not only *The Sinners* but virtually every other show being broadcast at the same time. But she didn't know how to work the complicated controls on the panel, so she settled onto the couch and watched Gordon's regular Trinitron—still much better than the small black-and-white set she had at home.

Nine o'clock came and went, and Gordon still didn't come home. Laura poured out some more wine for herself and watched the next CTC show, *Coronado,* and was getting thoroughly absorbed in a violent conflict between two sisters-in-law when she heard the front door open and Gordon come in.

She leaped up and started to go meet him at the door, but when she saw his expression, she stopped in her tracks. He looked exhausted, his jaw dark and unshaven, his eyes circled and sad, and he just shook his head as he threw his coat and briefcase down on a chair.

"What happened?" Laura asked, coming forward. She wrapped her arms around him and gave him a kiss, and for a moment he just held her, silently, burying his face in her hair and holding her close.

"It feels so good," he murmured, "knowing that no matter what's happened at CTC, you'll be here."

"I was glad to be here," she said softly.

When he drew back and looked at her, he was smiling. "You're watching *Coronado?*"

"Sure," she answered, taking his hand and leading him into the living room. "Why don't you watch too? Just come in, relax, and I'll give you a back rub."

"Mmmm. Sounds good. How do you like the show? I didn't even know you watched," he said as he sank onto the couch.

"Well, I felt it was an act of patriotism on my part," she said with a smile. "I mean, *naturally* I wouldn't follow that trash if it weren't for you."

He grinned. "Mmmm. I'll bet."

"It really is good, Gordon. I don't even watch *Coronado* and I'm all ready to tune in next week."

"I'm glad," he said as he slid his tie out from under his collar.

"You don't look very glad," she chided, sitting down beside him and unbuttoning his shirt.

He sighed and just shook his head.

"Gordon? Why don't you tell me about it? Does anyone else know what happened? What's bothering you, I mean?"

"Sure. Clay, anyway. He's been with me since you left." He sighed and looked into her eyes. "It isn't a matter of my letting 'people' know, Laura. It's a matter of my letting you know. You see, it might concern *you.*"

She swallowed. "Tell me."

"It may be more bad news about Jerry Manning, I'm sorry to say."

CHAPTER THIRTEEN

"Tell me, Gordon."

His dark brown eyes were full of emotion. "You never told me what kind of pictures Jerry took of you," he began slowly, quietly. "And I never asked, I suppose because I didn't want to know." He shook his head. "So much of this is my fault," he mused.

"Just tell me what you're talking about," she said, remembering even as she spoke the series of bathing-suit shots he had taken.

"Two of the, uh, women we reached tonight have discovered that their pictures have been sold in unauthorized ways."

"I don't understand."

Gordon reached out and took her hand. "One found hers at the back of *The Village Voice,* of all things. Her picture—of her in a bathing suit—was the come-on for a massage-parlor ad."

"Are you kidding?"

He shook his head. "I even bought a copy on the way home. She told me the name of the place, and there it is —or there *she* is—in black and white, for all the world to see. And, of course, it's not even a matter of what's showing and what's not. But she's a secretary at a law firm, now prominently advertising herself as a masseuse."

Laura swallowed. "You're telling me my picture is going to be in some kind of ad?"

"I don't know. I don't know what kind of pictures Manning took, Laura. You never told me."

Laura closed her eyes. "How could I have been so stupid? I just can't *believe* it. I should have *known—*"

"None of us knew," he cut in. "Obviously. And unfortunately."

"God, I just can't . . . You know, if I had thought about it . . ." She sighed. "But you know, I *did* think about it, Gordon. When he asked me to put the bathing suit on, I did think about the whole situation. But I have friends who've wanted to be actresses and models, and I've looked through their books at their eight-by-tens. And they have the same kind of pictures in their portfolios that Jerry took of me. I *thought* about it." She shook her head. "And that day, in his studio, was the day that Jerry seemed more professional than on any other day. *That* was the day I was most convinced."

"Look. I didn't know, you didn't know, no one knew what he was going to do."

She barely heard what Gordon said. For she was remembering that day, remembering the few weak protests she had made. She had reminded herself of her friends' portfolios, and that was that. What could be the harm in having her picture taken?

"Maybe it was just that particular woman," Laura suddenly said. "Which one was it?"

"Her name is Joanna Barnes. She's coming in with the others tomorrow morning. But I talked to another young woman this evening who had the same thing happen."

"That's right," she said glumly. "You did say there were two."

"Well, there was one difference. The second one was . . . personally involved with Manning, she said, and she had made the mistake of letting him take some nude pictures of her. Just for fun. And *she* didn't find them—she never would have known Manning had done anything with them—except that a male friend of hers saw them in a skin rag."

"So the gist now is that Jerry was in operation not just to pocket our so-called expense money, but also to sell our pictures."

"Exactly."

"I really . . . I can't even begin to react. I'm suddenly so tired. . . . And so tired of thinking one thing and discovering I'm wrong." She looked into Gordon's dark eyes. "I suddenly feel as if I don't know anything at all. As if I have no instincts."

He took her into his arms and held her close, resting her head against his shoulders and stroking her hair. "None of us knew," he said softly.

"You knew *some*thing was wrong," she claimed. "I should have trusted you. Instead I had to take this big stance because I thought you weren't being fair." She raised her head and looked at him with half a smile. "I had to be on Jerry's side because I decided it was a case of the underdog being kept in his place. What a fool."

"Don't blame yourself," he said. "Laura, none of us knew exactly what was going on. There was no way we could know. And there was no way *you* could know."

She shifted out of his arms and poured some wine for herself. "I know one thing, Gordon. If I ever see Jerry Manning again—"

"I don't think you will."

She looked up sharply. "What? Why not? What happened?"

"That was the other piece of news I had. We sent a man from the station down to see what he could find out."

"Yes, I remember."

"Well, we had him do a little legwork. And he finally found the super of Manning's building—the one he had his studio in."

" 'Had'?"

Gordon nodded. "Manning moved out all his things this weekend, apparently. Left his partner—some man he had signed the lease with—holding the bag for the entire rent."

"Oh, great. What timing. What about his apartment?"

"Gone."

"You mean he *moved?* He just moved all his stuff out in one weekend, from both places? That isn't easy."

"He didn't have much, according to Leif, the CTC man. The super of Manning's apartment building said he had rented the place furnished. The only reason he knew Manning was gone was that he happened to run into him and Manning was carrying out a television and a typewriter and a few other things like clothes."

"And that means he's gone?"

"According to the super, that's all he had ever brought in with him. Mostly clothes, actually."

"I don't believe it."

"Well, it's good and bad, the way I see it. Bad because it reduces our chances of ever finding him; Clay's theory is that he's probably on his way to L.A. right now. But it's good because it eases my mind about you, Laura. I don't think he would have uprooted himself like that if he'd intended to stay in New York."

"That's probably true," Laura said. "I mean, when you have to pay a real-estate agent a month and a half's rent, plus you have to give two or three months' rent to your landlord, you practically have to spend your entire life savings just to move to a new apartment. And I don't think Jerry has that kind of money. But I have a question."

"What's that?"

"Why aren't we doing more to stop him? Shouldn't someone else be brought in?"

"We're talking to the D.A. tomorrow or the next day," Gordon said. "Clay said it's very important to bring in as many people as we can at the beginning, to show it's not an isolated case and to encourage them to act quickly."

"But you're the head of a TV network," Laura said. "Clearly you're not some nut who just wants to waste the D.A.'s time."

"I know. But it still makes a difference. It'll be a much higher priority for them if they get the impression this is a scam that's taken in dozens of women. The other thing we're going to do is put it on the air."

"Really?"

"Our consumer reporter, Gloria Stern, is going to cover it tomorrow or the next day at six and eleven if we can get the story together by then."

"That's great." She sighed. "That makes me feel a lot better." She reached up and brushed the back of her hand against his scratchy cheek. "You look exhausted."

"I am exhausted," he said quietly.

"You know, I think it's great what you're doing—helping out as many of the women as you can. Clay made it pretty clear that you don't have to."

"Well, I'm not sure exactly what I'm going to do. If they have any talent, great; I can certainly hook them up with some legitimate agents and managers. Maybe even give them some work. If not, I still want to do what I can."

"I'm sure they'll appreciate it," Laura said.

"Well, I don't know how much, but I know it will make *some* kind of difference in their lives. What I care most about, though, is knowing you're probably safe. The more I've thought about it, the surer I've been that Manning must have reacted to the Rolodex business. And I don't like that at all. But since we don't know for a fact that he's left the city, Laura, I do think it would be a good idea if you stayed here."

She sighed and said nothing. She had been hoping he'd put the idea aside now that Jerry was probably gone. "I don't think that would be such a good idea," she said quietly.

He rubbed the bridge of his nose and spoke without looking at her. "Maybe this isn't the right time to talk. We're both so tired."

"Whatever you think," she said softly.

"Let's just go to bed and forget about it. We can talk in the morning."

She wanted to talk about what Gordon had suggested. Anything would be better than silence; but what could she say? She wasn't even sure he knew why he had invited her.

In the bedroom, as Gordon undressed silently, his back to her, Laura slipped between the cool sheets. Gordon was moving slowly, sliding off his clothes as if he didn't care about anything.

"Gordon?"

"Mmmm." He didn't look up.

"I don't know. I just think we should talk."

He slipped off his shorts and walked past the bed to the bathroom. "Why not just forget about it?" he called. "I'm all talked out."

She heard him splashing his face, then brushing his teeth. Damn. Were they going to spend the rest of the night in silence?

When Gordon came out of the bathroom, he was wearing a white terry-cloth robe—to Laura a very clear sign. And she thought, *This is bizarre; we're not an old married couple. He invited me to spend the night.*

Gordon got into bed and turned out the main light from a switch on his night table, then turned on a bedside lamp. "Damn," he said softly. "Do you know I have a script to look at tonight, on top of everything else?"

"Can't it wait?"

"Sure—if I want to do it that way. I can let it wait, I can let it slide, I can delegate the whole thing to someone else if I want to. But I'm convinced that when something bad happens—like this Jerry Manning thing, for instance—you can always trace its roots to some mistake you made somewhere along the line." He paused. "Obviously I've made a mistake with you, too, somewhere, sometime when I wasn't aware of it."

She looked at him in astonishment. "What do you mean, you made a mistake? What kind of a mistake? I'm here with you, aren't I?"

"That's not what I'm talking about. I always seem to be out of sync with you, Laura, or one step ahead—wanting more than you do." He sighed. "I told you once before that deep down, I feel that if I do everything right, I should be able to get what I want, or to know why I've failed. And that doesn't work with you."

She frowned. "But if you see things as in your control, Gordon, that means you're not taking my feelings into account. What about me and how *I* feel? My not wanting to stay here doesn't have anything to do with your making a 'mistake.' You asked me to stay here because you want me to feel safe. But I feel safe in my apartment."

"Look—let's just forget it, all right? We're both tired and we both have a lot to think about."

She sighed. She felt that they hadn't really solved anything, that they should talk more, but clearly he didn't want to. "Are you going to read the script?" she asked.

"Might as well," he answered, looking past her at the clock. "It's still early." He went out to the foyer to get his briefcase, and Laura went into the bathroom, where she knew there was a pile of magazines. Maybe if they read together in bed, in a kind of domestic calm, the atmosphere would lighten up.

Laura found a copy of *People* magazine she'd never read, and she'd already brought it back to bed by the time Gordon came in with his briefcase.

He smiled when he saw what she was reading. "Ah—into heavy literature tonight, I see. My favorite bathroom reading."

"There was a huge stack of these in your magazine rack," she said, flipping to the Contents page. "Hey. There's something about *you* in here!"

He looked at the cover and Laura grinned as she saw he was just realizing which issue it was.

He made a sudden reach for the magazine, but she saw it coming and leaped to the other side of the bed.

"Give me that!" he warned with a smile.

But she was off and running. She jumped off the bed and feinted right and then ran past Gordon, racing into the living room with him in hot pursuit.

"I'm warning you!" he said, laughing.

She leaped over to the windows behind one of the couches. The couch was a good barrier, since she could see which end he was headed for and just go the other way. Unless, of course, he leaped over the middle.

"Laura. You'd better give up. Right now," he warned, fighting a smile.

"Why? I'm going to read this," she said, quickly finding the article. "Here we go: 'Gordon Chase, new Young Turk down at CTC Television, promises "something different" this year, and by all industry standards, it looks as if he's succeeded. As one wag at another network quipped, "We're sick to death of him and his damn Midas touch, but what can you do? We just call him—" ' " Out of the corner of her eye she saw Gordon coming around the wall end of the sofa, and she took off toward the center of the living room.

But he had turned somewhere, and he caught her by the waist and spun her around, laughing and holding her against him. Surreptitiously, she clutched at the magazine, determined not to let him take it, and when she looked up into his eyes and he smiled one of his most magnificent smiles, she knew he was up to something.

Suddenly she felt a swift tug at the magazine, but she was ready for it, and she ducked back. "Don't you dare!" she warned. "You've got a script to read, Gordon!"

And she started to run off. But he caught her again. "Just where do you think you're going, Miss Dawson?"

"To the bathroom, if that's all right with you."

"Without the magazine."

She grinned. "With—*if* that's all right with you."

In one quick move he swept her over his shoulder, and a moment later they were lying together on the bed. "Later," he said hoarsely, uncurling her fingers from the magazine. "Later you can be my guest. But now . . ." He kissed her hungrily, stretching out his length on top of her, and she wrapped her arms around him and they rolled back and forth, round and round, reveling in a kiss that brought back all the times they had made love, all the pleasure they had shared, all their cries of happiness.

He tore his mouth from hers and gazed down at her with fire in his eyes. "I love you," he murmured. "I love you so much."

"I love you too, Gordon," she whispered.

And they came together with lazy pleasure, lingering over familiar favorite kisses and strokes, discovering new ones, all the while whispering "I love you's" that made every touch that much more exciting. And when together they convulsed in shattering bliss, the pleasure was deeper, fuller, more powerful than ever.

They had each been tired beforehand, both emotionally and physically. Now Laura was wide awake, but Gordon felt as if he were being dragged toward sleep.

"Don't fall asleep," Laura insisted, giving him a pinch on his buttocks.

"Yow!" he cried. "What did I do?"

"You were falling asleep."

He raised a brow. "Under the circumstances a rather appropriate course of action, it seems to me."

"It is not. You were going to read that script."

"To hell with the script," he grumbled into the pillow. "I'm going to sleep and that's that. After what we just shared, I don't want to read a piece of nonsense that's just going to make me angry. I'm going to hold you in my arms, smell that incredible hair of yours—what do you do, anyway, to make it smell like that?" he asked, opening an eye.

She smiled. "Trade secret. What if I told you and you told your next girl friend?"

"There isn't going to *be* a next girl friend. And I don't want to hear comments, questions, complaints, or anything else. Lights out and good night."

She smiled and turned out her light as he reached out and turned his out.

When he settled back into bed, he molded his body around hers and held her warmly against him, and soon breathing was the only sound in the room.

"One more thing," he suddenly said.

"You said no talking," she teased.

"Just one thing."

"Okay, what?"

"I love you," he whispered.

She smiled. "I love you too."

Later on that night, when Laura got up to get a drink of water, she found the *People* magazine she and Gordon had been tugging at and brought it into the kitchen.

There was nothing in the article about Gordon that she didn't already know, but it gave her pause. The pictures and text were so flattering and so glowing that they made her nervous; and as she looked at one picture, of Gordon running along the beach, she was amazed she was involved with him. She always felt just slightly out of place in his vast apartment, amazed when she walked into CTC headquarters that *her* boyfriend was in charge of all those people, and reading the article reinforced that same sense of uneasiness. When he had told her about Christine and how she had shared in his life, Laura had wondered whether she could fit into his life in that way. And she wasn't at all sure that she could.

CHAPTER FOURTEEN

The next morning Gordon was so cheerful Laura couldn't see how he could have been so upset the night before. He walked around the apartment with a secretive smile, a glint in his eye that told her he was definitely up to something and very, very happy.

"What are you up to?" Laura asked, looking at Gordon across the breakfast table. "What are you plotting behind those scheming brown eyes?"

He smiled. "Nothing that you need to know about."

"Does it have to do with me?"

He shook his head and sighed. "So self-centered," he teased. "She thinks everything has to do with her."

"Gordon!"

"It does have to do with you, Laura, but it's nothing you have to know about, as I said."

"Fine," she sniffed. *"Don't* tell me. I really don't care," she added airily.

Gordon smiled. "You are the worst liar in the world, Laura."

"Maybe that's why Jerry Manning skipped town," she mused. "If I'm as bad as you say, maybe he knew who I was. But I think it's just being around you, Gordon. I can't lie even when I want to."

"Good," he said, setting down his cup of coffee. "That makes one of us, anyway."

"You rat!" she cried.

"Oh, don't get too worried," he said easily. "It's nothing bad."

"Mmmm. I'll bet."

They left the apartment together with the understanding they'd talk at the end of the day. "And you still have the keys, right?" Gordon asked as they left the lobby and walked out onto the street, where his limo was waiting.

"Sure."

"Keep them."

"Are you sure?"

He shot her a warning look. "I'm not going to start again, Laura."

"Okay. You're right. Anyway, I have them."

"Good. So call me at the office later."

"Okay, I will. I hope you don't have too horrible a day."

He smiled. "You're as bad as I am. Where can I reach you if I need to, though?"

"Oh, just call my service. I don't know exactly where I'll be. I just have one appointment at two and then the network, but I may go out this morning."

"Have you thought any more about the countess's party?"

She shrugged. "I hadn't, with everything else that's been going on, but I guess I'd like to go. Why the hell not, right?"

"That's the spirit. Do you need a lift?"

She shook her head. "No, go ahead. I'm going to walk."

"Across the park?"

"Gordon, it's light out. And springtime. And it's early. Nine thousand joggers are already there, huffing and puffing all over the place."

"Well, okay. See you later." He kissed her and was just walking away when he suddenly said, "Oh, my God."

"What's the matter?" Laura asked with alarm.

He looked at his watch. "Oh. Phew. It's only eight fifteen."

"Why? What's the matter?"

"I was going to send Patrick to pick up one of the women I'm interviewing this morning, and I completely forgot to tell him about it. I had planned to take a cab to work. But she didn't want to be picked up till eight thirty anyway, so I can just go along for the ride."

"Who is she?"

"The first one I called."

Laura frowned. "Why did you tell her you'd send the limo?"

"It was a natural offer. She was the first woman I reached, and I wanted to be sure she'd come." He hesitated and smiled, and the smile grew to a grin. "Don't tell me you're jealous."

She glared at him. "I am not. I'm just . . . surprised," she said, grabbing at the first word that came to her mind. But it made sense, and she went on: "Clay said that you had to be sure not to bend so far backward that people think you owe them something."

Gordon stared at her. "I don't believe what I'm hearing. You, champion of the underdog, speaking out in favor of the network? Agreeing with one of the most conservative lawyers in town? Telling me to ignore the downtrodden?"

"I don't want you to ignore the downtrodden, as you

put it. I just didn't think you'd be riding them around in limos."

He picked up his briefcase and headed for the sleek black Cadillac. "Well, think again, Laura. You wanted a champion of your causes, and you got one. See you later!" And with a wave he disappeared into the car.

She smiled and shook her head. It *was* something of a transformation. And—she hated to admit it—she was jealous. Who knew what kind of woman this hopeful actress would be? With Gordon so determined to be nice . . .

Oh, it wasn't worth thinking about. It didn't bear thinking about. It was better to think about how Gordon was doing his best to try to make things right. Wasn't it?

Gordon asked Patrick to drive to 110th Street between Broadway and Amsterdam. They'd only be a few minutes late if Patrick drove quickly. After a few moments of looking out the window, Gordon settled back into the seat and began looking through the script he hadn't read the night before.

The night before. Somehow he or she or both of them had turned the night into something wonderful and unforgettable.

When Laura had told him she didn't want to stay with him, he had felt kicked in the stomach, as if the whole relationship were over. He had wanted to talk her into it, to yell, to convince her any way he could. And then he realized—what had he even offered her? A place to stay because he wanted her safe. An open-ended, vague invitation.

The whole thing had been a colossal mistake. He had

moved too quickly; he had given in to his emotions, something he knew was always a mistake.

No, he had to have a plan, a method, as in anything else.

And he seemed to have one in mind that might work.

Damn it, he wanted her so much. He had never felt anything close to this about anyone. And he'd do whatever he had to to make her his.

When the limo pulled up in front of a massive graying hulk of a building on the north side of 110th Street, Gordon looked out the window and saw a slim, pretty blonde standing at the building's entrance, looking ill at ease and out of place with the scraps of garbage and old newspapers blowing in from the curb only a few feet away.

"Patrick, I think that must be Miss Isaacs. I'll get out and see."

"As you wish, sir."

He knew the woman was Claire Isaacs the moment he opened the door to the limo. For in that short moment, as the young woman saw him out of the corner of her eye, she hurriedly smoothed down her bangs, licked her lips, and checked to see that her skirt was smoothed down and straight.

Gordon smiled and introduced himself, shook hands with her, and escorted her back to the car.

Right before Claire Isaacs got in, she turned back to the building, looked up, and waved. "My roommates," she explained as she got in. "Ooh. This is nice."

"Glad you like it," Gordon answered as he settled in and Patrick pulled away from the curb. "I thought this would be nicer than the bus or whatever."

Gordon had seen women like Ms. Isaacs hundreds of

times in the past. Pretty without being beautiful, they filled agents' offices on both coasts trying for parts they'd never get. They weren't character types, but there was just something missing—a spark, a flair, something not quite right. And once again his heart went out to Ms. Isaacs. For she had lovely blue eyes, beautiful straight blond hair, and a great smile, but her skin showed she still hadn't recovered from fierce adolescent acne.

"I'm sorry if I seemed a little distant on the phone yesterday," she said. "I was just so disappointed."

He frowned. "Hadn't you had any idea that something was wrong before then?"

She sighed and looked down at her hands. Gordon noticed that her nails were bitten down to the quick, and her skin was rough-looking and reddened, as if she had been doing some kind of manual labor or washing a lot of dishes. "I didn't want to think about it," she said quietly. "My roommates and I argued constantly about it. They thought it sounded like a swindle from the beginning." She shrugged. "I just didn't want to think about it." She looked up at Gordon. "How did you get involved, Mr. Chase?"

"That's a long story. Unfortunately, though, we haven't been able to contact Jerry Manning to let him refute any of our suspicions, and the more we look into this, the more unfortunate things we find."

Claire sighed. "I feel like such a fool. Five hundred dollars. Not to mention a really expensive lunch."

"That *you* paid for?"

"Well, he wanted to talk, and he picked the place, and I just assumed we'd go Dutch or that he'd pay. And it wasn't like I ordered the most expensive thing because I thought he was probably paying. I didn't order steak. I had an omelet. *He* had the steak. And Scotch. And wine. And even dessert!"

"Well, if it's any comfort to you, Miss Isaacs, we've tracked down a few other women, and you'll be able to compare notes if you'd like and at least know you weren't the only one."

"That does make me feel better," she said glumly. "I'd feel a lot better if I got my money back, though."

"Well, that's something we're going to look into. I hope you understand that if it were solely up to me, I'd give you the money. And I hope to give you the money. But if it turns out Manning swindled a thousand young women—"

"Five hundred thousand dollars!"

"Exactly. That's an amount that doesn't look awfully good on an annual report to the stockholders. However, that's one of my top priorities. I just don't want you to get your hopes up too much. As far as a friendly ear goes, though, and a friendly push in the right direction, you can count on me."

"I really appreciate it, Mr. Chase. And I'll do whatever I have to do to help catch Jerry Manning."

An hour later Claire Isaacs sat in Gordon's office along with Clay Brinkley, an assistant district attorney, Peter Monell, two of the other young women who had been swindled—Lisa Crane and Joanna Barnes—and the executive producer of the six and eleven o'clock news, Sean Claverie.

"We'll want all your statements again," Peter Monell said. "And some other details, of course."

"What are our limits in terms of a report tonight?" Sean Claverie asked. "Are we naming names? Places?" He looked from Peter Monell to Gordon.

"I say we go along with whatever the D.A.'s office and these three young women want to do," Gordon said. "Push it to the limits if we can."

"I don't want to have anything to do with it," Lisa Crane said. She had just told a harrowing tale of threatened *and* real physical violence, and right after the meeting she was due to go down to the D.A.'s office to file formal charges.

"I understand," Gordon said. "What about you two? Joanna? Claire?"

"I think I'd like to do it," Claire said, "depending on what I'd have to say."

"Just tell your story," Sean Claverie said. "We'd go over it beforehand and clear it with Mr. Monell, but it would all be in your own words."

"Joanna?" Gordon asked.

"What the hell," she said with a shrug. "Why not? I'm already on my way to having my picture all over half the newspapers in New York. I might as well get a chance to be on TV. Maybe I'll get some publicity. 'Doesn't really work at Secret Pleasures Massage Parlor.' That sort of thing."

The blood drained from Claire Isaacs' face as she listened to Joanna joke about the pictures. She had refused to pose in a bathing suit when Manning had asked her.

Five hours later the station's investigative reporter, Gloria Stern, finished the report, complete with shots of the outside of Manning's studio and apartment buildings, interviews with Claire and Joanna, and a good long warning to viewers.

When the taping was through, Gordon called Laura and left a message with her service to watch the six o'clock news if she could. And then he tried to salvage the small part of what was left of the day to do some of the work he was getting paid to do.

Laura had had an awful day. When she walked in the door, she was ready to quit, move back to Allenville, anything just to forget about her day. From the morning, when someone had spilled coffee down her silk blouse in a coffee shop, through the afternoon, when she'd had a difficult makeup consultation, and through her make-up session at CTC, her day had been a strain, and she didn't feel like seeing or talking to anyone.

But, forcing herself to stay responsible, she called her service just to make sure there weren't any important calls. "Just one call, Miss Dawson," the service operator said. "From Mr. Chase. He wanted you to watch the news at six o'clock."

"Oh," Laura said, surprised. "Okay. Thanks a lot."

Having missed half of the news show, she quickly flicked on the television set and caught the end of a segment about a midtown burglary. Then Brandon Bates, the anchorman, made the following announcement: "And tonight, our investigative reporter, Gloria Stern, will give us an exclusive story about a swindle that involved this television station, one man, a former employee of this station, and possibly dozens of aspiring actresses."

Laura turned the volume up and adjusted her set, and then waited anxiously for the story, surprised and impressed that Gordon had pushed it through so quickly.

Finally, Gloria Stern came on the screen. She was standing in front of a building Laura didn't recognize. "Tonight," she began, her hair blowing in the wind, "we bring you the first of at least two exclusive reports on a swindle in which CTC Television, along with perhaps dozens of young women, was the victim of one man. I'm standing in front of 615 East Eighty-first Street, home of Jerry Manning, a onetime employee of CTC's Sales department." She looked up at the building, a six-story, clean-looking building. "In this building and in Manning's studio, young women were interviewed, photographed, and promised jobs in television, without any knowledge of these promises on the part of CTC, and without any basis in fact. The young women received vague assurances that Manning would use his 'contacts' to get them work, but in the meantime they were required to pay fees, in advance, for Manning's services. The fees, from information we've gotten so far, were in the neighborhood of five hundred dollars, and in return for this the women received nothing—no jobs, no auditions, no interviews. Their portfolios, made up of photographs taken by Manning, were kept by their 'agent,' and in most cases the women either never heard from Manning again or had a good deal of trouble getting in touch with him, at which point he'd explain he was busy 'developing contacts in the field.' As we have pointed out in the past in our investigative reports, it is against New York State law for agents to charge up-front fees for their services. Here to tell us one version of events is Claire Isaacs, a presently unemployed waitress."

"Miss Isaacs, would you tell us how you feel about what happened."

"I feel awful," Claire Isaacs said, her eyes avoiding the camera. "I really didn't know I was being taken. Five hundred dollars is a lot of money. I hope they catch Jerry Manning—if that's his real name—and lock him up for a long time."

Gloria Stern held up a picture of Jerry Manning. "This is a blown-up employee I.D. picture of Manning," her voice-over said, "though a few of the women interviewed reported he didn't have a beard or a mustache when he had interviewed them."

The report then cut to Gloria Stern in front of the building that had housed Jerry's studio. "Here with me in front of 623 East Twenty-second Street, the building in which Manning maintained a photographic studio, is Joanna Barnes, an aspiring actress and dancer."

Joanna Barnes smiled broadly at the camera, waved, and mouthed the words "Hi, Mom!"

"Miss Barnes, I understand you visited this studio on at least one occasion."

"More than once," Joanna answered. "The first time I went, I paid the fee he asked for in advance. 'Standard,' he said. Five hundred dollars. The second time I posed for the pictures."

Gloria Stern withdrew the microphone and turned away. "Pictures that were later allegedly sold, without authorization by Miss Barnes, for use in advertising at least one massage parlor. We'll bring you *that* part of our report tomorrow."

They cut back to the studio, where Gloria Stern was sitting at the news desk, to the left of Brandon Bates. "Excellent report, Gloria. I'm looking forward to tomorrow's segment. If there are any other young women out there who have information for the D.A. about this swindle, what should they do? Is there a special number?"

"There certainly is, Brandon. They should get in touch with Peter Monell, assistant district attorney at the Manhattan D.A.'s office. His number is 555-6535. Or they can get in touch with me here at the station."

"Great. And thanks again, Gloria. Nice work."

Laura was just about to reach for the set to turn it off when the phone rang. She answered it cheerfully, assuming it'd be Gordon since the segment had just ended.

"Hello?"

Silence.

"Hello?"

She hung up and immediately took the phone off the hook so there'd be no possibility of the person's calling again.

But she knew it wasn't a matter of a "person" calling back. She knew, deep inside, that it was Jerry Manning.

CHAPTER FIFTEEN

"Gordon Chase's office."

"This is Laura Dawson. I'd like to speak with him, please."

"I'm sorry, he's in a meeting downstairs. Would you like to leave a message?"

"Uh, yes. Have him call me at his apartment in half an hour, please." She gave Gordon's number and then hung up.

She knew it was possible she was being irrational, but she didn't care. She just didn't want to be alone in her apartment. There was no doorman downstairs, only an ancient "locked" door that wasn't even locked half the time, and a buzzer system that was woefully casual. And irrational or not, she knew she'd prefer being at Gordon's at the moment, whether he was there or not.

She packed up her toilet kit and some clothes, then put the phone receiver back in its cradle.

Just as she reached her front door, the phone rang again.

She let it ring once, twice, three times.

Maybe it was Gordon. Maybe it wasn't Jerry. She had to know, just to find out if she was going crazy or not.

She set her bags down and ran to the phone. "Hello?"

Nothing.

She slammed it down and ran out of the house.

Half an hour later, she let herself into Gordon's apartment with great relief and waited for his call.

A few minutes later, though, Gordon came home, and Laura rushed into his arms at the door.

"Well," he said with a dazzling smile as he held her close. "I couldn't ask for a nicer welcome than *this.* I got the message you were here and came straight home. What did you think of the report? Did you see it?"

"Yes, yes. It was fine. Great."

He frowned. "You don't sound very enthusiastic. What's the matter?"

"I'm either losing my mind, Gordon, or Jerry Manning's trying to harass me."

"What? What happened?"

She told him her thoughts and suspicions as they walked to the living room together. "I don't know how it *could* be Jerry. Or why it *would* be, I guess. I've gotten hundreds of calls where no one says anything. But the *timing* of these is what makes me nervous. Right after he quit; then right after the story—I mean, the *minute* it was over. And then right after I put the phone back on the hook, which is especially creepy because it means he had been trying that whole time. Who would do a thing like that?"

Gordon shook his head. "I'm calling the D.A."

"Then I should talk to him, Gordon; everyone else is."

"We have enough without your testimony," he said roughly, stalking to the phone.

"Gordon."

"I don't want you involved in *any* way anymore, damn it."

"Then you can't call the D.A. You can't expect them to act on a specific complaint if the complainant doesn't even come in. They're investigating Jerry already; they can't send out a private force just to protect me; that would be ridiculous."

He sighed and put down the phone. "What do you want me to do?" he asked, his voice ragged with fatigue.

"I think we should slow down and think," she said. "I packed and rushed out of my apartment as if it were on fire; I wasn't the slightest bit rational. I mean, maybe it wasn't Jerry. Three phone calls don't prove anything. It certainly wouldn't prove anything to the D.A." She paused and looked up into his eyes. "There is one thing, though."

"What's that?"

"I *would* like to stay here after all—just for a bit, just until . . . I don't know, until we know a little more."

"You know what my answer to that is, Laura. Stay as long as you'd like."

"Thanks. Really, I just—"

"You don't have to convince me," he said, coming forward and taking her into his arms.

"I know. But I have to convince myself. I feel so silly —running like this. But the thought of my building— there's just no security. And *if* it's Jerry, he seems to know when I'm coming and going, because my service hasn't reported any callers who hung up."

"Would they?" Gordon asked.

"I don't know. If there were a lot of calls like that, I imagine they would. But I just don't know. I'd rather not take chances, though." She looked up into his eyes. "I really do appreciate it, Gordon. And I hope it's okay if I have my calls forwarded here starting tomorrow. And when we're not here, my service will pick up."

"Of course. Don't even ask, Laura. Arrange things whatever way you want. I'm just happy you'll be here."

She looked into his eyes and felt she had to make the situation clearer; Gordon was acting as if she were moving in because of romance rather than safety. "I want to keep it straight, though," she said softly.

He looked at her questioningly. "What do you mean?"

"About why I'm moving in. I—"

He took her in his arms. "Don't," he said gently. "It's not necessary. I know it's for your safety. I know that I asked you before and your answer was no, and that the calls were what changed your mind. But that doesn't mean we can't have a good time." He pulled her more deeply into his arms, and she settled against him, loving the scent and feel of his firm chest and the wonderful warmth of his hold.

"You're right," she murmured. "But I want to make it clear—when this Jerry Manning thing gets settled, I *am* going to leave."

He drew back and tilted her chin up. "We'll see about that," he said softly. "We'll just see."

"Gordon."

"I *said* we'll see," he teased with a grin.

The phone rang and Gordon went to answer it. "Gordon Chase," he said. Pause. "Hello?"

The look in his eyes was enough.

Laura sank onto the couch and bit her lip.

"Hello?" Gordon repeated.

He hung up and stood there, his hand still on the receiver. A moment later he was talking to Clay. "I know there's no proof," he was saying. "That isn't the point. . . . Then they should change their thinking, damn it. . . . No. Hold on." He covered the receiver and looked over at Laura. "Did you start forwarding calls here already?"

She shook her head.

"Not yet," Gordon said into the phone. "Yes, I see your point. . . . But how would he have gotten my number. . . . Damn. That's right. All right, call me if you have any more ideas. And thanks, Clay."

He hung up and came over to the couch. "That is *one* comforting thought," he said halfheartedly.

"What's that?"

"If it *was* Manning, which we don't even know, he may have been trying to reach me."

"Some comfort!"

"Better me than you. But, damn it, I just wish I knew if it was him. Then we could *do* something."

"You've gotten calls like this before, though."

"Of course. Perhaps fewer than most people because my number isn't listed, but even so. Everyone gets wrong numbers."

"How would he have gotten yours?"

"From CTC. Stu Whelan has it in his files, and so do a lot of other people."

"By the way," Laura suddenly said. "I don't know if this means anything, but Whelan's secretary was staring at me in the lobby yesterday and I thought it was a little strange. She was giving me the real evil eye."

"What? What happened?"

"It was after I left your office and I went down to the lobby and got a newspaper. I felt someone staring, and it really felt like a malevolent force. I mean, I could *feel* her looking at me. I almost jumped out of my skin because I thought she was Jerry Manning. Anyway, I just wonder if there's any connection. They did work closely in terms of office space, and he certainly was—or is—a flirt."

"I'll call her in tomorrow and ask her a few questions," Gordon said. "But in the meantime, Laura, I want you to try to get your mind off this whole issue."

"That's going to be pretty difficult if those calls keep coming in."

"Oh, I think we might find a way."

He drew her into his arms and for the first few moments Laura was completely involved in the pleasure of his long deep kiss. But then her thoughts dragged back to what she knew she should reiterate: that she was moving into Gordon's only out of fear and concern for her safety. She had said it once—no, twice—and Gordon claimed he understood. But did he really?

Laura stayed at Gordon's for the next three weeks, and in that time the calls from Jerry Manning or whoever—now being made to Gordon's number and Laura's service—dwindled and then stopped. The investigation by the D.A.'s office was continuing, and little by little, more and more women were coming forward. They were no closer to finding Jerry Manning, but the importance of the problem had receded for Laura now that she wasn't getting any of the calls. Gordon had interviewed Stu Whelan's secretary, Kathie Ellington, and hadn't been able to discover anything significant, but again, Laura didn't give it much thought: work was more important at the moment. Her session with Jasmine Cole at *Beauty Life-styles* was surprisingly easy and a smashing success, ending with the promise of much more work in the very near future. And Laura's private makeup work picked up considerably; people *were* telling their friends. All of which made it easier for Laura to give up her job at CTC for the seven o'clock news show, something she had wanted to do for some time now, since it was interfering with her private consultations.

With each day the importance of Jerry Manning receded, and Laura knew it was time to move back to her apartment. She felt perfectly safe, and she felt uncomfortable prolonging her stay at Gordon's now that the whole incident seemed so far away.

And so, three weeks after she had moved in, on a morning when they both had a little time to spare, Laura decided to announce her decision to Gordon.

"I think it's time I moved back to my apartment," she said as she poured another cup of coffee for herself.

His eyes darkened. "Why?"

"Gordon, we agreed that I was going to be here until the calls stop—"

"Is that why you're still here?" he cut in. "Is that all this has been?" He stood up and roughly pushed his chair back from the table.

"Come on," she argued. "You know it hasn't just been a matter of safety. I could have stayed lots of places and I chose here."

He studied her eyes, and she had no idea what he was thinking. Only moments earlier his voice had been harsh. Yet now his eyes seemed gentle.

"I don't want you to go," he said quietly. "I haven't been honest with you till now, Laura—at least not completely. But now—if you're leaving . . ."

She frowned. "What's wrong?"

He reached out and gently touched her cheek. "The

thought of your leaving," he murmured, shaking his head. "This whole time I've gone along with what you said and what you wanted because I didn't have any choice. I wanted you here on any terms. I wanted you with me. But take me as a lover instead of a protector now, Laura. Keep what we've had and throw out what we don't need anymore. Change the rules."

As he spoke, his voice and eyes and nearness were even more convincing than his words. *Did* she really want to leave? It was true that all the safety-related reasons she had stayed for were now gone. But now that he was pressing the issue, wasn't it also true that she had other reasons to stay? Wasn't it time, as he said, to put the past behind them and move forward? She loved him; she loved being with him—

"I'm not asking for a commitment," he said, interrupting her thoughts. "I just don't want you to leave. At least not without seeing your being here in another light, with me in another role."

She smiled. "I don't see how I can say no when you put it like that."

"Darling," he whispered, taking her into his arms.

As he held her close, she was glad she had said yes. For she didn't see him simply as a protector; they had been lovers the whole time; and moving out would mean making a statement she didn't want to make.

"I have an idea," Gordon said suddenly.

She pulled back and looked up into his eyes. "What's that?"

"Why don't we celebrate?"

She smiled. "Celebrate what?"

"You. Your being here. Your being here because you want us to be together."

"That sounds great."

"Let's make it a big one. Your friends, my friends, people we owe parties to. You must have a lot of people like that."

"Sure, sure," she lied. In truth, none of her really good friends ever had the time *or* the money to have formal parties. They got together for beer and music, a little food, and a lot of talking and dancing. And she was certain Gordon was *not* talking about that kind of party.

"Then let's do it. Do you like cooking for a crowd or do you want to get a caterer?"

"Well, I'm kind of busy these days, Gordon, so let's get a caterer."

"Fine. There's one over on Lex in the Seventies—Pierre DuVal is the name—that's very good. And flowers, the band, all the rest, should be simple enough."

She said nothing, but she didn't think he even noticed as he went on: "We can both make lists so you can get an idea of the number of people for the caterers, and then the invitations should be sent out . . . let's see . . . let's make it in two weeks. All right?"

"Uh, Gordon, I've never done anything like this before."

"Like what?"

"Given a big party like this—printed invitations and all that."

"Do you not want to do it?"

"No, I think it's a nice idea. This is a great apartment. But how about a little help? We'll split the work down the middle."

He hesitated for just a moment. "Okay. Fine. Or, actually, I'll tell you what: Vera, my secretary, loves doing things like this. I can have her do all the arrangements."

"That really isn't nec—"

"Of course it is," he insisted. "And I'm sorry; I don't know why I didn't think of it before. And I want you to remind me when I do that kind of thing again, Laura. I *have* a housekeeper; I *have* a secretary. If they don't want to do something, I can always find someone else. Technically, Vera shouldn't even plan the party since it's semipersonal business. But she loves doing it. So do you understand? Remind me. It's easy for me to forget that sort of thing. In my family, especially when we had our first house in Boston, my mother was constantly planning and giving parties. And of course my sisters were groomed for the role from day one, so I do forget."

"Well, the closest I got to being groomed or grooming anything myself was grooming horses," she said with a smile. "And I really don't know a salad fork from a . . . whatever else there is."

He searched her eyes. "There's something I don't understand about you, Laura. Since the moment I met you, you've been making a big issue out of where you come from, what you are and what you're not. Yet when I met you at the party, when I saw you from across the room, and then when I came over and talked to you, there was nothing about you that said 'I'm different' in that way, or 'I don't belong.' "

"I don't think *that,"* she insisted. "I'm just not *interested* in belonging to, oh, certain segments of society that think they're closed to outsiders. Like the countess's social circle. That's all I mean."

"Well, when we go to the countess's party, can I trust you?" he asked with a smile.

She pretended to look insulted. "Trust me? Why ever wouldn't you trust me?"

He narrowed his handsome brown eyes. "I seriously don't know if I can. It's like bringing an agitator into—"

The phone on the kitchen wall rang, and Gordon went to answer it.

Laura watched as he talked, his face etching with concern. He was so handsome, so masculine in such a relaxed way.

And as he spoke to whoever had called—obviously someone from the network, judging from the conversation—she loved his easy authority, the way he was handling an apparently thorny problem with such grace.

When he hung up, he came back to Laura and shook his head, as if he were unhappy or unsure about the call.

"What's the matter?" she asked.

"Oh, just someone who's been up all night worrying about something that doesn't bear worrying about. A lot of these producers are a little hyper and if they just got some sleep, they'd see things a lot more clearly. But I think I got him calmed down."

"I heard."

He looked at his watch. "Hell, the limo must be downstairs already. I'd better get going." He came up to Laura and kissed her tenderly on the lips. "But it's wonderful to go as long as I know you'll be here tonight."

She smiled. "I've been here every night."

"But this is a new beginning," he said, kissing her again.

She laughed and kissed him and said good-bye, happy once again that she had said yes to staying.

And she found as the days went by that their relationship blossomed. She thought that perhaps it was because she was seeing Gordon in a new light; or perhaps because she was simply beginning to relax about everything in her life; but for whatever reason, almost every aspect of their relationship deepened.

She did hang back in certain areas—they went out to dinner almost every night, and she didn't feel his apartment was anything approaching home; it still seemed like a way station, with a housekeeper who came in every other day and an aura that said the apartment belonged to someone else. But she loved being with Gordon. And he seemed just as happy.

And then one morning—the morning of their party—when Laura woke up, Gordon was smiling at her with special love in his eyes, a look that made her remember how he'd looked when she'd first said "I love you."

She smiled. "You look happy," she said.

"I am. How about you?"

"You know I am," she said.

He gently stroked her cheek and tucked a strand of her hair behind an ear. "I've been thinking," he said quietly. "We're so good together. So right. How about making it official?"

"You mean get married?"

He smiled. "What do you think?"

She was stunned. It was so soon . . . so quick . . . and she hadn't really thought of their living together as any kind of trial period. Of course, she *had* thought about what it would be like to be married to Gordon—but only as a fantasy, not as possible reality.

His smile faded. "Well. I see it isn't a question you've been waiting for with bated breath."

"No, no," she said quickly. "It's not that. It's just so soon. I hadn't really thought—"

"I see." His eyes searched hers. "Well. When would it not be too soon?"

"Gordon, I don't know. I'm not ready for marriage. That just isn't in my plans for now or—or maybe forever."

He frowned. "You never said anything to me about that."

"We never talked about it," she explained.

"Well." He glanced at the clock. "I suppose we'd better get up." He turned away quickly, afraid she'd see the disappointment on his face.

He got out of bed and quickly went into the bathroom. He turned on the shower—hot, as hot as he could stand it—and stepped in, then held his face up, letting the spray come down and hit hard.

He had never felt so robbed before, as if something he had just assumed was his had been ripped from his grasp.

Now he knew how blind he had been, just assuming that as his feelings deepened, Laura's were deepening too.

He had gone along with Laura's initial insistence that she was staying at his house only for safety, because he'd felt he had no choice. When he had convinced her to stay for love, his spirits had soared. And when he had asked her to marry him, he had obviously hoped too hard. He had even hoped they'd announce the engagement at their party tonight.

He had never wanted anything so much in his life. And though Laura hadn't said, "No, never," she might as well have.

How was it possible she had never thought of the possibility of marriage? How could she have agreed to stay on and not even considered the possibility? She had to have thought about it.

Which meant that she was just trying to be nice by not coming out and saying a flat no.

Damn.

"Gordon?" Laura was knocking at the door.

"Yeah! Come on in!" he called, trying to sound cheerful.

The shower curtain billowed out against his skin as Laura opened the door.

"Want some company?" she called over the sound of the shower.

He reached over and made the water less hot. "Sure. Why not?" he said. Did his voice sound as false to her as it did to his own ears? he wondered.

She gracefully stepped into the shower in front of him, and his heart turned over as he realized this would perhaps be one of the last times they showered like this together.

Wordlessly she wrapped her arms around him and laid her head against his chest, letting the water streak down her hair and over her face, holding him as if she'd never let go.

He knew what she was doing—trying to make him feel better, trying to undo. But it couldn't work. Not forever.

"I'm sorry," she murmured into the wetness of his chest.

And he wished she had said nothing, for her words made everything seem so final. . . .

She looked up at him and he moved back with her so the water wouldn't be streaking down her face. "I don't want this to be happening," she murmured, her lovely blue eyes brimming with tears.

"Change your mind," he said softly.

She closed her eyes, and when she opened them, they were sadder than ever—more eloquent to him than any words she could possibly say. "Why can't we go on the way we've *been* going on, Gordon? I've never been happier. And I love you."

"Go on for how long?"

She shrugged. "I don't know. Until the time is right for marriage."

"And if that time never comes?" he asked.

"I don't know. Then . . . maybe all the better that we wouldn't have made it official. And I hate the way it sounds, but I really think we *might* want different things. You want a different kind of life-style—a woman who's a full-time wife, who shares with you the way you said Christine did at first, giving parties and entertaining your business contacts, the kind of setup you grew up in. And that's not right for me at this point. If my career doesn't work out here, who knows? I might even move to L.A."

"You never said anything about that before."

"Well, it's just a thought. But that's the point. My life is totally up in the air at the moment." She looked into his eyes and sighed. "But I don't want to lose you."

"I think we both need to do some thinking," he said quietly. "Some very serious thinking." And he stepped out of the shower and wrapped a towel around his waist.

Laura turned off the water and squeezed the wetness out of her hair. But as she came out of the tub, Gordon opened the door, let a blast of cool air in, and shut it behind him without a word.

Damn. Why was she suddenly the guilty one? Gordon had made it very clear just now that "very serious thinking" might mean breaking up. And, damn it, why was that necessary? She loved him. She loved seeing him every day, being with him every night, knowing he'd be there for her when she needed him.

And at that thought, she had to ask herself why, then, was marriage impossible?

But she knew the answer. It went even deeper than what she had said to Gordon. Marriage, as far as she was concerned, was a lifetime commitment. It wasn't a matter of "making it official" after living together; it meant that those two people intended at least to *try* to live together as husband and wife for the rest of their lives. And just living with Gordon didn't mean that. Living with him was safe. She could object to anything, walk out any time she wanted, remain free in her heart and mind.

She heard Gordon's clock radio come on to an all-news station, and she wrapped herself in a towel and left the bathroom.

Gordon was getting dressed and didn't turn when she came back in.

"Gordon?"

He paused in the buttoning of his shirt and turned around.

"Do you want me not to come to the party tonight?"

"Don't be silly. Half the people who are coming are coming to see you."

That wasn't at all true, she knew. His list had consisted of more than eighty people; her list had had perhaps fifteen names on it that she had finally stretched to twenty out of embarrassment when she'd seen his.

But what hurt was that he hadn't said, "No, I want you to be there." He'd said *other* people would be expecting her. And that was a difference that hurt.

"Vera's done a really nice job of planning everything," Laura said.

"Mmmm. Maybe I should marry *her.*"

In the mirror, their eyes met.

"I'm just kidding," he said with annoyance. "Despite what you think, Laura, I *don't* hold party planning as one of the indispensable qualities I think a wife should have."

"That was just an example."

"Well, it was a rotten one," he muttered as he straightened his cuffs and pulled a tie from the rack. "If that's what you think I'm all about—"

"I don't," she cut in. "You know I don't."

"Then I honestly don't know what the problem is. Unless it's something you're not telling me. Which is certainly your right. Only it makes it difficult for *me,* that's all."

"I don't *know* what it is," she insisted. "I mean, when you say 'party planning,' that's just ridiculous. But you have to admit we are from very different backgrounds."

"So what? We've been over this, Laura. You have always been the one—the *only* one—who cared about that; *I* certainly don't and I never have. And you have these views of my background—gleaned from what, I don't know—that you seem to be subtly critical of. You're always talking about snobbery, but you've shown your own kind of snobbery at times. You judge my family, my background; you've never even met my family."

"I haven't judged."

"The hell you haven't," he snapped. "But even if you have, it doesn't get in *my* way. I can look the other way because I love you. Apparently that isn't possible for you to do." He straightened his tie and pulled it way too tight, then loosened it and grabbed his jacket. "I'll see you later," he said roughly, and strode out.

A few moments later Laura heard the front door slam shut.

CHAPTER SIXTEEN

This is crazy, she thought as she realized she was standing alone in *his* apartment, having apparently forced him to leave because *he* wanted to be alone. In an hour or so his housekeeper would be coming in, and a few hours after that, the staff that Vera had hired for the party. His staff; his housekeeper; his home. It wasn't fair to put him through this. She knew that. And so she began packing, gathering up little bits and pieces of her life that she had left scattered through his apartment—clothes, books, papers, shoes. Despite all the clothes and other things, though, she had always been a guest, never a real participant. She and the housekeeper, Katrine, were both people whose home it wasn't; Gordon had been the one whose home it was.

Knowing she couldn't just leave, fight or no fight, without a note, she sat down at the desk in Gordon's wonderful study and took out paper and a pen. And then she began writing, though she hadn't even planned what she would say:

Dear Gordon:

Please don't interpret my leaving as anything other than a chance to give you some room. I just thought it seemed crazy that if you wanted to be alone, you had to leave your own house. And maybe we do need some time apart.

I hope you know how much I've loved staying here. Despite what you think (and I *still* think you're wrong about this), I really do love being comfortable, and this apartment is wonderful. But that isn't important. What *was* important was being with you, and I really hope that doesn't end.

Don't worry about my going back to my own apartment in terms of danger or Jerry Manning. You know that the calls have stopped, so . . .

Also, I'll reprogram my phone so it rings at my house.

Anyway, I'll leave the keys in the foyer on the marble table (with this note). And of course I'll see you tonight.

I do love you.

Laura

She put the note in an envelope, wrote his name on it, and carried it out to the foyer, where she put it on the table he always threw his coat near. She had put her keys next to the note and was bringing her bags out to the foyer just as the housekeeper was coming in. She asked Katrine not to disturb the note and then she left, feeling strangely emotionless, as if she were merely leaving for an appointment downtown.

Half an hour later she walked into an apartment she had seen for only brief visits during the past five weeks, visits that had consisted only of picking up mail, clothes, and more supplies.

And the apartment showed her neglect: dust covered every surface, mustiness hung in the air like thick fog, and everything looked dingy and old and cheap compared to the furnishings at Gordon's.

She reprogrammed her telephone so that her calls would come to her apartment again, and as she hung up, she thought of those first mysterious calls that had driven her to Gordon's to begin with.

Maybe that had been part of the problem. She hadn't moved into his apartment out of love; it had been out of fear, and perhaps that had been the seed of a problem that had grown and continued to grow. She had moved in for one reason, and when they changed the rules, Gordon jumped one step ahead again.

She remembered how happy he'd been when she said she'd stay, how he had decided right then and there to have the celebration party.

How ironic that on the very day the party was destined to take place, they had had a fight and everything had shattered.

And suddenly she realized that perhaps it wasn't a coincidence. Perhaps he had chosen this morning—rather than yesterday or tomorrow—to ask her to marry him *because* it was the day of the celebration, because it fit with the mood and was almost an anniversary of sorts.

And suddenly, as she remembered the look in Gordon's eyes when she'd told him she wasn't ready, the weight of what had happened hit her with full force.

Gordon was angry. He was obviously hurt, but he was also angry. She said she wanted things to stay as they were, but did that guarantee that they would? She knew the answer was no. Once you wanted things to stay the same, they never did.

Getting ready for an 11:30 A.M. appointment, Laura

moved as if on automatic, increasingly nervous about the possibility Gordon would want to break up for good.

If he loved her, he wouldn't want to, would he?

She knew the answer. He was practical and he was also proud. If he thought she'd never change—and she couldn't guarantee that she would—he wouldn't wait around forever.

Her appointment went smoothly if not spectacularly. It was at the home of a lovely woman who lived on East 71st Street, a former customer at the salon.

Afterward, Laura went to the *Beauty Life-styles* office to meet with Jasmine Cole about their next shooting.

"I wanted to meet with you here, Laura, so you could look at the idea we have for the layout," Jasmine said, sounding strangely fatigued. And she looked uncharacteristically drab as well—totally different from her usual look, which was extremely polished and put together. "You'll see that we want to contrast the looks you can create using the same makeup—six eye-shadow shots here, six blush styles here, six eyeliner styles here."

Laura frowned. "Hmmm. Is there a reason you're separating the eyeliner and eye shadows?"

Jasmine smiled her first smile of the meeting. "Yes. I'm going dry, to be honest. I'm out of ideas and I'm trying to fill space."

Laura shook her head. "Then just blow up the pictures so they're bigger and do six total eye looks. Or do twelve. I can certainly do that. But separating them doesn't make too much sense. At least *I* don't think it does."

"Oh, *I* don't know," Jasmine sighed, tossing her pen across the desk. "I don't even *care* anymore. I've done the same damn things five hundred times already. It's just a matter of recycling. In case you hadn't noticed. You're awfully lucky you're not trapped, you know."

"In a job, do you mean?"

"Mmmm. I know I can hardly complain. I literally have one of the best jobs in the city. But I *am* rather tired of it."

"Can't you take a vacation?"

"Of course. Technically. But then what? Either I come back to twice as much work, or I can leave it to assistants who are just *waiting* for a chance to prove they're better than I am."

"Sounds rough."

Suddenly the look in Jasmine's eyes changed, as if she realized she had been too honest, or had given too much of herself away. "Of course, some of us have no choice," she said with a new brittleness.

"What do you mean?"

Jasmine raised a beautifully sculpted golden brow. "I did receive the invitation, Laura. From Laura Dawson and Gordon Chase? That's rather a big jump for you. Nice move."

"I don't understand."

"You've obviously moved in with him."

"We're just giving a party together," Laura said, seeing no reason to reveal the details of her personal life to Jasmine.

"I see," Jasmine said with considerable interest. "Thank you for the invitation, by the way."

"You're welcome."

"Christine wasn't surprised, incidentally."

"Surprised about what?" Laura asked, once again with the unpleasant sensation that she was being dragged into a conversation she'd rather skip.

"I told her you two were living together," Jasmine said. "And she wasn't a bit surprised. She said Gordon always was rather quick on the draw."

"Well, speaking of 'quick,' " Laura said, looking at her watch, "I *am* pretty pressed for time. So are we agreed on the makeup layout? We'll do eyes as one entity."

"Fine," Jasmine said. "By the way, though—"

"What?" Laura asked, a hint of impatience roughening her voice.

"Watch your man tonight, Laura. I was always interested by what Christine had to say about Gordon, and I liked him the one time we met. And I'm *very* interested in seeing him again tonight." She winked one of her gray eyes. "Don't look so shocked, Laura. I was only kidding."

Sure, Laura said to herself. *Women like you never kid.* But she *had* brought up an interesting point.

In the weeks that Laura had lived with Gordon, they had gone to a few parties, and he had always been absolutely magnificent to Laura, an ideal that none of her other dates had ever come close to approaching. Now there was a possibility that that would never happen again, that it was all over, just a memory she could cherish. Did she want to let that happen?

When she left Jasmine's office, Laura called Selena from a pay phone in the lobby. She needed to talk to her best friend, and even though Selena was coming to the party, she needed to talk to her right away.

"Come on up," Selena said when she heard Laura's story. "You're only ten blocks away. I'll take a break."

"Okay. Great."

Laura walked quickly up Third and soon arrived at

Selena's office, a small graphic-design studio she shared with other designers who were just starting out.

"This isn't very private," Laura said, looking up at the partitions that separated the designers from each other.

"What do you care? No one knows you. Tell me what happened."

Laura told her friend about the morning's conflicts: Gordon's proposal, her answer, her leaving his apartment.

Selena smiled. "Your mother would die if she knew you were throwing Gordon over."

"I'm *not* throwing him over! Why doesn't anyone understand that?"

"You *might* be throwing him over, Laura. You have to face that fact. You may lose him because he may not believe you'll ever change your mind. He obviously moves quickly."

"That's *his* problem."

Selena shook her head. "You can't think of this in terms of 'his' problems and 'your' problems. You can't blame each other, Laura. *Or* change each other. He's a powerful man. I'm sure he didn't get to be head of CTC by sitting around and daydreaming. Or waiting for other people to act. You're not going to change him in that area and you shouldn't expect to."

"I just resent being asked to decide so quickly. He springs this on me and all of a sudden I'm the one who's at fault."

"You can't honestly tell me you never thought of marrying him, Laura. I mean, for God's sake, you've been *living* with him for weeks!"

"I didn't think of it in realistic terms," Laura insisted. "It was just fantasy."

"Good fantasy?"

"Sometimes," Laura answered. "Sometimes not. I keep thinking of women I know who have thrown away their careers after marriage. They *say* they won't, and their husbands say they won't make them, but it happens. And some want that. But I don't. So I'm not ready, Selena. And what bothers me is that every time I think about other women—like other women who'll be coming to the party, for instance—I keep thinking, Uh-oh, I'd better change my mind and say yes to Gordon. Otherwise *they'll* get him."

Selena raised a brow. "That is a distinct possibility—for the future, I mean."

"It's no reason to get *married,* Selena."

Selena's phone rang and she had a short conversation about some designs she was working on for an advertisement. Then she hung up and looked at her friend. "If you're looking for advice, Laura, there's only one piece of advice I can give you. If *you* feel you're not ready—for whatever reason in the world—then you're not ready and you shouldn't get married. I wouldn't go so far as to say what I've heard other people say, which is that if you have to ask, if you have to question it, you're not ready. But you're not just questioning it. So my opinion is that you shouldn't. But then you have to take the consequences."

"That's what I'm so afraid of. And I don't see why Gordon has to put me in such a horrible position. It was all so great until this morning."

"All you can do is ask him," Selena said. "But if I were you, I'd wait till after the party. Why have another fight beforehand? At least now you're talking. And in the meantime, do some thinking. I don't believe that you moved in with him just because you were afraid of Jerry Manning. That doesn't sound like you at all. I mean, that may have been the reason you gave yourself, but since when do you run from things like that? So think about it. And go to the party tonight and talk to Gordon afterward."

Laura sighed. "I've certainly looked forward to other parties in my life more than this one."

"Well, if it *is* the end of your relationship, at least you're going out with a bang."

"Thanks," Laura said. "You're a real friend."

"Hey. You want sugarcoated optimism? Call one of those radio advisors. You want bitchiness? Talk to Jasmine Cole. I'm trying to be your voice of reality."

Laura smiled. "I know. I know. I just wish . . . oh, the hell with it. I guess all I can ask for is that things work out the way they were meant to work out."

"That sounds about right to me," Selena said.

The party invitations were for eight, buffet and dancing. The way Laura and Gordon had arranged it before the fight, she had expected to be at the house from late afternoon on. And though Vera had taken care of everything from the flowers to the orchestra to the food, with Katrine there to supervise, Gordon and Laura had assumed that Laura would be there as well.

Instead, at five Laura sat at home and tried to decide whether to call Gordon or not, to see if he still wanted her to come early. If she called him at the office, she'd have to explain what she'd written in the note. And she wasn't sure she was up to that. If he were home, though, he would have already gotten the note, and . . .

Damn. She had to do *some*thing.

She'd call him at home and if he wasn't there, she'd leave a message asking him to call her back.

Just as she was reaching for the phone, it rang.

"Hello?"

"What did you do?" It was Gordon.

"I—"

"What did you do?" he demanded. "I come home early, thinking I can help, and there's Katrine and the caterer and even Vera, and no you. Instead there's a note."

"Gordon, I—"

"That's a hell of a way to leave, Laura. A hell of a way to leave."

"I thought it was the best—"

"You're *so* good at figuring out what's best, Laura. You're so damn stubborn. I ask you to work for me and you say no, automatically. When *you* decide you have to, you ask if you can, and then you quit on me. I ask you to move in and you say no. Then *you* decide it's a good idea after all, and you move in. Then *you* decide you've had enough, and you're gone. I call that a hell of a way to make decisions about what's best. I—"

"I was doing it for you!" she cried.

"For me? For me? I ask you to marry me and you move out?"

"You said we needed time to think," she insisted.

"I didn't say anything about moving out, Laura. Don't try to make that into my decision when it was yours."

"I thought you'd want to be alone."

"You could have asked. Don't you think you could have asked? Do you ever think of bringing me in on any of your decisions? This is my home, damn it. I like to know who's living here."

"I'm sorry. Really."

"Hell. You should learn to pick up the phone and talk to me, Laura. Call; come to my office; anything. Just talk to me instead of . . . Oh, what the hell's the difference? You've made your feelings clear enough. Just do me one favor. Don't decide it's 'best' to skip the party tonight. Half the people who are coming are coming to see you."

And he hung up.

She closed her eyes and gently replaced the receiver.

And she knew that it would take a miracle to turn things around.

She imagined the party at Gordon's house: his living room filled with beautifully dressed men and women, the hum of conversation and clinking of glasses mingled with music from the band. And Gordon staring stonily at her from across the room. Talking with Jasmine Cole. Or, worse yet, coming up to her, ice-cold polite, and making cool small talk as if nothing much had ever happened between them. The final night of a relationship that had begun at a party that was much the same, with many of the same people. And with two people, once strangers, who'd be strangers again.

Lord, what had she done? She had obviously made a major mistake in leaving that way; that much was clear. But now what?

Gordon hadn't even wanted to *listen* to her; he hadn't wanted to hear one word.

She bit her lip and dialed Selena's number, and was just about to hang up after it had rung five times when Selena breathlessly answered.

"Hi," Laura said. "Did you just get in?"

"This *second,*" Selena breathed. "Hold on a sec. I have to put something in the fridge." The phone clunked down and Laura waited for what seemed like hours till Selena got back on. "So what's up?"

"Disaster," Laura said glumly. "Gordon came home and found my note and hit the ceiling. He called me up and just . . . he didn't even want to hear what I had to say."

"What are you going to do?"

"What *can* I do? I just can't believe things have escalated this quickly. I mean, in the space of a day—less than twelve hours—everything has just blown up. All he seems to care about right now is that I go to the party. And not because he wants to see me—I wouldn't be surprised if he didn't even speak to me the whole time—but because he says half the people who are going are my friends, or my guests."

"So are you still going to go?"

"Are you kidding? Of course. He's so furious about what he sees as my constantly walking out on things, and he's just looking for another example."

Selena sighed. "I don't know, Laura. I would go to the party and just play it very cool if I were you. Let him calm down, calm yourself down, and wait. If he loves you and you love him, you can work things out—despite this morning's fight. He wouldn't be so angry if he didn't love you."

"I suppose," Laura said uncertainly. "I just wish . . . oh, I don't know. I wish we could just be together without a thousand complications. Without any giant commitment and without problems."

"Well, you know from this morning that that may not be an option," Selena said. "But all you can do now is go, look great, act cool, and wait and see. What time are you going to get there?"

"Well, I definitely don't want to get there early and have to sit with Gordon at the edge of the dance floor."

"I meant to ask you about that," Selena said. " 'Dancing,' the invitation says. What kind of dance floor?"

"Oh, the living room and foyer were going to be cleared of their rugs. Apparently the previous tenants had put in some fantastic floor that's just perfect for dancing. But anyway I don't want to get there early, and I *can't* get there late or Gordon will be furious and just think I'm irresponsible. So I guess eight thirty. Does that sound right to you?"

"Sounds perfect. I'll get there around then too."

"Great. Well, I guess I'd better start getting ready. I look like a complete wreck, so it's going to take some time. But I'll see you there at eight thirty."

"All right, Laura. Take care."

Laura ran out to do some errands at the supermarket and the drugstore and then came back and took a long, hot bath. Then she discarded one "sure" outfit after another, discovering with disgust that she really didn't have as many great outfits as she'd thought. The party was *not* black tie, and Laura and Gordon had assumed that people would dress well but not formally. But nothing formal *or* informal that Laura owned looked good enough.

Her search was interrupted when the phone rang, and she answered it with some relief over getting to take a break. "Hello?"

Nothing.

Her heart leaped. "Hello?"

Nothing.

She slammed the phone down and closed her eyes.

Could it be? How could it be him again after all this

time? How could it be him when she had only just returned to her apartment?

But then, maybe it wasn't him; maybe it had never *been* him.

All she knew was that her heart was pounding and she had to get out.

She went back to her closet and settled on a black silk pair of pants and spaghetti-strap camisole with a matching jacket. Then she quickly made herself up, swept her hair up in a French knot, packed up a small evening purse with keys, lipstick, and wallet, and left her apartment.

"Don't close that door," came a male voice as Laura turned in surprise.

From the shadows of the hallway darted Jerry Manning, who in one moment had caught her by the wrist and jammed his foot in the door.

CHAPTER SEVENTEEN

"I've been looking for you," he said as he squeezed her wrist. "All over this city, Laur." His voice held a threat she could feel, an oily insistence edged with poison.

"Let me go," she murmured.

"Don't look around like that. And don't even think of screaming. The old lady across the hall's down on the stoop, and they know me anyway, those old ladies. They like me, too. So any kind of ideas you have, *Laur,* just forget about them and invite me inside."

"I'm on my way out."

"Oh, really? Gee, I never would have known, with you carrying a purse and leaving your cute little apartment. So your plans have changed."

He kicked open the door and with frightening strength dragged her back in.

She didn't know where her voice was, why she wasn't screaming, why she couldn't think. But a thousand thoughts were crossing over each other in her mind: He's just here to talk; it's natural he'd be angry; he's about to do something terrible and get away with it; he's been planning this for a long time; he's dangerous; he's not; you know him; he's a stranger.

But it was all happening too fast.

"You owe me," he warned, double-locking and chaining the door behind him.

She swallowed and said nothing, thinking about the fire escape outside her living room window. But the window was shut, and half the time it was so stuck it took ten minutes to open.

"You know what I've been living like for *five* weeks, Laura? Five weeks? Like a bleepin' fugitive. And don't look so surprised, *Laur.* I don't swear in front of girls. I have rules. I don't swear and I don't rat on friends. More than I can say for some people." He dropped her wrist and crossed his arms. "There. You're free now. Just don't leave my sight."

"What do you want? What are you doing here?"

"So many *questions!* So many questions for someone who never gave me a straight answer in her whole life."

"Jerry—"

"Did I say you could talk?" he snapped.

She said nothing.

"Did I? Huh?"

"I—"

"There you go again. You take a lot of risks. I guess that's the way you like it. Life in the fast lane."

She told herself to just stay quiet, to listen and try to understand what he was saying. And to try to get past him if she could.

He settled back against the door and looked her up and down. "I never sold your pictures," he said. "I've got them still, but I never sold them." His gaze settled on her breasts. "And you know I could have, Laur. I could have sold them in a minute. Especially a certain one I *really* like to look at—at certain times of the night. But you see, my nights . . . my nights aren't quite the same now.

Since I don't have an apartment, I don't have a studio, I don't have . . ." He shook his head. "You just didn't know. People like you, they just don't think." He shook his head again. "I know I made mistakes. Do you see me denying that? I don't deny it. I started something, and, hey, it wasn't that honest. I made some mistakes. I admit that. So then what? I try to get to a place I can do something: I work hard, I make a lot of calls, I bust my . . . I do the best work I've ever done in my life. I try to make something of myself, to advance. And then what happens? You know what I find out? You're some kind of spy, I find out. I find out Mr. Big Shot Gordon Chase doesn't like my business. I find out I'm going to be fired." He narrowed his eyes. "Even now you're trying to figure it out. I can see it in those eyes of yours. You want to try to figure something out? Figure out how you can live or do anything when your face is broadcast all over the city and people look at you like you're some kind of murderer. And don't look confused. I know you were *home* when that news report came on. You want to know where I was, Laur?"

She didn't say anything, afraid he'd get angrier if she talked.

"What are you, deaf? Don't you want to know where I was?"

"Where were you?" she asked softly.

"A motel. In Queens. They rent by the hour, you know? They don't care too much even if your face *was* on TV. And you know who was with me? Kathie. Kathie Ellington. You remember her, don't you? Cute redhead with the big green eyes. Smart girl, too. At least, she smartened up after I showed her why that would be a good idea." He shook his head. "Too bad she started the whole thing by writing to Whelan. Lovers' quarrels can be a real drag, you know?"

She didn't answer.

"Hey. I asked you a question."

"I—"

"You know all about lovers' quarrels, don't you? Or else you wouldn't be in this crappy little apartment instead of living with Mr. Big Shot, huh?" He shook his head again. "What we do for love—that's an expression, right? What you did for Gordon Chase and what Kathie did for me. She's the one who spotted you, you know. Miss Makeup. Miss Laura Dawson. That's how we finally made up. First she ratted on me but then she made up for it, warned me about the whole thing. But you don't really care, do you? Huh?"

"I need some water," she said quietly, her throat so dry she could barely find her voice.

He looked past her. "That's your kitchen in there?"

She nodded.

"All right. We can go in there. You can fix me something a little stronger."

He followed close behind her as she went into her small kitchen, a room definitely built for one. "Uh, do you want a beer?"

"What else do you have?"

"Uh, Scotch, vodka."

"I'll take the beer."

She took out a beer from the refrigerator and turned on the tap water, and Jerry started nodding as he stood next to her and stared.

"You look great. Really great, Laur. Fancy plans, huh?"

"I was going to meet someone," she said quietly. "And

I should warn you: if I don't show up, he'll be here any minute; we were meeting only a few blocks from here."

He grabbed her arm and whirled her around. "Don't you lie to me," he grated. "When are you going to get it through your pretty head that I'm not stupid?"

"I—"

"You think I don't know where you're going? You think I didn't *plan* this? Who's had five weeks to plan, Laura? Who's had five weeks without work, without anything but *time,* Laur—time to plan and time to look into things." He jerked his head toward the sink. "Get your water." He looked around at the tiny kitchen and shook his head. "What a dump. You must have made some big mistake to have Chase kick you out like that. Hurry up with that water."

She filled up a glass and turned off the water, and he led her out to the living room. "So what'd you do?" he asked as he sat down on the couch. "And sit down. I don't like you standing like that. And don't question me with those eyes. You don't have a choice here. Sit."

She sank to the couch, her knees suddenly shaky as she realized she had just missed a good chance. One good run—could she have reached the door? But he had locked and chained it.

"So what'd you do?"

"I don't see that that's any of your business," she said quietly.

"Are you kidding? Everything's my business. And I know things you haven't even thought of. Your big fancy party tonight. Guess he didn't want it to look bad, not having you there. But don't hand me any bull about anyone coming to get you. There's a hundred or more people going to that party, and your precious Mr. Chase isn't going anywhere." He reached out and stroked her arm. "So we've got plenty of time. *Plenty* of time."

Gordon looked up as he heard more guests arrive. Hal Jacobson from CTC and his wife. He smiled, gave a perfunctory wave, and quickly left the room.

Damn it, where the hell was Laura? He looked at his watch as he strode into his bedroom: eight fifty. Almost an hour late. She hadn't told him when she'd get here, but even so . . .

He sat down on the bed and rubbed his face, suddenly exhausted. Today had been one of the worst days of his life, a day he had begun with the highest of hopes, a day he'd thought he'd remember forever as one of his favorites.

All afternoon he'd wondered how he'd feel when Laura walked into the party and their eyes met for the first time. Those beautiful blue-green eyes he loved so much, that he had gazed at in passion and love, friendship and laughter. He'd see her, she'd see him, and then what? He still didn't understand how it had all turned so sour so quickly.

He knew that part of it had been his fault; he shouldn't have been so critical, so harsh, on the phone. But that was afterward—after she had turned him down, after she had moved out.

Now, after all that had happened, could they start over? He just didn't see how. Love apparently wasn't enough to keep them together: Laura was always finding reasons they were "wrong" for each other, always finding ways she could undo whatever he was trying to achieve. For every step forward he tried to take, she managed to find a way to move backward, or to shape things to her perspective. A party he had thought would be a celebration for them immediately turned into a source of argument, an example of how he wanted something "different" in a partner. She obviously had a deep fear of commitment, of agreeing to do things his way. And perhaps if he came to truly understand that, he could live with it. But had he ruined everything? Would he get another chance?

He thought about the trip they had taken up to Connecticut to see her parents that Saturday, and about what Laura had told him about her mother and father. Clearly she didn't want ever to be put into a position she saw as a trap. Her father and mother had had a very traditional marriage in which he had been the breadwinner and she had worked in the home, and Laura obviously didn't want to repeat the pattern. But why did she think he wanted her to? Hadn't he encouraged her in her work in every way since the moment they'd first met? Yet she persisted in thinking he wanted a different sort of woman, that she just wasn't "right" for him.

He winced as he thought of what might be the real reason for Laura's actions. Perhaps she just didn't love him enough; perhaps it was as simple as that—a case of unrequited love, a shared passion that could go only so far. He had been so caught up in his own feelings that he hadn't noticed she didn't fully share in them, that perhaps external circumstances were more responsible for their being together than love was. He had always believed, since she had first moved in, that the Jerry Manning situation had been nothing more than a catalyst, even a smoke screen; he'd believed that Laura had needed that sort of reason but that she'd wanted to be with him out of love. And that she'd *stayed* with him out of love.

And when she'd agreed to stay, his feelings had been confirmed.

But this morning it had all shattered. And perhaps it was time, finally, to face the fact that she didn't love him as much as he loved her.

"Oh, excuse me."

He looked up. A tall woman stood hesitating in the doorway.

"Hi, Gordon," she said softly.

He stood, feeling suddenly silly just sitting on the bed. "Hello. You're—?"

"Jasmine Cole," she answered, coming forward and extending her hand.

"Ah. One of Laura's friends."

"Yes. I haven't seen Laura, though. Isn't she here?" Her gray eyes were very direct.

"Uh, no, not yet. She should be any minute, though."

Jasmine Cole smiled. "I warned her about tonight."

"Oh?"

"I told her that if she didn't watch out, your time would be fully occupied, if I had my way, by me." She smiled again. "I'm a friend of Christine Kelly's, by the way."

"Really."

"Yes. I met you once last year at one of your parties."

"Ah. Yes," he lied absently, not remembering. He looked at his watch again: nine. "Uh, if you'll excuse me, Miss Crane."

He began to walk past her.

"Cole," she called out.

"Uh, yes, Cole," he said abstractedly. "And if you

were looking for the bathroom, there's one through there."

And he left the room. Damn it, where was Laura?

"So what do you think? Your boyfriend might be getting worried?"

"I'm sure he is," Laura said evenly.

Jerry had had three beers and she was praying he'd have three more. So far, he had been utterly mystifying, completely without focus when it came to his ideas on "revenge," as he put it. At one moment he seemed most angry with Gordon. But in the next second he'd focus on Laura all over again. And every time she even began to try to defend herself, he'd shut her up quickly, with a rough grab, a terse warning, or once with a slap to her face. And that was what frightened her the most. Jerry Manning had always struck her as a very physical person, the type who acted first and thought later. And he had obviously come for a reason. He had made it all too clear he had planned this night for weeks.

"He's giving some big party, huh?"

She shrugged. "I guess."

He grabbed her wrist and turned her to face him. "What is this 'I guess' business again? Don't you know who you're *talking* to? Who figured it all out, huh? Who's had five weeks to follow you around? Who's got a nice cozy contact at CTC who knows everything she's supposed to know and more? Who knew about the party without being invited? Me. Who knew when you got booted out of Chase's house? Me. Who knows what's going to happen to you tonight? Yeah, *now* I see some intelligence in those eyes of yours. *Me,* Laura. *I* know why I'm here. You don't know, and your Mr. Wonderful doesn't even know I'm here. I heard he thinks I'm long gone. Which is the way I wanted it."

"You're brimming with information," she said dryly.

"Hey, don't kid with me. You lost that privilege the day you walked up to my desk. Miss Temp Floater. Miss Hoover."

She swallowed and he tightened his grip on her wrist. "We have a lot of time to spend together tonight, the way I figure it," he said, a sickening suggestiveness lacing his voice. "Just you and me, Laur. Just you and me."

"Hi, you must be Gordon," a pretty, dark-haired young woman said as Gordon came into the foyer.

"Yes," he said abstractedly, watching the front door open. But it was just two people he didn't know. Laura's guests. And still no Laura.

"I'm Selena Johnson."

He looked at her again, this time with interest. "Laura's friend," he said with some pleasure. "The designer."

She smiled. "Right. Where's Laura? I can't find her."

"Late," he said, glancing again at the door.

"Well, I'm sure she'll be here soon. She told me she was planning to get here at eight thirty, but I guess she just couldn't get a cab. Or maybe she took a bus."

"But she did say she was coming."

"Oh, yes." Selena hesitated for a moment. "In fact . . . well, I don't want to butt in."

"No, please. Go on."

Selena shook her head. "I can't. Let's just say she'll definitely be here."

"I gather you heard about this morning."

Selena nodded.

"I just don't know what to do about that woman," Gordon mused. His gaze met hers. "Any advice for someone who's batting zero at the moment?"

Selena smiled. "You're not batting zero. She's just . . . I think she's scared." She paused and looked into his eyes. "I know she loves you."

Gordon sighed. "I just wish she'd get here. I want to try . . . to try to start over."

"Well, I think she'd like that too. But don't tell her I said so or she'll kill me."

"I've heard nothing but wonderful things about you, Selena. I'm sure Laura trusts you for a reason."

"Well, we go way back."

One of the maids opened the front door, and both Selena and Gordon looked up to see who had arrived. But it was just Stu Whelan and his wife, Tracy. Gordon greeted them and introduced them to Selena and then showed them to the living room/dance floor.

When he returned to Selena, he drew her aside and spoke softly. "I think I'm going to call Laura," he said. "What do you think? Do you think I should? I was so angry this afternoon." He shook his head. "I even hung up on her."

"I think you should definitely call her if you want to," Selena said. "Definitely."

"Then I'll be right back. But you should go join the party. You should be having a good time instead of playing Dear Abby."

She smiled. "I'm not about to leave, Gordon. I can have a good time a little later. I'm glad to talk to you. I feel I know you anyway."

"Well, good. I'll see you in a bit, then."

As he headed for the bedroom, he began to feel much

better about Laura. Selena was her best friend; they had discussed the problem, and Selena seemed quite confident that it could be worked out in *some* way, somehow.

Most of all, he wanted to make sure Laura was indeed coming, so that he could make up for the afternoon's call. He had been hurt and he'd acted in anger, and he didn't want Laura to think he was happy with the way things were.

He sat down on the bed and dialed her number and waited.

"Are you going to let me answer that?" Laura asked.

"What are you, crazy? What do *you* think?"

The phone rang and rang, and Laura counted twelve or thirteen rings before it finally stopped and the service must have picked it up. "All right, fine," she said with a shrug. "I . . . uh, that's fine."

He narrowed his eyes. "You think you're so smart. But who's got plans for who? I know what I want from you. You're in the dark."

Laura said nothing. Of course he was right. She still didn't know exactly why he had come, but she knew the reason couldn't be anything but bad.

"I'm the one who's had five weeks to plan this night. And I don't mind telling you it's been fun. I liked your voice when you said hello like that. Scared. Feminine."

She said nothing.

"The thing that gets me is, this didn't have to happen. You were the one who turned me around."

At that, she looked up at him. "What do you mean?"

"Hey, I was really into it. I thought I *could* make something of you. You think I don't have contacts? Okay, so I may not be buddy-buddy with Gordon Chase, but

I've got friends at the network. Stu Whelan's a good guy. I could have taken you somewhere. I *could* have made you a star. Then you turned it all to crap."

"You sold those pictures. Those women didn't appreciate that."

"Hey, listen—that isn't the end of the world for them, okay?"

"What about the money? They paid hard-earned money for—"

"Did I say you could talk? Did I say you could criticize?" He reached out and put a hand on her knee. "That's not what I came here for, Laur."

Gordon brought Selena into the bedroom and sat her down on the bed. "I'm worried," he said quietly. "What about you?"

She nodded her head. "I am too."

He looked into her eyes. "I need you to tell me whether she really intended to come, Selena. Are you sure she said she definitely was?"

"Definitely. Absolutely no question about it. Eight thirty, she said."

He sighed. "Then I *am* worried. If I thought she had changed her mind, then I wouldn't be, but this is her party too, and if you say she meant to come . . ."

"But you called her house and she wasn't there."

"I'm going to call again."

He dialed and the service answered. "I don't know what to do," he said quietly, after he hung up. "I just have this feeling."

"That something happened, do you mean?"

"Let's hope not. But what if she's sick? What if something happened to her?"

"I keep thinking about Jerry Manning," Selena said quietly.

Gordon gave her a look that made her even more nervous. "I'm going over there," he said.

"Maybe I should too."

"No, no, you should stay here, Selena, in case she comes, okay? I'm probably going for nothing . . ." His voice trailed off. "But I have to do *something.*" He sighed. "Do me a favor and keep an eye on things, all right? There's enough staff to handle everything, but . . . well, just be here for Laura. Let's hope she gets here while I'm gone." He shook his head. "I'm not a superstitious man, Selena, but I have an awful feeling," he said hoarsely.

And as he turned and Selena watched him leave, she thought, *There goes a man who's completely, obviously, totally in love. And terrified, even though he's trying to hide it.*

Gordon, meanwhile, was out in the street with his doorman, looking for a cab. He wished Selena hadn't mentioned Jerry Manning. He had thought the same thing but hadn't dared to say it out loud. And he had to admit it: there was a chance—a slim chance—that Jerry Manning was still around. And much as he wanted to drive the fear from his mind, he couldn't. He was scared. And in an uncanny way, he felt as if he could feel Laura's fear as well. He only hoped and prayed he was wrong.

Jerry Manning drained his fourth beer and tossed the empty can onto the coffee table. "So what do you say we go to my house?"

"What?"

"Hey, you don't think I'm going to stay *here* all night,

do you? With your phone ringing off the hook and you acting just a little too calm?"

"Well, if you think I'm going with you—"

He took hold of her wrist. "I got you in here. I can get you out of here."

Suddenly she remembered something he had said earlier; he had told her that the woman who lived across the hall from her was sitting on the front stoop along with other women from the building. Laura was sure this was true, since in the spring and summer they were out there every night. Which would give her the perfect chance. Maybe the four beers had dulled Jerry's thinking more than he realized.

But she didn't want to seem eager, so she sat and said nothing.

Jerry stood up, still holding her wrist. "You don't think I called you up and followed you around and did all this work to sit here and drink a few beers on your couch? Let me tell you something. I have two things left in my life: my photography equipment and my car. The rest turned to crap when you came on the scene as Miss Temp Hoover. Who knows? I might even call up your Mr. Great and get some money from him."

"You know he's having that party."

"So I'll call him tomorrow. Maybe have some fun tonight. Now come on." He jerked her up from the couch.

As the taxi pulled into Laura's block, Gordon pulled a wad of bills out of his pocket and stuffed them into the money slot of the partition. "Right here," he yelled. "Pull up right here."

He got up and made his way past the old women sitting on the stoop, and was just reaching for Laura's buzzer when he noticed the door was open a few inches, held there by a woman's shoe. He pushed his way in and started up the steps.

He heard a scuffle one floor above and picked up speed, skipping every other step as he vaulted up the first flight of stairs.

And when he reached the landing, he saw a hand on the banister of the next flight, and in the moment he realized it was Laura's, he heard a male voice and his heart nearly burst.

Then he saw it was Jerry Manning as they met at the bottom of the flight. And he didn't even look at Laura. He went for Manning's throat with a speed made of pure instinct and animal rage.

In the moment of contact, when his hands found Manning's shoulders and he slammed him back against the stairs, all the fears he had had about Laura's being in danger, all his feelings about the day, all his anger at everyone and everything made him react without thought, only with gut instinct and sheer speed and force.

He heard Laura cry, "Oh, my God!" behind him, and was aware of the terror in Jerry Manning's eyes for one brief moment, but then he knew he had him when Manning moaned in pain and weakened beneath him.

"Gordon!" Laura murmured.

"Are you all right?" he asked over his shoulder.

"Yes, yes. Oh, God."

"You'd better call . . . you'd better call the police," he said quietly. "And an ambulance." Manning was cursing and moaning, clearly hurt in some way.

"Laura—"

"Right, right," she said, and started up the stairs.

She moved as if in a dream, amazed at what had happened. And it had happened so fast. One moment she thought she was being abducted, dragged off in some car to God knew where by a drunken creep. And the next thing she knew, Gordon had appeared out of nowhere. . . .

Fifteen minutes later, as two ambulance attendants carried Jerry Manning off in a stretcher, Laura and Gordon stood talking to two policemen on the front stoop, with what seemed like the whole neighborhood crowding around to listen.

One of the two policemen had seen the CTC-TV report on Jerry Manning and was familiar with the case, and Gordon took that one aside while Laura stood and talked to the other.

A few moments later Gordon came up beside Laura and put a gentle arm around her shoulder. "Come with me," he said softly, turning her toward the building's entrance.

"What? What about—"

"We'll talk to them tomorrow," he said quietly. "They have all they need for now."

She looked at the two policemen, who were already dealing with the clamoring women from the building and the hundreds of questions they were yelling. "Well, I guess you're right," Laura said.

And she and Gordon went back into the building and started up the stairs.

"This all feels so unreal," she murmured when they got to the bottom of the stairs where Gordon had collared Jerry. "I just can't believe . . ."

"Shhh," he whispered. "I don't want you to think about it."

"But I can't *help* it. I mean, *imagine.* He was taking me

away!" She shuddered. "My one hope—and the reason I went willingly with him—was that I thought I'd be able to make a break for it on the stoop. I knew that Mrs. diPalma would be out there with her friends. But still . . ." Gordon held her tighter as they walked up the last flight of stairs, and by the time they got into her apartment, she felt shaky, her knees suddenly like limp rubber.

"Come over here and sit down," he said softly, leading her toward the couch.

She stopped stock-still. "Not there," she murmured. "Not there."

"Why—"

"I had to sit there for I don't know how long with him."

Gordon turned her to face him, and he looked down into her eyes with an expression she couldn't read. "Tell me what he did."

She shook her head. "I don't want to talk about it right now. I don't want to think about it. It wasn't a matter of what he did. It was what he kept threatening—the way he kept suggesting things, with words and with his hands."

"What with his hands?"

"Just—just—just hold me," she finally said, and he took her in his arms, and as she rested her head against his chest and he stroked her hair, all she could think of was that this was all that was right in the world, that this feeling of being in Gordon's arms was all that she wanted, all that she would ever want.

"Come with me," he murmured, leading her toward the bedroom. "I just want to hold you."

In the bedroom he held her close, then lay down with her on the bed and held her close again, just stroking her, soothing her, talking softly and bringing her back from the fear that had gripped her when they'd come back to the apartment. He was so gentle, so tender, and as she gazed into his warm brown eyes, she loved him so much she wanted to stay in his arms forever.

"I was so frightened," he murmured, stroking her cheek. "I just knew something had happened."

"Thank God you did. I don't know what would have—"

"Don't think about it," he said softly. "There's plenty of time for that in the future, when it's not so raw."

"I don't understand what made you come," she said quietly.

"I was waiting for you at the party." He smiled. "I wonder how they're doing without us? Anyway, I was waiting, and waiting, and waiting, because I wanted to undo . . . to undo as much of the day as I could. Just to tell you I was sorry about some of the things I said. . . . And I waited. Selena said she was sure you were coming, so—"

Laura smiled. "I should have known she had some kind of hand in this. She told you I definitely was going to come?"

"Yes, and it's lucky she did. Otherwise I would have thought you'd just changed your mind." He smiled. "As is your wont."

"No, that was one thing I wasn't going to change my mind about, Gordon. I wanted to show you . . . well, that I wasn't just walking out. And I wanted to see you."

"And Manning grabbed you in the hallway?" Gordon asked, recalling what she had said to the police.

She nodded. "But I really think . . . I really think it

means something that you came when you did. Don't you?"

"What do you mean?"

"Well, that things were meant to happen like this. That you were meant to save me." She reached up and brushed a dark lock of hair off his forehead. "You turned everything around," she said softly. "I didn't even remember we had had the fight until we came up to the apartment. It was as if you just undid the whole thing." She sighed. "Of course, I don't know if you feel the way I do. . . ."

"I love you," he said, his eyes shining with as much love as she had ever seen. "You know I love you. When I was waiting for you this evening, I knew I couldn't leave things as they were. But we can't just say they're gone . . . that we've undone them."

"What are you saying?"

"That I love you, that tonight made me realize even more than ever, if that's possible, just how much I love you. But we do have some things to work out."

Just listening to his voice, feeling his closeness, having him so near and so wonderful gave her courage to speak truthfully about her feelings. "When I was with Jerry tonight, Gordon, I had some time to think. He went through these really talkative periods and then he'd just brood, and I was so scared that I . . . my mind just wandered, sometimes thinking about you and what would happen, sometimes thinking about you and what happened this morning." She took a deep breath and gazed into his eyes. "I've never loved anyone as much as I love you. I can't question it anymore. I know I loved you way before I ever admitted it to myself, and tonight . . . tonight I had time to think about what has real meaning in my life. My family, some good friends, and you. Even my career, as much as I cherish it, is something I'd give up if I had to make a choice. But I know I don't have to. I'm just saying that there are certain things, and certain people, that really do mean everything." She put her palm against his cheek. "The feel of your skin against mine. The sound of your breathing as you sleep. Your smile. Your eyes. Knowing you're there for me. That you love me. It suddenly became so clear." She sighed. "I don't know why I reacted as I did this morning. I guess I really was surprised. And I was scared. But now I know . . . I know I do want to marry you. More than anything in the world."

He moved her hand to his lips and held it there, against his mouth, with his eyes closed, saying nothing. And she thought something had happened, that somehow he had changed his mind. But when he opened his eyes, there was nothing to question, nothing to wonder about. All that shone from his eyes was pure love, pure joy, pure happiness. And he brought her more fully into his arms, holding her tight against him, love deeper than any words could express flowing between them in silence.

And then he drew back and looked into her eyes and said, "I love you so much. You know what my answer is. You know I would never have given up, as long as I thought there was still a chance."

She sighed. "I really wasn't sure."

"I was angry today. I was so angry when I found the note. But I wouldn't have given up. Not as long as you kept looking at me as you're looking at me now."

"I don't think I've ever been so happy." She smiled. "What a *day!*" Her eyes widened. "And the party! We're lying here vowing our undying love while you've got a hundred people in your apartment!"

"Don't you think they can have a good time without us?" he asked, brushing his lips against her cheek. "The whole reason I wanted to give the party was to celebrate our being together."

"Mmmm, that feels good," she murmured. "I guess they *can* have a good time without us."

He smiled. "Of course you realize I'm ignoring something."

Her eyes flew open. "What?"

"This is just another instance, a major example, of Laura Dawson's stubbornness again. Once again I've asked you to do something and you had to say no until *you* could ask *me.*"

Her smile faded. "I wish you hadn't said that."

"Why?"

She shrugged. "It's not something to joke about. I've never felt so right about something in my life; I wouldn't want to think it's because I'm doing something that's part of a pattern."

He smoothed her brow with a gentle hand. "You are sure, though?"

"It just feels right," she said softly. "Everything just came together—all my doubts and fears and questions—and turned to love the moment I saw you. And that's why I think it was almost like magic, your coming to save me. It was like a charm that dissolved all my doubts."

"What about your lack of party-planning skills?" he asked with a skeptical grin. "Do you really think I can ignore that kind of deficit in my woman? In my wife?"

"Oh, in time," she mused, running a finger along his nose and over his lips. "In time you might, if you take certain other skills into consideration."

He took the tip of her index finger into his mouth

between his wet lips as his velvety gaze darkened with a lazy heat. Then he kissed her hand and moved his lips to her mouth and kissed her with endless pleasure, both of them reveling in the newness of their feelings. He drew back and smiled. "Our first engaged kiss."

"It felt nice," she said with a smile. "Didn't you think?"

"Mmmm. Needs more work, though." This time the kiss was deeper, an urgency simmering beneath the surface.

"Mmmm. Better," she whispered. "Should we try for more?"

"No question about it," he said hoarsely. And soon they were making love fully and deeply, truly amazed at how wonderful it was to know they *had* made a commitment to each other, that they loved each other enough to take a chance on love, a chance on each other, a chance they knew would be the greatest choice of their lives.

And when, at the height of their passion, cries of "I love you" filled the room, the magic that had brought them together made a bond that would last forever.

CHAPTER EIGHTEEN

Ten weeks later Laura woke up in Gordon's—now her and Gordon's—bedroom, sunshine flooding the room with light. It was a Saturday morning, and Gordon was still asleep, having announced last night that as a married man, he was going to start sleeping late on weekends now that he had a great reason to stay in bed.

He had changed even in the two weeks they'd been married: he spent less time down at the network, he laughed more, he was much more relaxed. He whistled as he got dressed in the morning, sang in the shower, kissed Laura whenever she was near. And she loved him more than ever.

She smiled whenever she thought of her first impressions of this wonderful man. She had thought he was arrogant, that it was a crime any man could make as much money as he did. Yet he was one of the kindest and most generous men she'd ever met.

She had resented him for "judging" Jerry Manning, had blamed him for basing his suspicions on snobbery. But she couldn't have been more wrong.

And though she didn't want to sully the sunny morning by thinking too much about Jerry Manning, she couldn't help thinking about what had happened with the case only four days earlier: Jerry had been convicted on charges of fraud and theft by false pretenses, with the sentence set at three to five years. Gordon had arranged for all of the thirty-two women who'd helped in the investigation to be paid back by CTC, and fifteen of them got small parts, as extras in upcoming CTC shows.

Laura smiled again as she thought about the young women coming up to Gordon after the trial. He had been uncomfortable in the glare of publicity that had surrounded the case, and he'd simply wanted to do what he could for the women without making a big deal of it. But to a small group of them he'd become a kind of hero, and he was still something of a media star at the moment.

"Mmmm," Gordon mumbled in his sleep, and Laura snuggled against him and wrapped her arms around him.

He immediately opened his eyes. "Hey. Are you trying to wake me up?" he murmured, managing to look playfully disapproving even though he was still half-asleep.

"Who? Me? Of course not." She wrapped herself tighter around him. "Must have been somebody else."

"Mmmm," he said into her neck. "I love you," he whispered.

"I love you too."

"What time is it?"

"About ten," she said softly.

His eyes flew open and he turned to face her. "Wow. I don't think you know how amazing it is that I can still be in bed this late."

"Oh, I know. I think it's great."

He brushed her hair back from her forehead and gazed into her eyes. "*You* were great last night—at that party."

She smiled. They'd gone to a party she'd secretly dreaded, given by a woman who'd reminded her a lot of the Countess di Lomazzo. But just as at the countess's party, everything had gone smoothly from start to finish.

And that was one of the most wonderful things she'd discovered about being married to Gordon. All her worries about roles and upbringing and background and status had all been so unnecessary. She was herself, he was himself, and everything else fell into place. And every time Laura looked back at the worries she'd had, she thanked her lucky stars she hadn't let her fears blind her to what she and Gordon shared.

Every day was better than the day before, and as she looked into Gordon's eyes shining with love, she knew it would be true forever.

LOOK FOR NEXT MONTH'S CANDLELIGHT ECSTASY SUPREMES: